WITH THE SNOW QUEEN

NOVELS

Of Such Small Differences
Age of Consent
Simple Gifts
The Far Side of Victory
A Season of Delight
Founder's Praise
In This Sign
The Monday Voices
I Never Promised You a Rose Garden
The King's Persons

SHORT STORY COLLECTIONS

High Crimes and Misdemeanors
Rites of Passage
Summering

WITH THE SNOW QUEEN

Joanne Greenberg

Arcade Publishing
New York

First Arcade Paperback Edition 1993

Grateful acknowledgment is made to the following publications, in which some of the stories originally appeared: *Tikkun,* "Stand Still, Ute River"; *50 Plus* (now *New Choices*), "Torch Song"; *Denver Quarterly,* "Elizabeth Baird" and "Like a Native"; *Rocky Mountain Magazine,* "Character Assassination" (now titled "That Bitch").

Library of Congress Cataloging-in-Publication Data
Greenberg, Joanne.
    With the snow queen / Joanne Greenberg. — 1st ed.
      p.   cm.
    ISBN 1-55970-110-2 (hc)
    ISBN 1-55970-192-7 (pb)
    I. Title.
    PS3557.R3784W5   1991
    813'.54—dc20   90-44191

Published in the United States by Arcade Publishing, Inc., New York, by arrangement with Little, Brown and Company, Inc. Distributed by Little, Brown and Company

10 9 8 7 6 5 4 3 2 1

BP

Printed in the United States of America

To Pamela Thayer Greenberg
Unearned Riches

CONTENTS

I gratefully acknowledge the help of
Steve Nicodemus and
John G. Martin.

WITH THE SNOW QUEEN

WITH THE SNOW QUEEN

I

"APPARENTLY this plague is worse than anyone thought," Berton said. He still read the news and now he folded the paper in order to read more comfortably. The epidemic was a feature article. It had begun in a place called Vézelay, in France, no one knew how. Sema put another piece of barley bread in the toaster. She didn't answer Berton because it had struck her with a pang of shame that she didn't care. It was a familiar scenario: terror, inquiries to the government, blame, emergency action. When the news had first come, she had thought, "What, another one?" Then she had felt the chill of isolation that the selfish and distracted feel in the face of great events. "Are you coming home early tonight?" she asked.

"I plan to. Luci's going to be away all week. I thought we could take her out to dinner before we see her off."

3

"I don't think she cares whether we see her off or not. This is her fifth trip this year."

"She may not, but I do," Berton said. "She's growing up fast and soon she'll be gone. I often think . . ." Then he shrugged and looked across at Sema, and smiled. "Some people can't have children at all."

Sema knew the one-child rule had been hard on Berton. She sympathized with him but had never really felt his loss. The rule had been made for good reasons; the reasons had been explained endlessly. Education, they called it. She had accepted the explanations with as little feeling as possible. Her life had been reasonable. There had never been need, urgency, a strong act of will, tragedy, or glory. Once, years ago, when she spoke of the lack of these things, the people to whom she spoke congratulated her. What good luck, what good health, what wisdom to escape such unpleasantness. She had grown up carefully, lovingly tended, had married, worked her necessary qualifying year-quarters, posted the proper papers, done what was expected dutifully, judiciously, and to the pleasure of her parents, Berton, and her friends. These were the ideals everyone had been taught to strive for. She and Berton were praised and her parents had died proud. When Luci was small, Sema's stifling had at least felt like disciplined usefulness. There had been the school volunteer work that had benefited Luci and her friends directly, in its limited way. By now the support groups were tiresome and her volunteering a makework that had no interest for her at all. She sat at the table after Berton left and wondered at her loss of self. She was a woman who had heard about a plague and lo-fatted another piece of barley toast without a sigh.

At eleven she dressed and went to Child Development Study Group, SSG16.7. The .7 group had been together since the women in it had gotten their pregnancy permits, fifteen to eighteen years ago. They had been through the laser treatments and one by one through pregnancy and delivery, early motherhood, and on and on. Their children were now all fourteen to seventeen years old and the problems they talked about, instead of being deepened by familiarity, seemed to Sema endlessly repetitious and endlessly boring. Most of the women had little in common besides their location: Sixteenth Suburban Service Grid. Although such support groups were supposed to be democratizing, they had not been formed by choice. People met, fulfilling the requirements. Sema had become friendlier with only two of the women, Luanna and Pat. Today she found the meeting oppressive. She hadn't read the chapter in the facilitation book: safe recreational drugs. She looked at Pat, who had knitted her way through these meetings. What could she have done had she taken up knitting — a toaster cover the size of Death Valley . . .

Pat raised her hand. "I won't be here next week. I have a pass from the Time Travel Division," and she pulled a blue computer card out of her waist pack. Sema had never seen one. She thought time travel was allowed only for governmental and official purposes. Hester, the facilitator, was too plodding to fake answers to the routine questions so they could talk about Pat's trip. Afterward, Sema and Luanna went to her. Special friendships with group members weren't encouraged, so they split up and met again later.

"It's still under lots of control," Pat said. She took out the blue card again. "This category is medical, second priority. You all know that I am . . . was . . . a carrier for Huntington's chorea, and that I was treated with recombinant DNA. It changed not only the particular gene but also some of the others. Without a print, Alicia won't be able to reverse her sterilization when she is ready. They didn't keep the records they do now."

Luanna wanted to know about the mechanics of the trip and Pat told them what she had been briefed on about the time car and the physical laws related to it. Sema tried to form her questions. She felt an urge to learn something, to hear something that Pat wasn't telling them. The feeling of eagerness and impatience was new to Sema, and disturbing.

"We've had three orientations, but those were about the laws they've set up to protect us and the people in the past we'll have to interact with. For example, we can't tell them we're from the future. We can't make racetrack bets — things like that. I'll only be staying long enough to get my records — a day, maybe two, and it's all very carefully scripted."

"Could you meet your mother or something?" Luanna had always been attracted by the bizarre. The group had often criticized her for it. It was what Sema liked in her.

"I won't, but apparently some people do. I don't think you can meet yourself, though you are *in* the body you had then, I guess. There are historians who go back to before they were born and have another set of physical laws to meet. They're very carefully controlled."

"Why?" Sema asked.

Pat looked puzzled. "The officer wouldn't answer when someone asked."

It flashed through Sema's mind that there might be such an exodus that no one would be left here — but she said nothing. Perhaps she was the only one who thought such things.

Pat was away for three weeks. When she came back, they took her out again, eager to hear about the things she had seen. Again Sema found herself impatient with the details — why was Pat dwelling on the clothes, the verbal styles, the news of the day? Something about the experience itself was fascinating to Sema in a way she hadn't experienced before. "Was there anyone going back for more than one specific — well — chore?"

"Well, the criminals of course — red card people, but no one like us."

That evening Sema told Berton about Pat's trip. "It's funny you should mention that. You know Bob Dutcher — I was telling you about his son —"

"The boy who had the accident?"

"Yes. There was a man from Channel Fifty interviewing Bob during lunch break. Bob had heard about their opening time travel for medical reasons. He applied as soon as his boy was out of danger. Two days ago they took the boy, without his back or leg braces, back to the time before the accident. He relived the time — his present self in his former body; he was free to unmake the act. This time he pulled over, slept off his drunk, lost six months in the relived time, but now he's back. He's no longer paralyzed. They're going to have the story on the holo tomorrow."

"If *I* could relive . . ." Sema said.

"But you're not paralyzed . . ."

"No, of course not," she said, but she thought, "Yes I am."

They showed that card, the blue medical passport, on the next night's holovision, and the Dutcher boy before and after, and his parents looking relieved and happy, welcoming him with tears. Time between is gained the way it is in space between time zones, the announcer explained; the boy came back six months older, the time he had picked up on his return. Time well lost, his parents declared.

Luci was watching the program with them in her usual desultory way, her attention split between what she was eating, talking on the holophone, settling and unsettling herself. Berton and Sema saw little of her, and Berton was so glad to see her at all that he put up with what Sema felt was her monumental rudeness and self-absorption. Now the girl sighed at the miracle and Berton looked at her in surprise. "Don't you think that's wonderful?" he said.

"I guess so." Her expression and voice were flat.

"The boy would have been paralyzed," Berton said.

"The government gets what it wants," and Luci sighed. "No medi-costs, the kid gets what he wants, and his folks get what they want. Everybody's happy. The End."

"Would you rather see the boy paralyzed?"

"No, and when the hemophiliac prince of Spain was little they padded him and they padded all the trees in the royal park, and all the sides of the buildings and all the palace walls and all the rocks so that even if he ran headlong into anything he couldn't hurt himself. We heard about that in Medical Policy Class last week, and nobody laughed but me."

"You laughed?"

"I laughed. You'll probably be getting a 16.4.M. form about it, and a meeting with my worker."

"Why did you laugh?"

Luci shrugged eloquently. "He lived with hemophilia and died of boredom," she said, "bore-*dum.*"

Sema felt rage beginning and suddenly it blew red and then white, all in an instant. The anger blinded her and dimmed her hearing so the voices of Berton and Luci went to murmurs, Berton's sound gently chiding, Luci's petulant. The crass, unfeeling little snip! What right did she have to talk so easily about padding, boredom, loss? The words in Sema's mind were like a sill over which she suddenly tripped and fell. Luci was spoiled and angry, but her anger had the same source as Sema's malaise. Sema remembered her own unconcern about the plague which was now raging through France and had all but closed its borders. What Luci was pouting and free to say, Sema was burying with guilt. She heard Berton give the same reasonable talk to Luci that he had always given, explanations about the reasonable plans of reasonable people. Luci wasn't accepting the reasons, and when Sema listened to her objections stated in so bald and parodied a way, she realized that only part of the emotion she felt was anger. The other part was envy.

She knew she should contact the Mental Health Agency. They would send out a family worker, who would turn the support group into peer counseling, and the worker and the group would mirror Berton's reasonableness into infinite prisms of reflection. This would get them noticed officially, listed, and it would end in marking Sema and Luci as officially "disturbed" and a potential source of trouble. This was a mistake she would not make. Instead, she would continue to ponder the escape of a trip like Pat's for a while. How long a stay would it take? A year? Two?

"If I went back," Sema said to her mirror, "it wouldn't be to escape but to relive," and then she realized that reliving a year or two would be of no help to her and it wouldn't help her to remake any single wrong decision. She would have to relive the time when all decisions had been made, and to live forward day by day from the time when a too obe-dient and passive daughter had sold her birthright for the easy approval of friends and the security dreams of parents and family. "If I went back . . ."

She said it to the mirror day after day for a year, and she said it to the stati-cleaner and the holovision as she looked at its box and to the walls without seeing them. "If I went back . . ." She said it in the road car and on the monorail. "If I went back —" She said it to the passport officer.

II

"You're only applying," he said, and stamped GREEN 25 on the form she had filled out. "You know you have to see a therapist about this first . . ."

Sema said, "Yes, I know."

"Is this passport to be from the Department of Corrections?"

"No."

"Psychiatric, then, or medical?"

"No."

"You're not a tourist — ever since that HV show —"

"No."

"Which section is compelling the trip, then?"

"None. I want to relive a part of my past."

"You *are* a Greenie; I haven't processed a Greenie yet."

"You mean no one has . . ."

"Not through this office. I've heard of it, though, people using travel permits for life enrichment." His face had become more alive; he was interested.

"There's no law against it . . ."

"No, it's got a category, but it's the lowest priority there is. I ought to tell you that even if our therapist recommends it, you may never get a place. The Time Travel people are beginning to say that the green category should be closed. You might be polluting the past, filling it with potential hazards, for no social purpose."

"I'd like to try. Where do I have to meet with this therapist?"

The passport clerk entered a number in the computer, printed out solid copy. "This goes on your permanent record," he said.

"I understand that."

He brushed the computer to activate.

"I've had conferences with your care-givers," the
Agency man said. He was short and bald. His name
was Mel. Sema felt in him, also, a hint of the incredulity about "Greenies" she noticed in the passport
officer. "They say you are not a danger to self or
others, and not abnormally attached to the past.
What inspires this wish in you?"

Sema had been raised with care-givers all her life.
She knew what they wanted to hear. She knew that
her reasons for making this trip were an indirect re-
proach to them and that she needed to say things
very, very carefully. The Welfare State had given
way to the Therapeutic State and the people who had
remained as earth dwellers were very careful people.
They had to be.

Sema told her life story. She did not say that her life
had been divided — wish on the other side of the
fence, need for continuity always before her. Her
parents had been in their forties when she was born,
the only permitted child. The one-child limit had
been absolute in those days, so strictly enforced that
even if a child died, no replacement was allowed. Her
every moment had been scrutinized, tended,
weighed. A sickness was cause for terrible alarm; a
small lapse in attention, reason for therapeutic inter-
vention. She grew up hung with duty, and the careful, watchful, should-and-shouldn't of every waking
moment, to be as much the charming, cherished girl
as she could be. Her life with Berton was comfortable, safe, and arid. When Geron, her father, was

dying of viral pericarditis, he had said, "I'm leaving
you in good hands, you and Luci." She wondered
why those words had been so disappointing. What
had she wanted him to say to her? Now with her
own daughter, she found she was preaching the same
safety, order, and responsibility because she didn't
know what else to do. The words came flat. Luci was
Sema and Berton's single, permitted child, but unlike
Sema, she had never sought to please or to conform.
Her rebellion came in a pose of sullen indifference
and studied irony. Sema realized her annoyance at
Luci was envy. The girl's attitude seemed like a direct
insult, an accusation of cowardice, a *declaration* of her
contempt. Fights followed, preachings, teachings, silences, glaring, rancor. Sema saw her own days
empty of meaning. Luci's contempt was her own.

She told the therapist none of this. Instead she spoke
rationally, calmly. "Luci is making her teen transi-
tions, Berton is happy and successful, and I will be
going into my middle-years soon. I'd like to return
and find the roots of some earlier interests that I
might use for socially positive training programs."
They were big on social utility.

"It doesn't sound like an unpleasant life," Mel
said, "not dedicated perhaps, not intense, but surely
not deprived in any way."

"I thought I might go back to the year I was eighteen and starting college. What if, instead of going to
college" (she was going to say mindlessly, instead she
said) "casually, I allowed myself to become interested
in a career, to follow that road and see what I might
become. I've read a bit about the technology. The
longer I stay, the farther back I go. When I am ready

to come forward, I will move into the time I have lost. To my loved ones I'll only be gone a week or two, and I'll pick up the time at the other end."

"The possibility of time travel has allowed us all kinds of social and psychological remedies," Mel said. "We haven't explored every one of these possibilities; the technology is too new, the experience too rare. You are a stable personality with a stable background. You are a good candidate for return on an experimental passport — Green Slash E. Few people have applied to go back for more than a week. Your application is for twenty years. That's almost a generation."

"I saw the boy —"

"Eventually we will do a great deal of remedial living." Mel steepled his fingers and rocked back. ". . . and while I see the value in it experimentally, I must advise against it. Without a pressing reason . . ."

"Are you denying me the approval?" Her heart had begun to pound.

"Oh, no, but I would think very carefully if I were you. Time travel has been used almost exclusively by the medical and criminal divisions. The criminal division reports great successes. People are now free to relive their antisocial acts positively. If the criminal does not wish to do this, the state can, for everyone's good, force him to unmake his criminal act."

Sema looked away and thought about Luci. Would they some day be able to put her in a ship and send her back to that moment in her infancy when stubbornness and rebellion began, and erase it, and bring her forward tranquil, dutiful? Would she be Luci then?

★   ★   ★

Mel's hearty voice called her back. "Civil libertarians objected at first, but their objections have had to change in the face of the need for public good. In a generation, crime will be eliminated; police and wardens will become social enablers, not agents of the state's punishment."

"I suppose I would give up a certain amount of free choice to achieve *that*."

"It's the psycho-medical applications that move me," Mel said, and leaned forward. "Soon, we will have all but ended suicide. The body is saved, gathered up carefully, and if the victim is below the age of sixty-five, is sent back for editing, remediation."

Sema felt a shudder but translated the move into something Mel would not notice.

"All this is by way of saying that perhaps it is *all* 'life enhancement' as it were."

"I will be going back to relive in the same way . . . the only difference will be that in the trip I will edit more of my life."

"Of course, your family approves . . ."

III

Berton was shocked and then wounded. "Why? You've been happy, haven't you? How could you have applied — gone ahead with something as important as this without consulting us first? What about Luci — our life together — I can't think why you've done this."

"In terms of your time experience, I won't be gone beyond the week it takes for lift-off and reentry.

I'll be brought back seven or eight days after the day
I left."

"That's not the point. The point is that you will
have left us, you will be gone — what did you say,
two years? You'll be building an identity, an experience, without us."

Sema had lied to Berton. Since leaving and re-
turning were the same, it could be done without their
knowing how long the stay was to be, and she had
doctored the papers she had given him to sign, blanking out the *0* of *20*. "My trip is not a criticism of you
or a demonstration against either you or Luci. This
is for me — another chance."

"But you'll come back two years older —"

"But then I'll be only four years younger than
you. I never could figure out why women are supposed to marry men older than they are. Women out-
live men. This way we're building hard widowhoods
for ourselves. Even if I stayed for . . . for twenty
years, we'd be more likely to die together than we
are now."

"It seems selfish to me," Berton said.

"Perhaps it is, but you don't realize what a value
there is in useful work. You went into metallurgy out
of no great love, but I think you feel challenged by
it. You're involved in a way of thinking. You con-
tribute . . ."

"So do you. The neighborhood — the home —"

"It's sleeper's work."

"You could go back to college . . ."

"I'm one year over the limit for career track. The
courses would be hobby track noncareer."

"What's wrong with that?"

She felt his sense of betrayal, that she was, in effect, wishing herself away from him, their daughter,

and the life they had made. She told none of her friends, hating their gossipy curiosity; years of courting the approval of others had made her wary and good at dissembling. She told no one she had doctored the printouts for a stay of twenty years. She talked to Luci last. Surely the courage of the act would engage her daughter. Luci took the news with complete indifference. Sema explained, asked for feelings, and was bewildered by Luci's anger.

"What do you want from me, a trumpet fanfare?"

"I thought you would be happy for me, encourage me. It's freedom we all might use, you, too, a generation from now."

"It's a way to talk over my head to people I don't know. Fine for you, but don't expect me to cheer about it."

"I might come back with some new ideas. You don't seem to like the ideas I have now."

"You might be a whole different personality when you get back, and that's not fair!"

"You try on a dozen new personalities every month. I thought you would be elated."

"I'm not. Other mothers don't abandon their children."

"Abandon? I'd be leaving for a week, two at most."

"Abandon in your head —"

"I will be doing what interests me, not forgetting either you or your father."

Luci pouted and sulked. So much for freedom of mind.

"Do you know who makes those trips?" Berton said a month later. He had studied. "— criminals and the mentally ill, society's misfits —"

"I'll be traveling with complete instructions and skin chips if I get in trouble or am unhappy where I am, but there won't be guards or the stigma of a red category."

"All our friends . . ."

"Our friends won't know I've gone."

They argued for days, probably to no purpose. The Green priority was so low, there might never be a place. For a dim possibility, she had alienated Luci, wounded Berton . . . He was deeply hurt. She had not expected that. Mel had said families gave no cheers . . .

We were building *this* life—" Berton kept insisting.

After weeks of wrangling and bitter silences, they decided that if the passport came through, she would go, and if it didn't, she would not try again. On the surface they lived their lives as before. Sema filled her time with Child Development Study Group and her usual work, being block captain for recyclables, and the organized visiting of sick neighbors. Time went by. There was still the brushfire war in Africa, the plague — it was, scientists now said, *Diplovirus Xanthus,* a variety of the same virus that had infected all the world's potatoes a few years ago and destroyed them. Could a plant virus be dangerous to humans? She listened, detached. Berton didn't mention the trip and neither did she. Each thought the other had consented.

The passport was delivered by computer like any ordinary letter and by a hard copy printout which told her that all the dates would have to be entered within one week and the trip would have to be undertaken within one month. Orientation was mandatory in three sessions. Contact numbers filled the screen.

It was suddenly real; the fantasy had been brought out of its retirement. "Well," Berton said, and then Sema said, "We decided, didn't we?"

"Yes," Berton said, "we decided."

"I'll be gone for ten days and I'll come back renewed."

"Renewed or new. Which?" he asked.

The first orientation was held at the passport office. Sema had asked Berton to come with her, but he had said, "This is your trip," and turned away. It wasn't anger — they had never been truly angry at each other, but she knew his disappointment was real. His hurt and Luci's resentment had so increased Sema's feeling of uniqueness in what she was doing that she was surprised to see a sizable crowd in the hall before the doors of the passport office's Time Travel Division. She turned to a nicely dressed woman near her. "I never knew so many people wanted to go back . . ." The woman was about to answer when two guards came down the hall escorting a line of shackled men. The other woman's eyes were riveted on the prisoners.

"Are they being *sent* back?" Sema asked in a whisper.

"Some are," the woman said. "Certain offenders go back voluntarily for minutes or hours. The serial killers and habitual criminals go back twenty years or more with retired volunteers so that the ages stay adjusted. Sometimes it works and sometimes it doesn't."

"You know a good deal about this," Sema said.

The woman sighed. She opened her purse and took out her validated card with the passport office's logo, the same Sema had received. The card was red. "That's a criminal . . ."

"Yes," the woman said, "Priority One. When prisoners . . . violent criminals, have gone back twice and still continue their behavior, their mothers are sent back under guard."

"Their *mothers?*"

"Yes. My son is that young man over there. I'm being sent back with him twenty-six years. I'm going back to have an abortion."

"Can they force . . ."

"Yes," the woman said, "for the public good." Her face showed nothing, but in her hand the red card trembled.

The orientation seemed to be mostly for the criminal priority. There were legal questions and everyone was told what he could and could not do. Each traveler was to be outfitted with skin-chip surveillance and a police captain told them what the penalties were for attempting to dismantle or remove these devices. Three historians with gray cards had a spirited argument with the official over the choice of landing place.

While they were arguing, the prisoners and some of the other people had begun to talk among themselves, uninterested in the problem. Sema leaned over to the red-card woman next to whom she was sitting. "I wish they would be quiet. That man is asking some interesting questions."

"They're protesting the involuntary part of this,"

the woman said. "You and those people, choose. *They* are — I am — being forced."

"How will you face what they'll . . . what's going to happen?"

"I don't know. I can't have a funeral for Jimmy; . . . three days from now he will never have existed. *I'll* remember him and that may be enough. I won't be able to validate him, his existence, in any way after this. My memory will be like a dream, or so they tell me. And there'll be therapy — lots of *therapy.*" She sighed.

The captain had begun to call people for their dimension tracks, printouts of time and place toward which the surveillance equipment would be beamed. "You will be contacted when your pattern is available. You will have seventy-two hours to make your arrangements." He paused and looked at a note. "Is there a green priority here?" Sema stood up. "The lines are full now. You may have to wait some time before you can be accommodated."

Sema nodded and sat down. The red-card men stared at her.

"Well — ?" Berton asked when Sema got home.

"Maybe a year." Sema tried to keep disappointment from her tone. She knew that her green status and its low priority proved to Berton the triviality of her wish. They went on as before, never mentioning the trip or its possibility. News items on holovision about time travel elicited no comments from either of them.

IV

The call came in June, much sooner than Sema expected. The computerized voice on her machine gave her validating number and said she was to prepare for a two-week lead time. The trip, green priority —twenty years — would place her in time span S. −20.40. The instructions said that on both sides of the trip she should arrange time for psychic reintegration. No one had researched the effects of extended travel; fifteen people had done it, but it was still experimental. Berton, if not agreeing, at least seemed reconciled. Luci was not. "You'll come back not caring." Luci had turned from her and walked away.

Sema knew it was time to tell Berton and Luci that the span was not two years but twenty. If the trip was a success, she would come back a woman of fifty-seven, fourteen years older than Berton, but not diminished by it, increased. Most people lived to their nineties — they would have three decades longer together and she wouldn't feel that she had thrown away her life.

Dear Berton and Luci,

I have a confession to make, one of cowardice, that my application was for twenty, not two, years. It went through. Why did I do it? I needed the time. It may not work out. I may turn out to be the same passive conformist I was the first time, but if that happens, I'll know the problem is not outside but in me, and I'll accept that, and come back in acceptance. If the trip does work, I'll come back with an interest, maybe even a passion, for something, that can only enrich all our lives. I can't talk to you,

Luci, and I know, Berton, how that hurts you. I think Luci is afraid of being like me, a woman lacking purpose and identity except as someone's wife and someone's mother.

Above all I want both of you to see this trip not as an act directed against you. I love both of you and I want you to love me, but the me I want you to love is a full human being, not a wife and mother by default and certainly not the grieving, contracted person you have had these last few years. I'll be older when I come back, and that may cause both of you some embarrassment, but I believe that what I hope to get from this trip will far outweigh the negatives, for all of us. If I didn't believe that, I wouldn't have worked so hard to go, suffering the loss of you, and the possible loss of your feeling for me. Your week, my twenty years — I hope the experience will enhance all our lives.

Your loving wife and mother,
SEMA

On the twenty-eighth of April, Sema reported, had her final briefing, and was fitted with her microchip devices. She and a group of red card holders and their guards went to the spaceport for boarding. That morning she had read the other side of Berton's newspaper for the last time. More news on the plague in Vézelay. The vectors of the virus had been found — skilled work by an agronomist . . . She hoped that this would be the last time she would feel the shame of not caring enough, of seeing the world as someone else's story. As they waited at the boarding ramp, her name was called to report to the podium. "It's not my low priority — I'm not being bumped?"

"Not that I see," the officer said. "It's a message. Pick it up at that computer."

Sema tapped her ID into the machine. It began to print. "If you have to go, go with our love. I knew you were going for twenty years and not two. They had it on the waiver I signed. It means you need this, or think you need it, a great deal. Luci moans and groans, but she loves you, too. B."

Prairie Village, Kansas, April. Time Span S. −20.40. She was Sema Stark and she was eighteen years old, and it was there like waking up after a nap, in a stretch into that former body. There was a breath, easy and long and then done, present, there. At first, as she had been instructed, she simply acclimated herself, watching, listening. School was out after graduation; there were few pressures. Geron, her father, and Dala, her mother, were now in vigorous middle age. She had forgotten how many activities they had enjoyed. She had forgotten, also, that their world-hopping years had come much later. She spent a day boating with them and liked it so much she asked to go again. They looked at her with unfeigned amazement.

"I want to hear more about your work, Geron, you never say much —"

"I didn't think you were interested," her father said.

She allowed herself to float along as she had the first time, but with better grace, serene. The present would change, was changing; new worlds, new dreams were forming in her moment by moment. She was eighteen physically and thirty-eight in her mind and experience. It was the emptiness of *these* years that would prevent her from living fully in the world she had left. Not this time — not now.

On the morning when two weeks of adjustment were over, she came to the breakfast table and put an orange and banana into the blender, watching Geron and Dala, who were reading the scope for the day's events. Her father used the morning's cool for planning. When the afternoon got hot, he would go downstairs and sit at his computer where he programmed and directed unmanned cargo in space. The hundreds of space stations he serviced were for the lively and adventurous who had left the earth. Their cultures had more leeway than those remaining. Because of its dwindling resources and delicate ecology, earth dwellers even then were careful people. Sema drank; the fruit mixture tasted flat. She had forgotten that the hydro-waste growth areas had not yet developed a way to make the flavors that would later be available.

"Geron . . ."

"What is it, mouse?" He turned from the newsscope and smiled at her.

"I'll be going away to college . . ."

Dala was smiling also, but there was something less enthusiastic and approving in her expression.

"I wanted to tell you," Sema said, "that I've decided to study this summer and apply for the career track in the fall, not the cultural one, the way I had planned."

They were surprised. "What would the study be?" her mother said. Dala worked in a linguistic bank as a translator-interpreter.

"I don't know — I thought I'd take one of the aptitude tests and find something that would give me a profession."

Her parents had been brought up carefully, as careful people. They didn't speak, but their obvious surprise was puzzling to Sema. Had she given so little evidence of her wishes for independence or self-fulfillment? After a while Geron looked at her and said, "The work is more difficult on the scholarly and professional tracks — you'll have little time for anything else."

She saw Dala looking at her searchingly. "You've changed somehow."

"I guess I'm maturing," Sema said.

When she thought about it later, Sema decided that the reason for Dala's skepticism might be that her high-school years had given no evidence of seriousness. Her friends were a bright but heedless group. Now, she found them silly and boring, obsessed with their looks and the minutiae of dressing and of boy-girl intrigues. It was a relief to slide away by saying, "My parents want me to go . . ." and "Mother says I have to . . ." She had no desire to waste precious time learning how to relate to other eighteen-year-olds. She had discovered, for example, Geron and Dala's library; there were tapes, even books, and computer programs that she found far more stimulating than Lula or Siri. The discovery surprised Sema, as her parents themselves did. Neither of them was as rigid or demanding as she had seen them to be. She had thought that they would protest her college decision. She had marshaled arguments for the more serious study, but nothing of the sort had happened. The other time, she had taken the cultural track, which was a sampling of the various branches of learning — college basics. There had been lots of social life and parties. Scholars were on a special track, learning advanced research techniques and an expertise in very limited fields. The professional tracks were somewhat broader, but as intense: law, medicine, science, social arts, economics, fine arts. Now that she had gone back to her eighteenth year to remake her life, and bearing the additional private weight of Berton's anguish and Luci's feelings of abandonment, she wanted to make the most of every moment of the twenty years she had won back. She was excited now, eager. She could hardly wait to move into the new life that would result in her changed being.

Through the summer, Sema steeped herself in Geron and Dala's library. There was such an intensity about her reading that her parents, at first gratified and surprised, became worried. "Too thoughtless," Dala said, "and then suddenly too studious."

"I'm catching up, that's all," Sema said, "please don't worry."

Her grades had not been good but her brainscan and interviews convinced the Admissions Department at K State to give her conditional acceptance in the career or scholars' track. The brain metabolism study showed dominance in Moench's Fold, so Sema went into the science program in botany.

V

Her first year was spent catching up and learning to study. She was closed in and very lonely. This was partly due to the dislocation in age. She had not expected to miss Berton so much, or in so many ways. She had been used to generous and regular love-making. Even though her body was now the body of an eighteen-year-old virgin, her emotional life was that of a mature woman; she ached for his hands, his closeness; she woke from sleep in that need. She was used to her maternal feelings, too, to guidance and teaching. She had been used to talking things over with Berton in the cooperative life of a married woman, not the competitive life of a student and adolescent. But the intellectual part of her existence, long suppressed, woke and stretched.

It became obvious that the minutiae of research and scholarship wasn't for her and she declared for the career track. Brain studies agreed with her own preference — eco-botany. The study might lead to the development of plants to stabilize depleting soils or new food sources for the huge human and animal population of the world. She studied microbial safety and symbiotic links. There was an urgency in this work that was felt by professors and students alike. The challenge inspired and excited her. Most of the vegetables that were being produced with recombinant genes were nutritious and keepable, but so bitter or bland that they had to be cooked with flavor pouches. Part of Sema's studies in the second year reminded her of nothing more than a return to housewifery. Her experience as a cook years in the future got in her way.

*   *   *

She knew, for example, that the powdered celeriac her teachers were praising would not succeed as a substitute. It would not because it *had* not. She regretted all the energy they were wasting on its development. She had not anticipated the impatience and frustration this would cause her. Most of the daily news was irritating, too; people worried about things that would not mature into actual threat and trivialized what would later be seen as serious. After a while, she stopped reading newspapers and watching holovision. There had been warnings during orientation about behavior which might change macrohistory. Her own age was worried about her making stock purchases or affecting the news. The Monitoring Agency might as well have left her to herself for all the financial advantage she took of her return. In her orientation they had also warned her about the effect of the ordinary impact of her life on other lives. She had been warned to keep her circle small. This, in addition to her demanding studies, kept her from friendships. She was smooth and pleasant. She glided away.

There was danger in any involvement; it was as though she had a terminal illness with uncertain years to live. She studied, immersed herself in ecological science, habitats, microclimates, and plant anatomy and physiology. She began to understand and be awed and excited by the complex relationships between plant and plant, plant and parasite, plant and insect. She discovered a creative wit in herself based on the knowledge she was gaining, a way of seeing other relationships that drew enthusiastic praise from her professors. Now and then one of them gave her a job to do, researching or reporting for his own on-going work. This was a relief to Sema because her free time was barren and needy.

Part of her protection from the contaminate world came from a maturity her body did not show. Her schoolmates were mostly kids to her and even the studious ones had the green blush of immaturity: self-centeredness, like small whirlpools drawing inward from their orbits. The older students, absorbed by present trends and politics, could be acquaintances but not friends. Her knowledge of the future made prediction too tempting, so she stayed away. She did draw closer to Geron and Dala and their friends, and she came from school as often as she could during her first and second years to be with them. With each visit, her respect for her parents increased. It was another surprise.

During Sema's third year, Professor Ana Bently asked her into the research office. "Seth Pritchard is coming to us this summer on a co-university grant. He and I have developed a variety of rice that's grown with little water and during a very short season. We need students to plant, care for, and observe this rice and other experimental grains in several altitudes and microclimates. The project fits into the Field Summer, but it's in Colorado and will continue there for several years. Can you be available for that time?" She said she could.

Dr. Pritchard came out to K State to organize the project. He was younger than Dr. Bently, a dark, gentle man — Sema thought he must have some Spanish or Mexican blood. The field camp was at

Cripple Creek, and she left Kansas for the Colorado
mountains late in May. She and some graduate students set up the camp. There were to be control crops
to work with and two other crops of newly developed barley and millet. When Seth Pritchard arrived,
the project came alive with his enthusiasm and energy. The group did as much in a day as it had done
in a week. Who would volunteer for the control
work? He looked around, his expression whimsical.
No one raised a hand. They all wanted the exciting
new part of the project. Then Sema said, "I'll do it."

"Good. We'll all be sharing every part of the project formally and informally," he said. "It's all new —
we've done beautifully in the lab but Mother Nature
is not a doting parent. I'm banking on the success of
this rice. My students think the barley has the biggest
potential. Of course, no one knows."

Sema bit her lip. Someone did know. She said,
"Whatever happens, it's good to be part of this project." He smiled. A graduate student guffawed and
Sema thought, "You don't know about wasting a
life. I do."

They worked soils on all kinds of slopes and in valleys. Seth and Ana dug and planted along with their
students. In the simple environment of the camp,
with no newspapers or holovision for Sema to guard
against, her usual formalities relaxed and so did the
distance between the other students and the professors. Sema opened up to the full enjoyment of her
present life. When not at work, they swam in the
river and fished and read and wrote. Seth taught
Sema and three other students some basic rock climb-
ing and how to sing two or three songs in Romany.
His people had been Gypsies. "Shut out," he said,

"something my grandmother did — I don't know what." But he taught them the words of the songs carefully. Sema realized that he never would have shared so much of himself in the formal atmosphere of school. When asked about her own background, she told a story or two about Geron and Dala. Sometime later, Seth said to her, "You speak of your parents with affection. That has a pleasant sound, nowadays. The one-kid world isn't easy."

"They're good people."

"You seem more mature than the usual college junior. I notice the others confiding in you — like an older sister."

"Field Summer fever," Sema said. Seth laughed, but the laugh was gentle.

Even with the reversible sterilization they had all undergone, custom forbade unmarried sex. Field Summer put young people together in the high and beautiful mountains with a crisp iridescent air and a sense of otherworldly remove. Lovesickness was epidemic. Sema, unattached and uninvolved, was a good confidante. Though she looked no older than the other juniors, there was an undefinable air of centeredness and poise about her. Ana began to look to her for help with camp problems. The three of them were often together; they worked well.

As she had suspected, the alternate grains, the new barley and millet, were proving more adaptable than the rice. As unthinking as Sema had been, even she knew that everyone would be using the new grains in another decade; everyone would eat barley flour products, especially after the tuber failure that would come late in the next decade with *Diplovirus Xanthus* —

★   ★   ★

But Diplovirus was ten years in the future and Seth was eager for his new strain of rice. Sema wished she could tell him why the rice wouldn't work. Time after time she stopped herself from the forbidden words: I *know* — I've *seen* — we *will use* . . . look at the *barley;* look at changing the taste of the *millet.* Your *real task* is . . . Instead she watched him waste his energy and enthusiasm on the wrong parts of the experiments, saying only, "The alternative grains are doing exceptionally well."

She thought her closeness to Ana and Seth would disappear after the summer, but there was data to collect and evaluate and Seth asked her to come to Greeley and work as his assistant at the university. She could finish her schooling there.

When she called Geron and Dala to tell them, she realized in the middle of a sentence that her enthusiasm was as much for working with Seth Pritchard as for the project itself. Her parents were proud and pleased.

"I underestimated you," Geron said. "Forgive me. You seemed to be . . . until the spring before college — so giddy. I always felt I had to watch you and guide you or you would do something foolish."

"Don't expect my name to appear on anything that's published," Sema began.

"We don't care about that," Dala said. "I guess I'm seconding your father. You seemed, as he said, until the spring before school, so diffused and yet so restless. Here you've found a focus . . ."

Had she really appeared that way to them, all those years ago, restless, diffuse, giddy? She had always thought it was they who had limited and thwarted her. She turned back to her work of packing. In a week she would be working out of Greeley at the university there, studying and being an assistant to Seth. If only she could move him subtly toward the work on which he should be concentrating.

VI

Her future-now-past, Berton and Luci, were fading for her. She hadn't realized that having no contact with her husband or daughter meant that every hint of them, every word, memento, reminiscence would have to be purged. Paradoxically, there might be a Berton *here,* in this world, a man of twenty-five working in Germany doing metallurgical studies in alloy rebonding, falling in and out of love, in his own words, daily. She wasn't informed enough about time-warp and time physics to know if he was there. She did know that she dared not try to find him and that the life she had had was moving farther and farther from her as she came closer and closer to it. In seventeen years she would have to go back to the life she had left, but, she now realized, profoundly changed. She could remember having wanted that.

And she yearned to talk to Berton, to see him, to be reassured about the turn her life was taking. She was falling in love with Seth Pritchard and worry about it made her restless and unable to concentrate. She thought about him all the time, not only as he lived now, but as he would be later, in her world to come. Would he be alive then? Would he have realized his dream or found another? In ten years he would be

unable to apply as a father. He was now thirty-six
years old, she knew, and had been divorced. She pursued her studies diligently, all the better to keep her
mind off Seth. On the afternoons in his lab, she
worked with formality, seeing that they were never
alone together and that their conversations were
never personal. Subtly, she urged the millet and barley studies forward. She had to acknowledge her feelings for Seth to herself, but she never allowed herself
the slightest action. In that way, she thought, the
longings would die naturally. After the project was
over, she planned to move back to Kansas, where she
could take any one of a dozen research options somewhere else, and her lines with Seth Pritchard would
spin out and snap and be gone. Then she could get
back to the world she had laid claim to at such cost.

The next summer they went again to the field camp
in Cripple Creek. They had a different group of students. Ana was staying back at K State to conduct
lab experiments on the rice gene. The presence of
two aggressive and misfit seniors and Ana's absence
subtly changed the tone of things from a model like
a family to one like a tribe. The other students, used
to excessive order and control, were unable to react
quickly to what was happening.

At first Sema thought the change was in her mind.
Isolated and suffering, lovesick herself, she knew she
would be seeing desire all around her. It was almost
a musk hanging in the air. Without the accustomed
structure and constraints, the two young men became arrogant in their freedom. There were dares
and fights and pairings and weeping at night in the
girls' tent. The evening fires, where the year before

all the students sang together and told stories, were this summer attended only by Seth and Sema and the few celibate-for-principle and the cast-off or unchosen among the students. Seth was baffled, then angry. "This isn't supposed to be happening." At last the students themselves began to voice their confusion and anxiety. Sema was relieved and went to Seth with a group of them.

"It's Hauser and Ballantine," one of the girls said, "the rest follow." The others admitted they were afraid. They talked about approaches.

When the question came around to Sema, she said, "I think it's gone too far for meetings. I think you need to call the university and order the suspension of the students from *there*. It isn't as though they hadn't been warned or don't know that what they're doing is wrong."

"Could ten of us run the plots?" Seth asked. "If not, two years' testing is down the drain."

"I think we could, until the school sends more people." There was a sigh of relief from the students.

Later Seth said to her, "What made you so sure we could do the work without those two?"

"I'd been thinking how to allocate the labor. It might mean mini-camps at Windy Gap, and the Overlook — four and four, and then we'd meet on weekends . . ."

"I'll call Ana tomorrow. It will be difficult —"

"I think we can do it."

"You're no older than the others . . . but —"

"I am somewhat older."

"No, I've seen your records —" and he caught himself too late to change his tone to something lighter. Of course he had seen her records — he had

had to fill out and sign her application for assistant-
ship — but his tone said that he had remembered,
considered . . . She heard from her own loneliness,
respect, and affection, his words and his stopping of
the words. He had noticed — "All the students on
field placement —"

"Yes," she said. "My parents gave me more responsibility than most children have." The words
sounded flat in her ears. Had she hated lying so much
in her old life? She had always felt guilt and discom-
fort in her evasions to her acquaintances, to Geron
and Dala, to Berton. For years she had dissembled
about contentment she didn't feel, but those were
evasions — these were outright lies, and the lie was
thickening like plaster in the mouth.

The ten of them worked happily and very hard on
the project. Sema was grateful for the busyness. It
kept her too exhausted to think about Seth and the
mistake he was making on his rice, and his hands and
his eyes and his smile, his having thought he knew
her age so quickly, and the now obvious struggle
against his preference for her.

Then it was August and in the uplands of the Rockies
autumnal colors announced themselves on the north-
facing slopes. Aspen went yellow overnight, mountain maple turned delicately pale gold before their
eyes. The noons of heat were captured in the cold
upland breezes of late afternoon. Summer field camp
was coming to an end. They were lighting their last
evening fires. In two months Sema would be forty-
two, and she knew she had not thought hard enough,
not imagined deeply enough, what her fuller life
would mean. She and the time travel people, even
the therapist, had been interested in *things,* in lies to

be told and jobs to be gotten where there would be
no publicity, in prescience and stockmarket ventures
and macrohistory. They had, none of them, talked
about friendships, loving, about being a colleague, a
rival, taking up the threads of a world and being
woven in, of belonging. They had talked only about
not belonging. Already she was more intellectually
alive than she had ever been. She was reading, thinking, integrating, meeting as colleagues people at
work, intent, aiming for the heights of their profes-
sions. In eco-botany she and they were planning
world change, its basics, from what people would eat
to their habits of work. She had begun; she would
continue. All of her intellectual purposes were being
realized, but neither she nor her advisers had understood that the intellectual and emotional parts of
life, when it was lived as it should be, would merge.
The day was lived in a world, and that world was
peopled.

Now she had to sit at the fire and weigh the in-
tangibles of her experience. Her life as a time traveler,
green category, was meant to be twenty years of celibacy and minimal human contact. She had been
warned against entanglements, even close friendships. She had been sent back to find herself profes-
sionally while she looked spiritually and psychically
toward home. Now she realized she had changed
homes.

Berton may have predicted all this. He had not given
it voice because he would have been too frightened
of sounding jealous and sentimental by saying,
"You'll fall in love." She had fallen in love with this
place, this life, and was now hoping against hope to
escape from investing life in the life she was living.

★   ★   ★

Seth came to the fire and sat by her. The others had gone to the shelter momentarily. He had been visiting their camp, checking. "Three more days," he said. "Thanks to you we'll leave on time. The plots have all been harvested and there will be all the lab work to do — making flour, cooking, eating — all the tests, and of course the chemistry —"

"Yes."

"There will have to be three visits back to the site here through the fall and winter to analyze the ground and the stalks and to plan for next season . . ." She said nothing, giving him no help. "Would you like to come along?" he said. "We'll be gone only the weekends — two or three weekends and during vacations — you won't miss classes."

"Can't you get Ana?"

"Ana is going to do the Kansas plots. We'd be alone, unless you aren't ready . . . or couldn't. This is hard for me. I'm telling you that I want us to be together."

"I'm only a student," Sema said. She wanted to say, "I'm older than you," but didn't. Long ago she had counted the difference in their ages — seven years.

He spoke quietly, unused to being personal. "I don't approve of professors falling in love with their students. It happens, though. When it does, I blame the teacher if there is an affair. The teacher is older; he has the power and is the guide. I've been attracted to students two or three times but I never acted on the emotion. I laughed it away. This time it's different."

He was so blunt and sounded so tired of wrangling with his feelings that Sema knew they were past the time of dissembling. She looked at him but couldn't see him clearly. He was only a shape on the other side of the fire. Her eyes had filled with tears. Here comes another lie, one more evasion. She took a breath and heaved the half-truth forward.

"I came here to work, to find a career and meaning for my life, not to fall in love. I'm already married. My husband is . . . abroad."

"You've been at school for four years — two Field Summers —"

"Yes."

"Do you go back . . . vacations, holidays?"

"No, we're separated. I don't see him, but falling in love was not part of . . . not what I wanted . . ."

He nodded. She saw his eye-gleam, the fire reflected in it as he moved his head, nodding.

"It happened against my will."

"But it did happen," Seth said.

"Yes," and she let her head fall so she couldn't see him.

"You can't have been married long," he said after a while.

She said quietly, "I am older than I look. I'm not twenty-one, and I am married."

"I don't want to hurt you in any way," he said. "I've told you how I feel — tell me how you want it to be." His voice was soft and very gentle. They stared into the fire.

There was a sound behind them. The others were coming. Sitting where they were, across from one another, there was no feeling of the others intruding. Sema was happy at this. Seth sighed and welcomed them to the fire, saying, "Have you ever wondered why we're sitting here burning wood to carbon instead of using heat bars? My back is freezing and the front of me is half burnt . . ." They laughed.

Mari, one of the girls, said, "Man does not live by heat bars alone."

"What does man live by?"

Luke said, "Fire has a different feel to it than heat from a heat bar — something ancestral. My folks have one of those electric fireplaces."

"The smoke keeps the insects away," Jinn said. They all laughed.

Sema thought: "I will not live a celibate intellect for sixteen more years. I will not live without befriending because I hate lies, not loving because Berton is at home for two weeks alone and wondering where I am." When they were moving into their Ream shelters for the night, she passed Seth and said, "Yes, Professor. Yes."

Very quietly so only she could hear he answered, "Thank you. You've become . . . very . . . important to me."

VII

IT IS UNLAWFUL

1. To carry artifacts of any kind to or from past time points.
2. To travel without disease inoculation and appropriate time in decontamination procedures.
3. To contract debts or make agreements that run beyond the trip duration, mortgages, wills, etc.
4. To contract in marriage, to bear or sire offspring.

5. To engage in social or political group activities conducive to the alteration of macrosociology or macrohistory.
6. To attempt to persuade or dissuade person or persons into courses of action conducive to the alteration of macrosociology or macrohistory.
7. To wager, purchase, inform, advise regarding the future, economically, politically, scientifically, or medically; to predict, forecast, or auger.

There were a dozen others. She had learned them, signed them, agreed to them easily in the headlong pursuit of what she had seen herself becoming, and the speed of her transition blurred for her the day by day truths of loneliness and loss.

She and Seth met on weekends, discreetly. They were careful, but they did not have to worry about Sema's becoming pregnant. Both of them had been patched for sterilization, Seth without having sired any children, Sema as a nubile girl. Luci had been unmade for her as easily as the murderous son must have been unmade for the red-card mother at the orientation, now four years ago.

At first they worried about their sterilization patches. The chemical, a rebonding hormone, sometimes produced pain with intercourse, and both Sema and Seth stopped taking libido-suppression pills. They were anxious until they found themselves free of the negative side effects. Sema had learned that life was even more narrow and stringent here than it was later to be. Some food was still rationed, travel was restricted, and the housing shortage was extreme. Seth had a small apartment in faculty hall. They could meet only off campus on weekends.

But they were deeply in love and well suited to one another. She needed his sweetness, he relished her enthusiasm. Years of teaching the career track had made him cynical, and as he watched the long dying of his rice project, he was cheered and bolstered by her delight in all their accomplishments, and her joy in the simple facts of living and working.

As she and Seth became closer, Sema had to struggle more and more with keeping the rules she had signed, the breaking of which would mean return and prosecution. She had been marginally guilty of "advising, informing, predicting." She as much as told Seth that in the future it would be the minor grains, the barley and millet, altered in texture and flavor, that would create the plenty they wished for. She could not tell him why it was necessary to hurry the project. Soon *Diplovirus Xanthus* would all but eliminate the potato as a food.

As she spent more time with Seth and invested feeling, passion, love more and more fully, Sema began to wonder about what her skin patch — it looked like a mole on her shoulder — was monitoring. She tapped in information by means of a code she touched to the skin patch, but that was about location and health, checking in. They would monitor her area for outward manifestations — newspaper articles, real estate transfers, legal records. They couldn't monitor for all the things against which they had warned her — persuading, dissuading, loving, befriending, intimacy, acceptance.

*   *   *

After a year of seeing one another, Seth asked Sema to get a divorce and marry him. She lied yet again, telling him she had already spoken to her husband. She had never told Seth his name or where he lived. She spent a long weekend away, thinking, and when she came back, told him that she had asked for but not received her freedom. "There are legal entanglements but not spiritual ones," she said. She did take Seth home to meet Geron and Dala, who liked him even though he was a good deal older than Sema. She had asked Seth not to mention her former marriage. She had also lied to her parents about legal problems Seth had with his former wife. Lies and more lies, more and more painful because she told them to people she loved. The next semester she and Seth moved into university housing as coviviants, a common-law relationship, which did not confer legal or childbearing rights.

They were whole and happy together, united by love and work, excited by the urgency Sema knew and Seth guessed at. They felt themselves at the heart of vital events. A year went by and then another even more quickly. The long vista of twenty years, once seen as almost a lifetime, had closed to fourteen, to thirteen. Sema took her master's in eco-agronomy and began working on her Ph.D. Their apartment was a meeting place of excited agronomy students, and she and Seth were colleagues in projects that were widening in scope and importance. They understood one another's moods and patterns of thought, they filled their off hours with laughter and fun. At last Seth stopped work on the rice and threw the program's efforts into the secondary grains on which they had had great success. She used her doctoral thesis to introduce the recombinant, tasty, non-doughy barley thriving on land so arid it had never supported a crop before. Seth introduced a millet that tasted like sweet corn.

A quirk of Sema's behavior puzzled Seth. She would not allow her name to appear with his as collaborator on any of their articles or monographs. She refused to be pictured anywhere. "I don't want my husband to make demands," Sema said. "It will be safer for us if I have no public notoriety whatever."

"He can't enforce such a condition — you have a different life, now."

"You can't know how true that is," Sema said, "but the less public my life is, the better. It's a very small price to pay for real freedom."

She began to feel a restlessness in Seth. "Is it the project?"

"No."

"What, then?"

"I thought coviviant was good enough; we were together, *are* together and happy, happier than I thought two people could be — Suddenly, it's not enough."

"Why not?"

"I want a marriage, a family, our child, a permanent . . . a *life* together."

She couldn't tell him that she now had only eleven years left in his world. "I'm still married," she said, "you know that."

"We're together. We have every expectation of staying together. Why not go to your husband and face him with it."

"I have. The situation isn't reasonable. He has his own motives."

"Why don't you ask him here, let us meet with him and talk it all out?"

"That's impossible."

"Why?"

Lie, another lie, gagging the throat but big enough to stop the inquiry. She told Seth that her husband was in organized crime, in a Family, and that enemies of the Family could hurt him through her. If she stayed quiet, remained married to him, and made no public stir, she could do as she pleased, love whom she pleased, live as she pleased, all under his protection. She had already had her allotted child, the safety of whom might also be compromised if she filed for divorce or tried to remarry. "We are separated and there has been no contact, although I miss . . . the child."

"Can't I even know his name?"

"No; even that's too dangerous."

She left him no way to prove or disprove. He loved her; he trusted her, but she would give no names, no corroboration, and her story never changed. There followed the darkest months of her life. Seth was living in silent pain. There was nothing she could do to ease it.

VIII

And the years kept closing: ten, nine. She had her doctorate in ecological agronomy and a project that was a lifework of world importance. There were invitations to present at universities in Europe and Asia and grant money available to extend the millet and barley projects. Barley would soon be as versatile as soy beans and would be grown everywhere. Sema and Seth continued to live and work together; she waited for his grief to die back to sorrow. "We could have had a child and lost it," she said.

"I know." He believed her because of the look he saw in her now and then, a look of regret, of sadness, sometimes of grief. They found themselves huddling together in their moments alone, sitting close as consoling mourners. They brought one another little gifts, flowers, toys, they sat wordlessly together at their open window watching the night come on in an abstracted way none of their students would have imagined.

"I keep dreaming about it," he said on one of those evenings, "about our being a family. In the old days they had big families, you know, and if a child died they'd have another."

"Don't make it hurt more than it has to."

Eight, seven. They had recombined the barley to a harder kernel, the millet to a variety of flavors. The stalks turned out to have special qualities as cattle forage. Secondary problems were emerging, secondary benefits also. *Diplovirus* appeared suddenly, taking Sema by surprise. She had thought to work to prevent it, but because of the new grains she and Seth and others had developed, the potato-dependent countries of the world were saved from starvation. The U.S., Russia, and China shipped the grains all over the world and seed grain was planted in every ecological combination. There was talk of a Nobel prize. Six years . . .

Later that year, Meyers and Poor announced discovery of the Luria Layer. Time travel experiments began. The first volunteer time travelers went and came

back. There was an immense excitement. Seth and
Sema, busy with their work, were only passingly interested at first, and then Seth thought he should sign
up for a trip. "Think of the possibilities in extinct
grasses. I could go back to Paleolithic times and recover . . . There's no telling what could be com-
bined . . ."

Everyone began to speak of time travel's potential.
"Think of the vacations!" Calabrese cried as he un-
packed his lunch at the lab. "Imagine the trips, the
education . . ."

"Think of knowing — really *knowing* — what Jesus looked like, what he said . . ." Betty Barnes
said.

Sema remembered the quiet mother at the passport office holding her red priority card. "I think if
we all got together *now* we could keep the state from
using time travel to regulate human behavior," she
said.

Calabrese, Betty, and Ida Jones, who had come in
with him, stared at her in amazement for a moment,
and not understanding what she had said, went on.
"The government would probably limit the number
of vacations. You couldn't have the Crucifixion overwhelmed by Easter tourists or more bystanders at
Ford's Theatre than John Wilkes Booth could fight
his way past."

"Think," Sema persisted. "If you were in the family of a murder victim — would you be bothering
about vacation trips?"

"I suppose I might want to go back to remake an
event like that," Calabrese said, "and if I did, what
would be the harm?"

"The state will have a compelling reason to control time the way it now controls housing, employ-

ment, and childbirth," Semá said. "Don't you see
how law might force prisoners to relive their moments in crime, unmaking crime, and in the end,
forcing abortion as a form of crime prevention."

"What?"

"I think time travel will mean more choice in
some ways. I think it would be wonderful in some
ways — freeing — but much less wonderful in others," Sema said. "Individually, it might give great
opportunities, but wouldn't it be natural for the state
to use time travel as a way of unmaking horrible and
then tragic and then perhaps simply unfortunate
events, and if the unmaking didn't work, of unmaking the people who caused them?"

"What would be wrong with that? We practice
abortion if the one child we can have is a child we
don't want. You can't expect parents to accept that
their only child might be a criminal."

"Sacrificing a fetus is not the same as unmaking a
growing person. For the community it would be as
though he had never been, but for the parents, because *they* would remember him, don't you see — it
would be murder." The people in the lab looked at
her with incredulous wonder.

The papers carried stories and queries that both trivialized and lost the issue. Would we meet ourselves?
Would time travel be the fountain of youth? Sema
tried and failed to organize oversight groups at the
university. There were religious people who did not
want to accept time travel at all. They were the only
ones who came to the meetings she called. At first
she was gratified by their acceptance of her points,
but instead of oversight they wanted prohibition.
Travel in time was sinful, it arrogated God's view to

man's eye, it ruptured His set course of things. The rest of the country seemed to accept the idea uncritically but as a toy. Sema wrote a speech anonymously. It was reasoned and, Seth said, convincing and eloquent. She took the risk of having it presented at the first International Convention to Legislate and Control Time Travel. The speech was received with polite disinterest. Sema didn't think it safe to go, but Neva Ronson, who gave the speech, said that the delegates were too busy setting rules for international agreements that would keep the nations from using the Luria Layer to try to remake the past at crucial political moments in order to affect the balance of power. Seth was surprised at Sema's strong feeling on this issue and her venture into politics. He had never known her to do so much as read a newspaper or watch holovision news. He thought it might be her attempt to deal with their private grief, a sublimation of the pain she felt at their stunted hope of being a family. Sema let him think it, but it gave her pain that the man she loved was so blind to the possibilities of the new discovery. For Sema, it was Year Five.

Then one day he came to her in a fidget of hope. Even his voice had changed. "Lanier and his wife don't want children. They'll substitute for us."

"What?"

He thought her sudden pallor was shock from happiness. "John Lanier talked to me at lunch. They *want* to remain childless. They're willing to let us have a child as theirs. I told them you have had a child and were permanently sterile. They're willing to go through the process. They'll appear in court and sign a dedicating deposition. It's a hell of a sac-

rifice because it means permanent sterilization afterwards for them — they won't be able to change their
minds after we've taken the child." She looked at
him. She saw he had been crying. "It's our chance,
Sema — it's our chance to have a family!"

"Would the state let a coviiant couple have a
child?"

"That's the point — I looked it up. Since neither
of us is reversing sterility, there's nothing to stop us
from having ten kids if we can get them produced by
other parents."

Sema sat in the dustmote sun that came through the
solar garden window. In five years she would have
to go to back. Geron would die next year; Dala
would move to Malaysia beyond Sema's power to
wound. The wounding of Seth would be total and
forever. She would, one day, disappear. There would
be no trace. It seemed that before her disappearance
there would have to be other wounds. The agreement they would make with the Laniers would be a
legal document and Sema was expressly forbidden to
sign such a document, which would be registered
someplace, spotted by monitors. Even if she talked
Seth into signing alone, there would be abandonment
of a child. She had already abandoned Luci, not in
time but spiritually, and she had told Berton by her
choices that life with him had not been full or satisfying enough for her. If he thought so before she left,
he would know so now — as soon as she set foot on
the ground at her return, the hated, inevitable return
to her former life. Her directive had been to cause as
little harm as possible, to make so small a ripple in
the world she was visiting that when she left, little
would be disturbed. Seth wanted a child. In five years

he would be alone, having been left with nothing of her but memory. If there were a child, he would have that child and an identity as husband and father. In normal life mothers died . . . Normal life . . . In five years she would have to return to normal life. It was a life where her present expertise would be unusable. Education at her advanced age was leisure enrichment. She wouldn't be able to get another doctorate and work in the field. She would be the old Sema, and there would have to be more lies . . .

Seth misread her silence. "I can hardly believe it myself, but it's real. I feel like dancing, like singing. I feel like making love."

They did, he with a passion she hadn't known he had. She, too, had read those old stories about people in the past, people who had not had to reverse sterility to have children. Everyone knew how harmful overpopulation had been, but there was something joylessly careful about the way everything was done, now. The state was producing risk-free, etiolated people, tiptoe people, uncomfortable in their planned world. Soon they would be unable even to commit suicide. There was crime now. Soon that would be banished by time travel. No one would mourn the passing of crime, but choice would be dwindling with it. There would soon be acquiescence only. Sema was moving into her own times inexorably. Five years. In five years, she would have to leave this world, having caught up to her own.

She lied. Simulating joy was more difficult than any lying she had ever done. They went to the Laniers and were rhapsodic, so rhapsodic that they forgot the legalizing forms. She told Seth they could wait until the baby came.

There followed months of Seth's hope and Sema's dread, waiting for Halun Lanier to become pregnant. There were bills and examinations and promises and then Halun did get pregnant and was sick and was spotting and was swelling and might lose and might not and then there were lies and more lies and Halun's vacillations and Seth's anguished fear that Halun would want to keep the child and nights when *she* lay in bed awake and listened to Seth walk the floor.

Ulu was born, officially to the Laniers, and decreed to Seth. They had a child. As coviviants they couldn't get married housing so they lived tight as mice in Seth's apartment, the third room half study, half nursery. As coviviants Seth took official claim for Ulu and Sema did not have to sign.

Year Four. The International Academy of Agronomy gave its highest honor to Seth for his work on recombinant grains. Sema again refused to be listed as co-recipient or to be photographed or interviewed or to go to claim the prize and its money, but now she was able to excuse herself on the grounds that Ulu needed her at home. Year Three. Year Two.

In spite of the pressure, Sema was happy with Ulu and with Seth's obvious delight. She kept the dark boundaries as far away as she could. Only in dreams — a picnic in a sunny field ringed by storms, a festive house surrounded by police — was the anxiety beyond her control. She sang to Ulu and told him stories — many that she had told Luci, whose favorite, when she was six or seven, was *The Snow Queen*. She would never know Ulu at six or seven, and once or twice it made her cry. She told Ulu the beginning of the story, how the imp broke his mirror and the pieces went into the world and got in people's eyes and how they then saw the world as ugly and distorted. Ulu liked the story and sometimes laughed when she used it as a metaphor for his bad moods: "That angry mirror piece is in your eye today."

How wide and plenteous the twenty years had seemed, stretching ahead of her; how distant the end had once been. Now it was two years away: May 3; the coordinates ready to be tapped in — not Kansas anymore, but Fort Collins, Colorado. Ulu and Seth and Sema were a family. Sema had tried not to love the tiny baby that Halun had with symbolic dignity placed in her arms. The little boy he had become, had broken her resolve. The loss was inevitable and inexorable, but their living together, Seth's joy and Ulu's obviously loving and happy personality, made the knowledge almost unbearable. Ulu would be almost four when she left, and Seth only fifty-two. Sometimes she thought she would tell him that she was a time traveler. It would mean breaking the law and, if he were angry enough to report her, possible legal action. Everyone knew about time travel now. The physical experiments had been done and the first criminals had already been sent back experimentally, for revision. Social costs were being discussed at last. That therapist — she had forgotten his name — had even mentioned the reviving — pre-viving, really, of suicides. In a few years, people who wanted to end their own lives would have to vaporize or scatter themselves or disappear to make their deaths irreversible.

On a winter morning, awakening from another dream of approaching menace, Sema realized that she would have to begin planning her disappearance, her change of times — of worlds. In the orientation it had looked easy — disappearance after time spent so invisibly that such disappearance affected no one. But she had achieved, loved, she was all but legally married, all but a legal mother, and now the only way she could leave Seth without his feeling hideously misused and betrayed would be to die. If she told the truth she would reveal a twenty-year span of lies, evasions, and deceptions, about who she was, the very self she had given him. Having set the lie, she had no choice but to live by it, and that would mean to die by it, to fake her own death with another dozen lies. For a month, during which she went every day to the university labs and studied reports on Seth's barley and millet, she was holding up the possibilities, turning them this way and that, watching them bite into Seth in her mind, watching him suffer her disappearance, her suicide, her murder. She decided against simple disappearance. She couldn't allow his sorrow and loss to be compounded by mysteries, searches, official denials. With a faked death, he could marry again; another woman would be happy and lucky . . . Then she turned that over, figured it, mulled it, while her unseeing eye looked down lists of germination rates in a new millet. Since there could be no body to identify, it would have to be a death so obvious that no one would bother trying to look for a body. How? It wouldn't be death by suicide; she couldn't give him that kind of pain.

How could she provide a body murdered or dead of
natural causes, which would be taken for hers? Missing — presumed dead. Suddenly, idly, she thought
about *Diplovirus*. What was to happen? Wasn't that
plague, that coming plague — hadn't that been
linked . . . ?

There was to be a plague with thousands of deaths,
and it would be associated with the *D/X* virus,
though no one at that time would know how. That
virus had attacked potatoes, and because of its extent,
the rotten tubers had simply been plowed under in
most of the places where they had been grown. The
soil had been tested in the first and second seasons;
the virus had not remained in the soil; the land had
been declared safe for other cultivation. Still, the
plague was coming; she could not intrude on history
by trying to stop it or even by giving a warning, but
she might find a way to disappear in the panic and
confusion of its early days. There would be mass
burials done in panic — If her death were there, it
would be a sad thing, but it would be a death in the
line of duty as it were, and without the accusation of
suicide or the terrible uncertainty of a disappearance.
In the meantime she might use her expertise to build
the records that would bring saving knowledge that
much sooner.

It would mean leaving Seth and Ulu almost a year
and a half before the time she had set to go. It would
mean more lies and more secrets, fabricating excuses
at the point where history became news as she moved
into her true present. Think. Accept. Plan. If only
she hadn't been so vapid and careless, so ignorant and

self-absorbed back in those future days, she might have listened better, remembered more.

She raised the issue casually at staff lunch. Seth had been talking about altering quinoa in flavor. She made herself laugh. *"I'm* loafing. The exciting part of my new set has been done, but I've been thinking about something . . ."

"About what?"

"The potato." The room changed. Some people laughed. Every agronomist had a theory of how the situation could have been handled or how the potato could be reintroduced. "Join the club," Calabrese said, "Every potato they plant still gets D/X."

"I wasn't thinking of agronomy," Sema said, "I was thinking of genetics. I was wondering how we could change the genetic picture just enough to fool the virus."

Seth looked dubious. "I thought we had decided to limit our work to the five grains . . ."

"Certainly, but no one I know uses your methods, or the triggering. I think we might extend the methods we've perfected here . . ."

"Aren't there lots of people working on the potato already?" Calabrese asked. "Genetics and all?"

"Yes . . ." Sema wanted to throttle him. She tried to keep her voice from being too urgent, "but not with our methods. I've been reading some of what they've been doing . . . the French, for example." It was another lie — she didn't have a clue about French D/X research, but the story had to be begun, the parameters and location set.

Seth was looking hard at her. Then he smiled. "I've been down this road before," he said. "Sema

has an instinct about things and I learned long ago
not to argue with it."

She smiled at him in as much relief as pride, but
then sorrow rose up in her so suddenly and with such
intensity that she almost wept aloud before them all.
She coughed to hide it; she wanted very much to
make her disappearance as bearable . . . tears again.
She thought: "Let's see how clever I can be at aban-
doning." She coughed and anger drove the tears
away. She answered, "I never *knew* . . ."

"No," Seth said, "but you felt something, and
you feel it now."

"Yes, I feel it now. It was a 'hot potato' and we
dropped it — we studied the *D/X* virus but we didn't
look at the genetics of the tuber. All the research
money went with the dramatic part of the problem."
Marge LeRoyer, who was sitting next to Calabrese,
asked where she planned to set up the part of the lab
dealing with the tubers; space was at a premium. "I
didn't say this to worry anyone. We are doing the
grain project and will continue to do it. I only want
to play. . . . I won't be using lab space or changing
anyone's lives. I think my knowledge might even
help the grain project." No one agreed; she could see
it, but the words had been said, the curtain had risen.
"I will not grow potatoes in the sink," she said. They
laughed and the moment passed, but not before she
had looked around at the people with whom she had
worked, and the man she had all but married and
whose life she had shared so completely. In a year
they would be sitting around this table in varying
degrees of sadness, or feigned sadness in Marge's
case, and talking about her death. There was very
little time . . .

★   ★   ★

She had not fully committed herself to the plan with its unbearable loss of fifteen months. "Decide!" she cried aloud one morning. Ulu was at nursery school and Seth had gone to meet a colleague. She was supposed to be preparing a paper for presentation at an international convention. "Decide!" the next day and the next, "Decide!" She remembered that Seth was home. He heard her through the closed study door and came. "What is it, are you all right?"

"Oh, yes," (damn the despair in small rooms!) "I can't get this idea properly written." She knew that on the other side of the door he was smiling, his face alight with sympathy for her problem. She had the almost overwhelming urge to run to the door, open it, stop lying into his dear and loved face, and tell him how Time Future was too rapidly becoming Time Present.

"Time is not a river," she said, "it's a wall."

"Don't worry," he said, "you'll find a way."

She did. She would endure the fifteen-month loss to give Seth her accidental, sudden death, a death without a body but also without the pain of having to find a body. She combed her memory for the half-heard details of a nineteen-year-old event that had yet to happen and for which no corroboration was available. France — Vézelay — They would first confuse the mortal illness with something caused by contamination of a stored wheat crop. If only she had known then . . . been an agronomist; she would have had a detailed memory. If only she had been more than half alive; if only she had given a damn.

The outbreak would come early in April. She would have to begin to set up her disappearance in Vézelay to coincide with its coming. The timing would need elaborate care. Seth would have to get vidmail every few days — then, right at the time of the outbreak . . . She would have to escape, find a hiding place where she could alert the time travel authorities with her ID patch and code, and wait for the time shuttle to come.

Sema began to make her plans. She wrote to the Institut Agronomique expressing interest in an obscure and not very original study she had dug up about viral-genetic immunology in tubers. Was the D/X strain the same everywhere? Could it be cultivated in grain? She wrote to and received an invitation from the University of Paris for a three months' study. There was no sign of the virus in the soil and they were doing no ongoing studies at present. She wrote that there was a grant, quite a large one, for such a study — agro-babble, dollar-babble . . . the plans took most of the summer. When would she like to come? March — just at the beginning of the growing season. Sema had never officially appeared as Seth's co-author, but people in the field knew who she was and what her lab at Fort Collins was doing. They were delighted.

IX

She said goodbye to Seth, not for the first time. Field visits and studies had separated them before. She had read to him from the Institut's letters as though their questions were statements: "We think there may be a link between the grain, the potato, and the virus. The secondary grains have been grown in all the locations studied." "I want to go over and look at what they're doing," she told him, "and if something looks good, I'll tell you right away."

"With so little to go on, I don't know why you think their study is important," he said, and then he kissed her, "but I've learned to trust your instincts."

"They want the plant connection to be someone of — what did they say — big reputation."

He crossed his eyes at her which had always made her laugh, and then said, "I know you've had something on your mind for a while now."

"I have been a little moody."

"I wonder if it's disappointment over this time travel business. I was wrong about the future of my recombinant rice, but I learned how tough it is to feel — to *know* you have a truth to give and to have people look at you with — with —"

"Incredulous wonder — shaking their heads."

He laughed, "Yes."

She could see he was letting himself be comforted by her. There was worry familiar on his face. He had been teacher, friend, lover, husband . . . Between his eyes and nose where the glasses sat were two wrinkles. When he was worried . . . "I'll be back before you know it."

Sema got to Paris knowing enough about *D/X* to talk to the French researchers. *D/X* was amazingly versatile, but even she couldn't understand the link to the outbreak that she knew would come within the year. Soils were clean, or appeared to be; yet a farmer put the seed potato into a garden or hill of soil anywhere outside a lab and it turned to mush within a month of first producing leaves. What was really going to happen in Vézelay, she wondered, and how could it be studied? Had the virus mutated in some way?

Unfortunately, the Institut's experimental plots were west, not south, of Paris, and for the first month it seemed she would never get to Vézelay; she was so far from the plague area she might as well have stayed in Fort Collins. She went back twice to visit Seth and Ulu for long weekends. The visits were sweet, full, and happy — the happiest days of her life. Having decided on the death she had planned, she allowed no worry to touch her. The crowding in their three rooms, Seth's occasional depressions, university politics — she put all these aside. They went to the park, the museum, the zoo — to Wild World and Water World and rafting and dancing. She ate well, and she spoke less about her project than she would have, saying only, "I have a strong feeling about the importance of what we're doing over there. When it starts being obvious to other people, someone will be picking up my travel checks, so why should we worry about money?" She discovered that she could tell Ulu sophisticated stories if she told them bit by bit, adding a little each time — all her favorites, Snow White and Rose Red, stories of Theseus, the whole of *The Snow Queen* — bit by bit, Gerda's long exile seeking her playmate in the Snow Queen's empire of ice and her final rescue of him.

"You needed this new project," Seth said to her, "you're so much more relaxed and happy than you've been lately."

★   ★   ★

Sema did not read the French newspapers but back at the project she heard the news from LeClerc, a colleague who had shown no previous interest. An organization of personal rights activists had formed to protest the "reconstituting" of suicides for remedy. LeClerc quoted to her, reading: then he smiled at her, "I did not think deeply on this. You were telling us of this at the convention last year — that time travel would not be simple tourism."

"Yes."

"I owe you an apology. I thought your worry silly, then. I had no idea . . ."

Seth also sent a vidletter with kind words about her prescience. It gave little comfort. Days were bleeding away.

In November, Sema began spending much of her time in and around Vézelay. She took soil samples of all kinds. The area was mountainous and rugged. Root and tuber crops had been grown there for centuries. It was a poor area, never overfertilized. It supported sheep . . .

She thought of sheep liver fluke — a process of stages — intermediate hosts . . . Time was passing. Where was the key?

At Christmas people from the Institut went up with her and Valliant, one of the directors, said, "I see you are interested in this region — would you like to start some small plots here?"

Sema tried to keep the excitement from her voice. "Yes, I think I would. The microclimate is very different from what we have at Flers . . . I want to study what grows here." She had wanted to fly back to Seth and spend the evening and day with him, but her acceptance of the plots dictated her attention at Vézelay.

It was Christmas Day, and Sema was gathering droppings, sheep, goat, deer, dog, cat, and sending them to the Institut for testing for D/X. The director questioned her with increasing disbelief. The slow pace and low priority of her study were infinitely frustrating. A bomb was ticking. Death would come in April to hundreds, and in a way to her. For twenty years she had watched intelligent people walk by the important events of their times and pick at the trivial ones, giving themselves no way to examine events in the light of what they had already learned. It had so anguished her that until the time travel issue, she had stayed away from all public discussions and the news.

By February she was full time at Vézelay. The Institut had furnished her with an assistant whom she sent on careful but routine collections. She collected insects, ants, beetles, and flies. "Look for a fungus or a parasite with the virus," she wrote, underlining and in red. "The virus could still be in the ground." There was no evidence of such a thing. Since the potato failure, nothing had happened in any of the studies of soil or water.

She arranged her own study area to be far from her assistant's; she felt an overwhelming need to be alone because she would often burst into spontaneous tears or rages and she wanted the freedom to cry, mutter, curse when the mood took her. Sometimes she sat for an hour or so with no more change than a face allowed to relax into misery without evasion or the uttering of another lie. It was the only relief she could make for herself.

Time was getting short. Sema became haunted by the future. She could no longer bear to visit Seth. She sent a vidletter every week trying to plead work without letting him see the desperation on her face or hear the urgency in her voice. Nothing was coming in from the Institut. She had an urge to send Seth a sealed letter to be opened at the outbreak of the plague. That was self-destructive. She sent cheerful vidletters instead, describing the land and the project and the people at the Institut. She had to remember that working on the virus was secondary to her planned death, a death for which she had already sacrificed precious time.

In March she received a type-print letter from the Institut. "Anomalies in your ant samples. Collect more specimens, specifically . . ." and there followed a list of varieties of ants. Sema called her assistant and they began working the fields in and around Vézelay.

It was early spring. The first flowers came, crocus and snowdrop, and soft green hazed the trees. They collected ants from fifty fields in grids in all directions and the lab wanted more. "What is it?" Sema cried into the holophone.

"It's something; we don't know what. The ants you are sending from south sides are thirty percent anomalous — there's also a fungus some of them are carrying."

"For God's sake — are you going to get people to look at them!"

"Yes — now we will. Collect on these grids and send us soil samples, too, and the new shoots that come up — mushrooms also."

March became April. Winged seeds blew in the air and spiders sailed downwind on long lines tenting the sky to the earth. The earth broke open in the rain and sprouted wild chive and primula. Sema breathed in springtime. This very springtime in which she, twenty years ago, had felt so desiccated and hopeless, now seemed infinitely precious and time dripped moment by moment, dew-mornings and dew-fall nights, here and gone.

She was spending parts of each day in the town, now, waiting, hope versus knowledge, for the first news of illness. The weather was holding — warmer than usual, people said, and the crops would be early. Sema was also on the holophone to Paris almost daily. What was the fungus? Was it a D/X carrier? Seth's vidletters were puzzled and hurt. What had happened? She had spent a month away from them and her tapes were so impersonal. Did she want him to come over? Funny, he said, with all the forms of communication, we are still mysteries to one another. She sent a vidletter with all she really knew.

"I'm sorry I have been so absorbed. I've been tense and yet there's nothing specific to report. I'll be back with you all summer — I don't want Ulu to forget me. I don't want you hiring anyone who speaks Romany better than I do." (family joke) "Answer to your question is yes — they've found something anomalous. I was doing soil studies but now I'm helping out on this. If I sound removed, it's because I'm at sea. The fungus may be very important. It may be a link with D/X . . ."

★   ★   ★

April 15. She sent her assistant back to Paris on a wild goose chase that would save him from whatever was coming. The lab was silent. The town was peaceful and happy. Sema walked the hills, trying to think of what else she could do. The outbreak would come — she began to worry that she had mistimed it.

April 16, 17. Soft rains fell, soft mists rose. The nights were luminous with moonlight. It was almost possible to hear the roots stretching, finding, nudging the earth aside with gentle, forceful fingers, deeper. This country was hard and dry, but the hardening would come later with the hot winds from the south. Now, it was all green haze and the deep inward pull of breath as the earth awakened and the rains sank into it.

Mme. Laurier, the postmistress, was ill. Sema went pale at the news. Mme. Laurier recovered. La grippe.

And then. Sema had had the idea of a day-by-day building, of one person, two, five, becoming ill. This was a manifestation like flood or earthquake. She came down from camp on the morning of the nineteenth and saw the people in the streets, weeping, hysterical, or standing mute and stupid with shock. In their homes were the dead, a taking sudden and violent. She went to the post office to make her call to the Institut but all lines, computer or holophone, were overloaded and no calls were being put through except those to government agencies. In the street, a truck with a P.A. system was cruising. Teams were on the way, the voice said, panic is to be avoided.

Residents must go to their homes in case the illness was contagious.

Sema's first thought was to go to the homes where the ill and dying were — she might ask the question others wouldn't come to until months later when the close witnesses had died and other memories faltered. She felt invincible because of her sorrow. She realized the impracticality and danger of what she thought to do. She did not wish to die. She did need to set her presence in Vézelay and begin the lie of her death. She went back to the post office and spent an hour trying to get the clerks to find a way she could place a call to the Institut and one to Seth. She went to several officials about procedures to seal off the town — people were still thinking in terms of a violent food poisoning and there were rumors of all kinds.

When she had made her presence felt, Sema went back to her hill camp and activated the comp patch with the small reader she had been given. She gave her ID number. A pause. She activated the early-return code. Verified. She activated her new location number. Pause. She was hit with sudden panic. If she put in the wrong number or the wrong series, she would have to spend her fifteen months as nameless and stateless, a wanderer somewhere, unable to stay. On the reader, verifying numbers began to appear, a place, a time. There would be a wait of some hours and then she would know if return were possible at present. She sat on her hillside far from the dying town, far from her husband and child, and grieved.

X

It was time to remember Berton and Luci, to search for them in detail, to untie herself from Seth and Ulu, from Seth's jokes and habits, their private language as they worked. He had been quieter, shier, when they first married, but a slow secret humor had emerged over the years and an ability he had never known, for play. . . . According to the rules she had read and the agreement she had signed, she would have to return or Luci would be unmade, Berton could never have met her, and history would be changed. Like the time picked up on a cross-country trip, the flight would activate the former past and put her back into it as she flew, aging, as she flew, the present woman into the former life. She had signed papers, made meaningless promises to forgotten authorities twenty years ago. . . . The twenty years she had just lived so intensely were now officially to be dropped like clothing. The copter came. She was lifted off on a night without stars. The ship took her in. Time was. Time is.

Sema lay unable to move. She had forgotten how violent the buffeting was. She wept in the restraints, unable to wipe the tears away.

Then they hit the Luria Layer. At first the memories were easy — childhood, girlhood — as the time was regained. The old realities reasserted themselves: college on the general track, meeting Berton, marriage, Luci, the laziness and self-pity of her past life. Her decision to go back. Then there was a wrenching implosion as time is collided with time was. Darkness. She felt herself being torn apart. She woke, sick. She was Sema Stewart and she was fifty-eight years old.

★   ★   ★

She had a pounding headache. The attendant came and sat by her. Other passengers were being picked up from other assignments. Some wept, some were jubilant. None was a green card. None had been twenty years away. "We don't see people like you very often. A year or two and then even the Greenies come back."

Sema sighed. "Headache," she said.

"Your bones are hurting from the rapid aging, but headache — I don't think it's only that. You should know why it is — you should have been briefed. . . ."

"Yes," Sema said, "twenty years ago." Her voice sounded miserable to her own ears, bereft, lost as a child, a kind of shock.

"You look pretty bad. I don't *have* to give you a tranquilizer, but I think you should have one."

"That's all right; I need to face this. I need to know . . ."

"I've seen a few Greenies — I'm sorry — green priority passengers. They're more anxious than any others about their returns."

"Have you ever seen a twenty-year Greenie?"

"No — I never have — I think they're going to close the category."

She tried to calm herself, to speak through the headache and the pain in her joints.

"Listen, when I left, there was a plague. It was in France. Thousands of people were killed. Has it spread? What caused it — do they know what caused it?"

The flight attendant shrugged. "I don't watch the news much. I guess if it had come over to America, I'd know it."

*   *   *

She rode in time and remembered how, in Andersen's *Snow Queen,* Gerda, the heroine, went to the Snow Kingdom to rescue Kay. When they came back they were old people, having given their lives to the Snow Queen's hospitality of ice. She was coming back to two strangers with whom she must live. Denver-Boulder was a megapolis of ten million, with Fort Collins at its northern rim. Hers was to be a life entirely different from Seth's. She would never see him or Ulu again. When would he have heard about the Vézelay outbreak?

As they flew, the plague was becoming a reality, becoming known, taking its outline. She wondered what was happening, had happened in the ten days she had been away. When would Seth find out she was missing and presumed dead? She wondered if she had guessed right. He was at home now; when she got back to Denver, she could pick up the phone and call him, and hear his voice and destroy him with the truth for the first time and then she might be caught and prosecuted for violating all the contracts she had signed. It meant prison and probably the end of the green passport provision for some other dreamer who wanted to remake a life.

Thirty-eight to eighteen, and now she was fifty-eight. Fifty-eight wasn't very old — people stayed at work until their seventies, but achieving an identity again — starting over would be impossible . . . she sighed.

Berton met her at the spaceport. They were both stiff and reserved.

"How was the trip?"

"Fine." He shook his head and she had to laugh. She had aged twenty years and she felt as if her bones had been shattered.

"I have some bad news for you. Your early arrival — it was impossible. I was gratified that you wanted to leave early — that sixteen months, even — well, that you wanted to be home — of course they couldn't give it to you — you were here then and that time can't be relived. It's two weeks and two days after you left."

"Physically, I ache all over. Mentally, I feel numb."

"They said you would."

"When I left — there was the diplovirus —"

"That was last year. It has had little flareups here and there, but nothing like Vézelay, no."

"Why? have they found the connections? are they spraying? is it the fungus?"

He looked bewildered.

"I'm sorry," she said. "I just came from there."

"Sema . . ."

"Yes?"

"Do you want a divorce?"

"No, but you may. I've been such an awful liar. I lied to you about being happy and to Geron and Dala when I was growing up and again when I went back and to other people, lots of other people."

"You were married there, weren't you." A statement in a flat voice. She nodded. "You weren't supposed to . . ."

"It was never official. We adopted a child, too. I don't want to lie anymore. I'm tired to death of lies."

"Were you happy?"

She nodded. "I've made a hell of a mess."

"I'd say so. You could have had the life you

wanted here. You could have taken training, done what you wanted to do."

"I didn't know what a mistake I had made — how little I had given myself, until after Luci was born and after thirty-five they wouldn't have let me go for professional track. I was an agronomist."

"You were?"

"The barley everyone eats, the millet. Seth Pritchard and I." She could barely speak. She saw he was impressed.

"I'll want to hear —"

"Will you, really?"

"Yes," Berton said. "I've thought a lot about how it must have been for you, a talented, bright woman —"

"Where's Luci?"

"Out with friends. She's still angry."

It was cool in their home. They lit the electric lights, which were mellower than light bars, and made a softer glow in the room. She liked this house. Berton had designed and built a nook with an electric fire mimicking a fireplace; he had gotten an old-fashioned grate and wired it up, an antique system, but one at which they were comfortable sitting, summer or winter. They sat there but did not touch. Berton said, "Now tell me who you were . . . are."

It was a remarkable act of charity. She told him about Geron and Dala in the long summer of reacquaintance, and Berton smiled. She told him about her eco-botany studies, the excitement of being at the cutting edge of research, the rice project, her frustration, and the final turning of the study to the secondary grains. "The barley — all those products — not the products, of course, but the research that made them possible."

"You were . . . are . . . an important person, I mean, in science. World class."

"In our own circles, I guess I am — was." She told him a little about Seth and Ulu and the *D/X* plague in which she was supposed to have died.

"Then your coming back early was about them, not about us . . . I hoped . . . I thought . . ."

"That I was unhappy?"

"Part of me hoped you were, yes. Part of me was annoyed, I guess, thinking you might have been unhappy there, too, and would come back doubly frustrated, angrier . . ."

"No, I couldn't think of a better way to leave everyone, so I picked that. I'm a person of some discipline, now, of some — will —"

He laughed. "You always had that."

"I never felt I did."

"I know, and now you're back here in a life you said you never liked or wanted. How is it now? What can we do?"

She thought a long time and then said, "I gave you a hell of a time."

"I married you for love. You married me because I was a good match, I think."

"You were. You still are. I thought, waiting in Vézelay for the plague to come, that I might go back into eco-botany at a different place, a lower place. The study itself has gone on while we were specializing in grains. I could do eco-botany and never meet a grains person. Maybe I could do something that would be useful in a minor way — I've lost my degrees, of course, and at this age they wouldn't let me do them over, but there are classes I could get into, and I'm good enough so that someone would use me as an assistant even without credentials. Certainly it's worth a try."

"Would you hunt for Seth Pritchard?"

"What use would it be? It's illegal and would be too painful anyway. I would probably stay with genetic work on the potato or on fruit. Seth has all the grains to explore — it would take two lifetimes. Our conventions and meetings would be at different places; seeing him would be unlikely."

"I'm willing to wait for what we both feel in a month or a year," Berton said. "Let's rest and be patient for a while."

She studied him. "I underestimate you, don't I? I keep doing it."

"You underestimate yourself, or did. Do you want to go to sleep now — you must be exhausted."

"I am, but I —"

"Use the bed in the loft, or Luci's. She'll stay over at Kit's house." They didn't kiss but she looked at him quietly again. The guest room in the loft was serene, impersonal. She slept long and deeply.

The next day, too impatient to obey the time travel instructions about resting for two weeks, Sema got up and went to the three local universities where she picked up catalogues on agronomy and eco-botany. She was recognized at the University of Colorado when a professor walked by where she was waiting, stopped, stared, and then said, "Aren't you . . . Sema Pritchard — I thought . . ."

"I'm Sema Stewart. We're . . . we *were* second cousins, named after the same great-aunt."

"You look a lot like her."

"Look again; there's a twenty-year difference."

★   ★   ★

After getting the catalogues, she went to the university's library to read about Vézelay and the *D/X* plague. The librarian looked at the access coding. "Local papers didn't carry that as fully as the national ones; try the *Nation Times;* that's probably your best source . . ."

Sema sat before the scanner coded for Vézelay, *D/X,* plague. There were the first releases, items from the day after the first news of the plague — chronologically sixteen months ago. By the second day there was a fuller account, numbers coming in, hysteria in the town, symptoms. The authorities had decided to quarantine the town. Epidemiologists had . . .

A piece had come up on the scanner and she had seen it was short, so her hand was pushing the pass button as she read, automatically; then she stopped and had to press review again and she read:

> AGRONOMIST DEAD IN SEARCH FOR WIFE
> Seth Pritchard, renowned plant geneticist and eco-botanist, died yesterday in the emergency facility at Vézelay. His wife, Sema Pritchard, also an eco-botanist, had been in the town on a study when the plague erupted. Dr. Pritchard had gone to Vézelay to locate his wife and had been told that she might have contracted the illness. At the time, the contagious nature of the disease was insufficiently understood.

She went dizzy and faint and found herself struggling for breath. There was a long wait before her vision cleared. She kept thinking that unless it did, she wouldn't be able to read the article, but she was also aware that she was now deep in a psychological response against reading it. She waited. The clearing was woefully long in coming.

> Pritchard had spent the day trying to trace his wife. He collapsed in the evening but because of the hysteria of the community, it was many hours before he was taken to the facility where he finally expired. It is assumed that his wife, Sema, was among the first victims of the plague and is one of the 30 or 40 unidentified bodies awaiting disposition in the cordoned area of the town soccer field, where the dead have been taken.

She read more, doggedly. The research the doctors had done was being examined by virologists. A later article on Sema said that her linking of the outbreak to *D/X* had been a leap of genius, but that the link would have to be studied and that would take time. A fungus carried by an ant had already been found to harbor the virus; plant-animal vectors had been found before but this one might yield, etc., etc. It was no use trying for calm by reading, by trying to understand. Seth Pritchard had died over a year ago. Ulu would have been adopted by one of thousands of childless couples who would want him. Perhaps even the Laniers had come forward as his natural parents. She couldn't seek him out or have him in this world. Her first need, her need now, was a place where she could go to cry. The library had a restroom. She went there.

In Andersen's *Snow Queen,* the old people, once children, hold hands together in the world to which they have come home; innocence in youth, peace in old age. She had promised not to contact anyone in her old life, but she had planned to follow Seth's career. This meant that once again, yet again, she would be only half invested in a present like Kay, the Snow Queen's boy victim, and half looking, like Gerda, for the missing part of herself. The cold she now felt was the Snow Queen's cold; numbness, evasion, forgetting, the covering, equivocating snow. She might go westward up from this campus for a few miles and be able to see into the ranges where snow stayed all year, like time stopping.

OFFERING UP

THE wind blows all night. It howls down Chinaman's Gap and through Whiskey Gulch and over Victory Pass hell-bent. Our monastery lies supine beneath the beating on its little shoulder of upland under the gray knees and breasts of the mountains. The chapel is protected by the refectory and barn but the chapter house and cloister with the dormitory bear the wind's full force, funneled, aimed, channeled like a fist through the gullies between the mountains. I look at the brothers' faces next day at Mass and see mirrors of my own grainy-eyed sleeplessness. Is the anguish the same? I know two in whom it is.

I'm the brother who does most of the shopping. Today I leave after breakfast and am back at four. When I turn off the highway and take the bumpy road to our gate, I think about its metaphor. The road is savage with mud in winter and spring and there are always washouts and dangerous ice. In summer it bakes and chokes the rider with dust as soft and per- vasively gritty as ground glass. After this long, bumpy ride, four miles, the traveler senses a lift in the land and then comes the gate and beyond it, the welcoming spread of the field and the chapel, the guesthouses and chapter house, the harmonious clus- ter of all of them — the distant view allows no sight of patching, staining, weathering — it all looks rested, quietly breathing, at peace.

There's an electronic system at the gate now, saving us from having to call a brother from his work. I press the button and speak to Brother Herb in the office and the buzzer sounds, the gate opens, and I go through. For discipline's sake, we don't use an automatic closing device. Gravity swings the gate open and we have to get out of the truck to close it. I have learned from Brother Herb's voice that he is not having a peaceful day. Does the wind keep him trying to pull up sleep around him? In this commu- nity, where we hope to reach God, there is never, not ever, an escape from man. In the world outside, a friend's loss of faith, selfish impulse, annoying habit, stroke, illness, loss of capacity are misfortunes which usually signal withdrawal. Here there is no re- lease from a tiresome brother or one whose illness renders him wretched. Your narrow-eyed judge is saying his office three steps away from you and will be there at Compline and there again at Lauds and at Matins when patience and love are still sleeping even though you are standing up and uttering the words of praise.

★   ★   ★

Brother Herb's annoyance has been partly caused by me. "You were supposed to have been back an hour ago."

"They didn't have Matt's prescription ready. I had to wait."

"Dale was ready to do the tune-up."

"Perhaps there's still time." I get back in the truck and drive it over to unload. Herb's officiousness irritates me, and during the evening walk, I will recite the Veni Sancte Spiritus, I'll get to the part that says, "bend what is unbending" and I'll think of him and wish I didn't dislike him so much.

I pick up Brother Peter, whom I still think of as being new even though he's been here five years and is a professed brother, and we go from area to area unloading. Flour to the locker, lumber to the shed, Matt's prescription to the refectory along with all the other personal shopping I've done for the brothers. The Limbate inhaler I got for myself, Tim, and Johnny is in my jacket pocket, a little bulge that makes me nervous. I want to go up to my room and hide it, but there's no time. I'll have to wait until recreation at least before I'm able to get away. It is the fourth inhaler I've gotten. Like booze and cigarettes, Limbate, legal out there, is not legal in here. Like booze and cigarettes, there would be talk about a brother buying some, and they know all of us in Granite. I had to go to Aureole where they don't know me, and I went cursing and came back cursing the thirty extra miles, which was why I was late.

In the secular world, they'll tell you the stuff is not addictive. Considering our experience, I'd have to

disagree. Studies in physiology don't cover it. I think
we addict to whatever will free us from our para-
doxes, from the shock of difference, between what
we wish we were and what we know we are. I realize
I'm addicted; my hand shook perceptibly when I
reached out for the inhaler from a stack of them and
took it. I was breathing hard, too, and had to make
a conscious effort to calm myself. The stuff is forbidden and I use it anyway, and I watch it beget other
wrongs. Rotten meat doesn't summon a single mag-
got only.

We try to limit the harm. Brothers are forbidden to
enter one another's rooms; Tim and Johnny come to
my room twice a week when the brothers are supposed to be sleeping. That was my idea, and using
was my idea. Johnny found a discarded inhaler cap
in my trash and came to me. Tim intuited something,
God only knows how, and so we three are changed.
The sins multiply. We're what no brothers should be:
secretive, frightened, rule-breaking, and the monastery is not what it should be, at least not for us.

Why don't we stop? I don't want to and the others
don't either. I swear to myself that I will stop. The
inhaler, which I keep in a little sling in the closet,
belongs to the three of us. There are nights when I
could break it, shatter it under my knees as I pray,
but it isn't mine alone, and keeping it is a privilege,
a favor to me. Twice I let Johnny keep it and the
insecurity and loss of control made me a nervous
wreck.

After Pete and I deliver all the shopping, I take the
truck over to where Brother Dale is supposed to be

waiting. He isn't there and I don't see him until mail call and recreation. I give him the story about Matt's prescription, which he seems to accept. There are three hundred doses in an inhaler, although the last fifty or so seem weaker. We use it twice a week, except during Lent — I know how ludicrous that sounds. With two breaths in a dose, and the three of us using, we get a new one every five or six months; well beyond what suspicion could attach to for consistent latenesses or especially long trips to town. Today is Wednesday and I want my two breaths — I think of cheating, doing it tonight, lying down on my bed alone. I know if I did that, I'd do it every night as some people on the outside do.

In the moments when we go to clean up before supper, Johnny calls me with a question and I answer it, and his eyes ask and I smile and nod imperceptibly. He'll tell Tim. This is the worst of it, when I bring the new inhaler in and have to get rid of the old one, when we sneak around like kids, signaling over the heads of the brothers, when there are pounding hearts and guilty looks, justification and fear. Tomorrow it will be routine, and for almost half a year we'll be ordinary brothers, working, praying, living monastic life as authentically as we can, considering.

The night chant is my favorite. It's the Salve Regina, haunting even in English. We come out of chapel still singing it and into the night, to the dormitory. The sky over the valley is huge and on moonless nights, so thick with stars that the sight catches and makes us weep, sometimes. Only the oldest brothers use flashlights. I like to hang back and let my feet find the path, past the loom of the outbuildings and refectory all the way to the chapter house and dormitory where we end the day.

We are in Night Silence then. I try to do as much as I can in darkness, going about my preparations by feel. There is neither light nor heat in the dormitory; we use Coleman lamps and heaters which we carry — a little self-denial, that we don't come into a room already warm for us.

There is a crucifix on my whitewashed wall on which Jesus hangs exhausted. In the old days there was a nail below it on which a scourge hung and on certain days, the brothers were required to use it as they recited the penitential psalms. On sleepless nights, windy nights also, they must have had a go at the old Adam: wish, desire, guilt, recrimination. We don't do that any more, or pray kneeling on a rope or on pebbles. Our underwear is bought downtown and not sewn here of rough burlap. We are enjoined to imitate Christ in his virtue, not in his suffering.

I think the whips didn't work. The effects must have lasted no longer than the pain itself at its most intense, and there is always the danger of addiction to pain as to pleasure. The nail and scourge are gone; my back is unscarred but there are the sleepless nights under the scourge of the wind. It drives before it all the wrongs I did great and small, and the recrimination that confession is supposed to silence.

We wake before dawn for Matins. The wind has died; the air is gray and soft, a sweet air for February. In the pre-dawn, our singing has the abstracted quality of the sleep-talker. I love this hour almost as much as the last one of the night. Later I realize that for hours at a time I have forgotten about the inhaler, and that it is Thursday, that at the end of this day, we will use it, all three of us.

Perhaps the others only seem to be untroubled; their faces are serene as they pray. Maybe I seem that way also, although inside I am waiting, alert, eager, but never out of sight of fear. The monastic day leaves no room for private discussion, or any discussion among the three of us. Recreation is time for general talk only. The rest of the day, except for the demands of work, we pass in silence. There are things I need, urgently need, to talk over with my fellow users. It has to be done in typical monastic style, by a combination of luck and planning that will give us time alone.

I work in the bakery. Though it's only February, we have begun to stockpile the tinned rum cakes we sell at Christmas. The work is hard but neither unpleasant nor mindless, and unlike the brothers who are in the laundry or cooking, we are merry. Now and then we sing. I've been happy in this life; its purpose and dedication have uplifted me. Celibacy doesn't bother me much when I consider what married sex was like for my parents and what the abuse of chastity is doing to my sister and brother. When I burn, I remember that.

After recreation, I go to Father Abbot — it's Don Kinear now — and I talk to him about the brochures we send with our cakes. By the time we finish, it's time to make the evening walk, checking everything for the night. We lock up. We have Night Prayer and the Salve again; these motions are to quiet the soul, to still it. My heart is beating with expectation.

In my room, I wait restlessly past lights out. The monastic day allows no waste of time. Even recreation is purposeful. Now I hang in limbo and wish the time away. It's 9:00. It's 9:30. It's 10:00. There is a single soft knock and the door opens and Tim and Johnny slide in silently and go down on their knees. I don't know why we take our Limbate this way. I go to the closet, moving the clothes back, find the fourth hanger, and take the inhaler out of the sling. I bring it over, kneel with them, and give the inhaler to Johnny, who is on my right. I hear him using it: shake, one breath, two. Then Tim, the shake, one, two, and then it comes to me, smoothly in my hand, and I shake it and hold it before my mouth, barrel up. I breathe in, once, twice.

There is the usual anxious moment because Limbate is tasteless and odorless and I always wonder if I'm not breathing a dud. It takes almost three minutes for the drug to reach the limbic area of the brain. We wait with no other thought and then I hear Johnny sigh and then Tim and then the relief moves through me. My memory remains intact, available, but shame, chagrin, regret, self-hate slide off and what I remember is memory only — my spirit is lightened, gentled, unashamed. Tim gets up, touches my arm in leave-taking, and slides silently away. Johnny follows. I go to bed and to the untroubled sleep that Limbate does not initiate, but allows.

Its critics call it chemical lobotomy, but Limbate doesn't change the moral or ethical sense; it only stills the voices of recrimination for thoughts and acts already done. It doesn't help in schizophrenia, except that part which connects to regret. For people fixated in shame and remorse, Limbate is the drug of choice.

When it first came out, Father Abbot — it was Stu Miller then — took me and Andrew and two brothers from the house in North Carolina, to Denver for a day of lectures on it — its pharmacology, side effects, etc. We sat in the back, a line of brown habits looking very medieval, and listened to speakers telling us what Limbate did and couldn't do.

Some people would use Limbate every day, more would use it only after traumatic or tragic events, twenty percent would never use it because they didn't experience gnawing regret for past acts, or not above a momentary pang. It amazed me to learn that so many of us have no night haunts, no long sighs, no tears wept and wept again for a word said amiss or a word not said at all. "Who are those people," I asked the psychologist, "those happy few?" He looked at me quizzically, I remember.

"Some of them might be doing time," he said. Regret may be a way of teaching lessons learned in no other school.

Then I sat in the line of brothers and ached and wondered if they bore the weight I did. Absolution after confession is supposed to establish the regret and then deal with it. Hard work, prayer, simplicity of life are supposed to thin out the forest in which regret wanders, without purpose. During the day our lives work well. We pray, work, simplify the essentials. At night, it's every brother for himself. Armies of recriminations stream across my undefended borders: the son I was, the brother, the friend.

★   ★   ★

In the end Limbate was forbidden. I started about four years ago. I had been shopping. I was in the denims and dark shirt we use for ordinary trips outside, this one to Gold Flume for some special hardware. I found myself in the drugstore — the inhalers were on a rack. I lifted one off and read the label and then I just took it, paid for it along with the other things. I was trembling, and like a thief I sat in the truck and used it to banish the guilt of using it. Then I hid it and used it after lights out once a week.

But for Tim and Johnny, I think I would have stayed a Sunday night user — except for Lent. They wanted it twice a week. I caved in. We're all part of it now and time has gone by. We need to talk about what we're doing, how it's changing us.

My father was a cripple. The word is not fashionable today. We use "disabled," but he was more than that; his crippling was of more than body, although severely enough there. He had had polio as a baby and his back was bent like a bow to useless legs. His tongue was vicious — I know there must have been pain, but I don't remember a day when he wasn't giving pain to us. I hated him — I hate him still and for my mother, who bore it all, cowed and patient under his verbal lash, I grew to have an even more virulent scorn. I hated the cruelty and filth in my father's mouth. He was a great characterizer of people and experience, including sex, and his view of the world was ugly and brutal. Of his intimate life with my mother, he spoke over and over again until the acid scorched and ate away some spiritual lens in us that registers the beauty of people and things. Decency and beauty were illusions to him, and I was years here before I could see anything except through that lens. Hating my father, how did I learn to imitate him so well? Wounds I've given others still remember me, open-eyed under the wind or in the pre-dawn. It's confession without absolution, penance but no peace; until Limbate's chemical and temporary forgiveness.

On Friday the wind comes again, this time like revenge itself. Its gusts are ferocious and long. I'm saved the pain of remorse in plain fear. I hear noises I never heard before, rending noises, and we are struck in the night with what the wind has torn away from other things. What things? I hear brothers' voices, see the light of their lamps coming and going past my door. What can they do? It's too dangerous to go out and we know that the barn where the animals are is more protected. I lie in decent fear, free from indignity, and wait for morning.

It's a blessing in disguise. The pumphouse is gone, walls and roof. The pump is all right — these winds are not northers and there was no freeze. I'm delegated to go into town and get lumber for repairs. I ask for Tim and Johnny to help me pick it up and load it. Yes. We will have two hours up and back to talk.

They are relieved. I see it in the speed with which they follow me to the truck. No questions are asked. We don't begin to speak until we have gone through the gate. Johnny starts. "Have either of you guys confessed this?"

"No," I say. Tim shakes his head. We are not remorseful or anguished now, because it's Friday and the drug is still in our systems. Guilt is at bay and will be until some time between tonight and tomorrow morning when it will sift slowly back into our awareness.

"Anybody do any extra penance?" Tim asks. We nod. We've been so isolated we haven't been able to ask even such basic things of one another. Relief floods us. We laugh. We don't tell one another what the penances are — private penance in a monastery is a very private matter — but it warms us to know that we share our response to the sin and to the extra sin of not confessing it. We ride in silence for a while but we are under pressure to speak. It's unlikely that we will have another chance to be so free.

"What do you suffer from most," Tim asks, "the little stuff or the big stuff?"

"Little," I say. "The casual, tactless remark, the shoving in ahead of a brother at the sink, reverting."

"Reverting?"

"The man I was before I came here." We laugh again. The reason for becoming a brother is supposed to be loftier. The world-escapers don't usually last, but we all know. . .

"You're lucky to have only that," Tim says.

"Sufficient unto the day," I say. "It's all I need."

"I was young and as unaware as a chicken," Tim says. "I lived in Denver and worked out at the airport. I had a sporty car, apartment, clothes. Next door was a young married couple, Ginny and Bill. We used to go out drinking. We all did a lot of drinking, snorting, toking, in those days. They would fight sometimes. She had a vague idea it was wrong, that they should be saving, building something. I would hear it all through the thin walls. After a particularly bad fight he left. She cried. The next day I saw her in the hall looking half dead. She wanted to talk, she wanted sympathy. I listened. She was going to wait. A week went by, two weeks. I told her she shouldn't stay in, crying. "Where can I go?" "Come on up to the mountains — I'll take you to a great jazz place." We went. We both got smashed. She cried some more — I was a wonderful friend, etc., etc. In the boozy bloom, sympathy flowed, we both cried. He had abandoned her. Abandoned. It was dramatic stuff. Those mountain roads are not easy when you're cold sober. When we crashed, I was thrown out first, two feet onto a soft shoulder. She went flying out the passenger side into thin air and off the cliff. They found her six hundred feet down the gully." We waited. The telling hadn't been easy but it had been possible, which I don't think it would have been without the Limbate. "I went home; she went to the morgue. The next day Bill came back to patch things up. There was nothing left of Ginny but my story. He got drunk and stayed drunk for two days. He came to my apartment and called me a murderer and then went to his brother's in Longmont and got his brother's gun and shot himself. They gave me two years probation and suspended my license for six months."

"Is that what you go over?"

He nods. "Detail by detail. I make and remake their lives and my own. I do the drive over and over. I do the drinking again and again, drink by drink."

Johnny and I hear Tim with some surprise. We had known none of this. Monastic life is concentrated in the present. We are still for a while, then Johnny says, "*I* had no big events. I was in foster homes — six of them. Two were hell. Plain hate might have been better to feel, but I remember what went on with shame. I used to be such a whining, begging kid. I cringe when I think about that and wonder if he's still inside me, that helpless, pleading victim."

"We're telling this to one another," Tim says. "Who else knows it?"

"In my case, there isn't that much to tell," I say. "A hundred ugly, cruel remarks. I deal with them in Confession but they won't be absolved and go away." We ride on in silence.

Then Johnny says quietly, "Lent is coming." We don't speak. After a while he says, "I don't think I can make it without help this year," and we are deadly still.

It's not as easy as I thought it would be, talking in the truck. I'm driving, partly concentrating on the road, and we don't have much time. Here's town already and the wood to get. I had thought the urgency would help, but it doesn't. I head for Krohn's Lumber and Hardware. "Did you make the list?"

"I was supposed to do that on the way," Johnny says.

"We'll stop here and you can do it."

Johnny used to do carpentry and cabinetwork. He figures quickly from the measurements he took and I realize that although I know a good deal about him, having lived with him for eleven years, there are big areas in his life that are closed to me because we don't talk much about personal pasts here. It isn't forbidden; now and then someone will share a letter or memory; I know that Tim gets boils and that Johnny has violent nosebleeds when he is emotionally upset. I never knew about Tim's accident or Johnny's abusive foster fathers, though, and no one knows about my father, piled in his wheelchair, saying ugly things in that soft, oily voice . . . I stop the thought. I'm sweating with a rage Limbate doesn't touch.

Lumber. Hardware. Lots of people are out today. The wind hits hard on the east side of the town and some people from the outskirts are regulars at the lumberyard the morning after a big blow. Our wait is long. On the way home, Johnny says, "I don't think I can do Lent this time; not without help. I don't think I can take forty days."

"We've done it before," Tim says, "and we can work so hard that sleep will sandbag us." His voice is hollow, tough, and sounds studied. He must have been saying this to himself for weeks.

The truth is that we are all afraid. We sit in the truck and tremble, thinking about the forty nights with no Limbate. "We'll have to take what we get," I say, "and the nights only come one by one."

"Let me discipline myself," Johnny says. "I'll keep the Limbate in my room during Lent and I'll use it only when I need it, and . . ." "NO!" I find I am shouting, "No! It's mine; I buy it. I take the risks getting and keeping it. I carried it through the gate in my pocket . . ." They are staring at me and the truck is on the wrong side of the road. I bring it back and then pull over and turn off the ignition. I am shaking with anger. "Buy your own," I say.

"I can't," he whispers. He puts his hands over his face. We hear his voice between them. "If I did, I'd use it every night."

Tim is quiet. "We're in an Order," I say. "We chose the life. It's a life full of restrictions. No booze, cigarettes, girls, lobster dinners. Limbate. We don't use Limbate."

"But we do."

"Not in Lent. We decided . . ."

"You're so pious, I can hardly stand it," Tim says to me.

I put my head back against the seat and feel weak. "I have to sound this way. Things have been going through my mind, things I haven't thought about since I came in. I wonder about trying to get so tired I can't think, about copping doses when you're not there. It's Lent. We're *supposed* to feel remorse."

"I'm not ready; it starts next week . . ."

"Then we'd better get ready."

We sit in dead silence. There is only the sound of our breathing; no car passes. Then Tim begins to recite the De Profundis and we join him and I turn the key and start up. We go home in true monkish style: pouring our pain into those ancient receiving words.

Lent comes. In the solemnity of the season monastic practice is more rigorous. There's little leisure, no recreation. Many of the brothers have personal penances of total silence. There is a set of fasts and many of us do voluntary ones as well. We have more work, too, cleaning the entire monastery for Easter, building by building, room by room; inventories, repairs. I have a calendar I check off day by day of the forty; unnecessary, since Lenten liturgy does that for us. It reminds me of a space-shot countdown.

On the tenth day the wind wakes up, Lent-hungry, and roars down on us from the west-northwest. I lie in bed reliving a fight with a friend in college, my fault. It led to hard words on both sides, his unremembered, mine vicious and cutting. I said personal things; I stripped him. My father had used our secrets against us — things said in confidence or learned from others about us. I had sworn never to do that and I seldom did, but the cruelty in what I let myself say frightened people about what I knew, and after experiencing what I could do, they were never easy with me again. The words come back in the wind. I hear them over and over, harder to bear because in the closet is a hanger and on the hanger is the Limbate and two breaths of it will still the regret.

It must be two o'clock. I hear a sound. The moon is down. I sit up in bed and try to clear my vision. I get up. It's bone-gnawing cold. Someone is here, in the room. I hear the closet door slide quietly. I go to the figure I now see faintly, a person my size. I touch him on the back and hear his pulled-in breath of surprise. He starts, then sways. It's Johnny. "I have to use the inhaler," he says.

He and Tim have seen me get it, but since it has always been in darkness, neither of them knows exactly where it is. "It's freezing," I say. We are whispering; I don't know why. The rooms are private enough to allow all the coughing, muttering, and groaning that people do at night and still be unheard. "Please, Johnny . . ."

"I need it. I can't stand this."

"Please," I say. "Get in bed; you'll freeze out here. Go on. Now."

My urgency and command get to him. He is in my room; he has been compromised already by coming, and if anyone finds us the result might be expulsion. He goes to the bed and gets in. I plug in the small heater and get under the blankets at the foot of the bed; we are sitting side by side under them.

Johnny laughs, I think at the edge of tears. "Caught in bed together . . ."

"During Lent," I add. He has begun to weep, tiredly. He has wept earlier, I think. "Listen, Johnny; the inhaler's not here. I buried it when Lent began because I didn't think I could take knowing it was here. It's in a little box under the chapel side of the bakery."

There's a long silence and then Johnny says, "No, Marty, it's here. I know because I've used it twice."

I'm shocked. I sit trying to sift thoughts that won't yield reason to me. Then anger comes. I get up and stand in the still chilly room. "If you don't get out of here now, I'm going to smash the inhaler for plain spite. You gluttonous cheat! I've been hanging in what I thought was at least a shared suffering. You were lying . . . you . . . " I bite back the words.

"I need it," he says simply.

I walk over to where he is and whisper into his face. "You gutless, chinless, dribbling wimp. Your foster fathers must have had a hell of a time beating you — who can beat Jell-O? We *decided;* suck-finger —"

"*You* decided," he says, and then gets up and leaves.

Two hours later we are up for Lauds and I am feeling poleaxed, ruined inside. I sing the morning chants and pray the prayers without looking for Johnny, although, of course, I know where he's standing. He has spoken to me in confidence and I've used it in anger. Then, I think he had it coming. He deserved to know what he was doing by breaking faith. Limbate is a luxury, not something we deserve, and he betrayed our trust.

The breakfast table is silent but this morning the silence is anything but peaceful. Anton and Carl are nodding off, Del is yawning. Everyone looks surly or pouting. We have given up tea and coffee as our group penance. As with Limbate, the first few days went by on a sacrifice-high. We were psyched up for our denial and we felt clean and proud. We were happy that our monastic practice was in keeping with the more rigorous practice of the past. But the days are daily and by the ninth or tenth, flesh and spirit begin the long exhaustion of withdrawal. I want coffee, I want Limbate, I want my bread buttered. I want a heater in the chapel. I want sleep. Without these things I am angry and self-pitying. I am a creature I despise. By which the Rule means to teach us on what fragile stalks our pathetic virtues are balanced.

I am still righteously indignant. After morning work, Father Abbot asks me to pick up a big order in town. Many lay people spend Good Friday through Easter with us on retreats, and we are getting the guesthouses ready. Toilet paper, towels, soap, sheets. It's cold. Before I leave I go back to the dormitory for a jacket. In my room I go to the closet and take my jacket and turn. The floor. There are drops of blood on the polished wood. One, two, three, four from the bed, five, six, seven to the door. I blew up at Johnny. I lost my temper, but the cause was just, I was severe . . . he bled. He is my friend, brother, accomplice, and he bled with the horror of what I said to him.

As this dawns on me I stand blinking at the unmistakable drops and then move through the door and follow them, one, two, three, four down the hall. They stop suddenly and I have a picture of him in the darkness realizing he was bleeding, pinching his nose, and then guiltily, as I do now, wondering if the blood he has already dropped would accuse him. I get a rag and clean the floor in the hall. The blood in my room I let stay.

It's always something of a jolt to leave the monastery for the outside, even to shop. In the old days, brothers used to go in twos, less to keep an eye on one another than to provide the monastic reality even in the person of one other brother. It's no longer possible; the order has shrunk and while this has its advantages in the sense of fraternity and spirituality, every brother is vital to the running of the house. We can't afford time taken in town.

Lent, with its pinched belly, sleepless eyes; Lent, with no coffee, no tea, no cocoa, no Limbate, is absent in Granite. People look easy and rested. The merchants who know us by name joke with me, and when we talk about the wind they do it from the comfort of Ascension without the suffering that precedes it. For them, Easter is still a month away.

I'm riding back when exhaustion hits. I've been sleeping as I drive and nearly go into the ditch. I pull over and am out before I know it, and an hour later I go sheepishly back to face Brother Herb. The sleep did me good. Going into it I decided what I would do that would allow me to clean up the blood and apologize to God for the whole Limbate mess. I will do a vigil.

There's a list on the bulletin board outside the brothers' entrance to the refectory. Some brothers want their vigils in chapel and yet alone. Now and then there's a note about special intention: for world peace or against hunger, and there'll be many brothers doing it. I pass by the list and look to see if tomorrow night has been checked off. To keep the penance private, there are no names, just check marks. The night is free. I put my check mark opposite the date I want the chapel to myself. To complete the requirements of privacy and modesty, we go to the dorm after late prayer and then come back. We also leave the chapel before Lauds and return to the dorm so as to come in with the brothers at early prayer. Father Abbot is not a believer in holiness one-upmanship.

I feel good about doing this vigil. There's only the problem of the Limbate. We promised we wouldn't take it during Lent. I don't want to add suspicion to the sin of wrath, or temptation to their pain. We live close here and clues are read almost subconsciously in the way it must be for many married people. Tim and Johnny will know when I won't be in my room. I go and get the Limbate, stick it in a plastic sandwich bag, go to the bakery, and bury it in the stored flour we won't be using until after Easter. I'm ready for my night of prayer and penance.

I come into the chapel and quiet myself. I have planned each of the six hours carefully. In each I will offer a different group of prayers and I hope to accomplish a specific as well as general confession and contrition and to receive absolution and healing.

I begin by lighting the candles for my father and mother, hours one and two, and for my brother and sister, hours three and four, for Tim and Johnny and myself, hour five. In hour six I hope to close the vigil and experience the peace for which I am struggling.

I pray for my father, trying to accept his cruelty without consenting to it, to put it in the perspective of his pain, his twisted body. I struggle for this height, achieve it for a moment, and then slip away from it into self-pity. Still, it was there, a moment's freedom from personality and my own pain and into a wider place where forgiveness is possible. I pray for my mother, my confused, cowed mother, who mistook my father's rancorous sarcasm for brilliance. I do the Stations of the Cross. I say some of my favorite portions of the Penitential Liturgy. I pray for Annie, my sister, and Claude, my brother, seeing them as clearly as I can in all their early-blighted possibility. I begin to cry. I see Tim and Johnny, whom I know better than my parents and in some regards not at all. I pray for myself.

Seen in comparison to my parents' life, to Annie's and Claude's, my life seems ordered, decent, productive. Like the monastery in distant prospect, there is simplicity, and peace. It's only when one comes close that the weathering is seen, the stable-muck, the signs of disarray.

I kneel and then lie facedown, cruciform, my head toward the altar, and recite the Miserere. Then I begin to tell God, to speak out of the heart of myself. I tell Him about the Limbate, about how we've fought it and how Johnny has been misusing it and how I hate him for it. Is Tim sneaking into my room, too, to get extra hits on it? Will I draw in a breath three months from now and breathe no ease from the nozzle and feel cuckolded, betrayed?

I am in our traditional posture of utter surrender. It isn't the humility of kneeling; it is complete yet the words coming out of my mouth have no smallest measure of submission in them. All the pain, all the anger, the pent-up remorse and sorrow, helplessness and rage blow through me like the night wind down Whiskey Gulch. I let it come. It howls out of me, nothing like what I planned when I planned this vigil or conceived of doing when I knelt and then went down to full length to mark the hour of the death of selfishness and the rebirth of selfhood.

I cry myself dry. I have accused everyone for whom I have come here to pray. When I stop and am finished at last, I realize there's still an hour before Lauds. I get up on my knees and then stand and turn. There is Father Abbot, still on his knees where he has been since . . . when? There are black flashes and I begin to lose balance and he's up and supporting me.

"I'm sorry, Martin, I didn't check the list and I came . . . you seemed overwhelmed — I thought . . ." and then, "Come on," he says.

I have destroyed myself — destroyed all three of us. Father knows, and what he knows is not under the seal of the confessional. He will call a meeting, chapter, probably all the brothers. They will judge us. We may be sent to other houses. We may be asked to leave the order altogether. I don't want to leave. This is my home. This is Tim's home and Johnny's. I can't beg or protest, I can't speak at all.

I begin to dream; it's the way of people whose exhaustion has left them unguarded, the odd, irrational thought walks in without being stopped and searched. What if rats got into the bakery and found the bag of flour stored there and ate their way in and ate the inhaler. Evidence destroyed and a rat with regrets but no remorse.

The wind has picked up. I can hear it experimenting with some wood that's stacked near the barn. It comes through the passage between barn and chapel, bakery and dairy house. It goes everywhere, inspecting, nosing out sin, and now it's found the dormitory where some brothers are not sleeping and there is its whip — remorse . . . remorse.

THAT BITCH

THAT bitch! Look at me and see if I ain't someone with an appearance, even though I'm short for a man, and thin — skinny even. With my overalls worn through to my behind in places and my underwear doubling for a shirt, you'd look at me and look away, but hell, you'd know I was there.

Walking down Federal in this clean, small town, you'd be shocked to see me coming toward you very slow like someone learning how to walk — 'cause lately my balance ain't been too good. Then you'd think, I'll bet that's the town drunk. You wouldn't say it out loud, but if you did, it wouldn't bother me. It's what I am; nothing more for most people, now that the bitch won't have me in the town she made; in the book that's got the town and all the people and my life in it.

After thinking me, naming me, seeing me in her head and writing me down day after day, real on the paper, standing, walking, part of this town, a man with his own purpose, my God, a man with enemies, the bitch read the thing over, all of it, sitting there looking through them bug-eyed glasses of hers, and then for no reason she drew a big X over my pages, and that was that. Later, she hunted out, page by page and line by line, the parts where people talk about me, because yes, I did pick fights and ruin things when Adam tried to find work for me, and I did walk through town muttering, they said, talking to myself. Line by line she blacked 'em out with a thick pencil, and I was unwrit, unmade, never been.

I yelled at her out of the story, "I been part of all this! Elia and me, we started the store Adam owns now! I was part of the foundation of the family you're so damned interested in, and the town. I'm sixty-seven and I been here since 1913!"

She made a gumpy face and she said, "Elia is a minor character. He's been dead five years when the story starts. You throw the weight off; the balance of the story is wrong with you in it."

"Balance of the story — what the hell do I care!" I was yelling up out of my mind and up off the page. "I'm some way alive. This is my only chance to be alive, to live the awful life you give me!" Then I done something I ain't proud of — I started begging, and for that I won't forgive myself or the bitch, even if she makes me the main character in some other book, writes a whole damn book about me!

"I wish I could keep you," she said, "but it's just no good this way," and she drew a last line through the part where Adam and Grace was talking about me. Grace is the town's two-bit philosopher, and she was ruminating about what towns like Gilboa do with their failures, people with weaknesses bigger than Doc Mellinger or Pastor Dodge can handle.

That's where I went first, to see Doc. He lives on Tulip Street, one of the oldest streets in town. Tulip is one block north of the Methodist church, which is on Haas. Doc lives one block off Federal, which they named for the brigades of Union soldiers formed on it during the Civil War. How could the bitch make it all so real — name the streets, give each a description, explain what kind of people settled the town, be a damn highway engineer making overpasses and exit ramps — and then take a person created as careful as any of them things and kill him, draw a line through his life?

I looked at Doc in a new way, now that he was a character and I wasn't. Once you get a name and move around, once things happen to you, you get seen by the writer even if it's quick and vague, and you get all the parts other people have. I noticed Doc was even missing a little finger, which ain't in the book but must've been in the bitch's mind somehow, along with his paunchiness and the look of having slept in his clothes. What he lacked was something else, a kind of strength or energy I couldn't name. I told him my story, how she crossed me out.

"I know," he said, "you gave a quality to the town, a dimension. She got around the problem by introducing a very minor character towards the end of the story with some of your less attractive qualities so the balance could be kept."

"Balance. I got killed for balance?"

You know what that fat bastard done? He shrugged his fat shoulders — looked at me and shrugged. Our town healer.

Why did I go there? I guess I wanted him to be as strong, to be as mad, as I was. Why couldn't I get all the minor characters together and protest? There'd be lots of people — relatives and neighbors she mentioned without even the decent blessing of names, people driving through town, people in the new development and at the shopping center. Them people wouldn't be minor characters to themselves. I figured they would be mad being trapped in one or two descriptions — just put down like that: Carl, the wife beater; Lucille, the whore; the two little girls; the man at the bank. Think of it, a life like that, with no other place or purpose. But if they was mad, they was too weak to show it. I haunted the town for three days, looking into their faces and watching 'em turn away.

The third day it came to me. I was in the drugstore, though I didn't have nothing to do there. I went to the phones to see if I could look through the phone book and find someone to help me. She'd never thought about a phone book, so there wasn't one there, but there was a dime in the coin return. Not enough for a cup of coffee, but enough for my weight on the big old scale they had. I got change and went and got on. One cent. The machine was still weighing. There was a mirror back of it, and up on the platform I saw myself there.

Scale didn't register. I had figured maybe it wouldn't, but I was still visible. I stared at me in the mirror. God, I was like a savage. The hair was wild and long, strawlike, not white but colorless. The face was like leather gathered up in pouches, and the eyes stared back at me in rage. I opened my mouth and the mirror-man gaped at me. It come to me then that I had never asked myself why I was so angry and so strong. I was a minor character like dozens of others — four pages, mentions and all. The bitch had cut me out in half an hour without having to move a single thing or pave over a hole in her precious plot. And yet, I still had features and a form and I was stronger than some of 'em still living in the story. Why?

Memory, that's why. I was in from the beginning. I remember Elia, who started it all when he come to Gilboa. I remember Adam being born and Grace coming as a bride, all the main characters important to the story. The background of it all was seen through my eyes, and the bitch couldn't change that because she had thought it that way first. I thought I saw something in that.

Over the bank — that's the corner of Federal and Haas — is the lawyers' offices. I went up there and walked past Rita Neri, their secretary, right on in to see 'em. It was a shock.

The bitch had never got around to giving 'em names or personalities. Rita, their secretary, is a friend of Grace's, the so-called heroine of the book, and Rita is pretty and full of detail, but the lawyers is just "two lawyers in offices over the bank." They wear three-piece suits, tweed; or the same tweed, like twins. They got the same shoes and the same brown ties. They got the same height and the same weight, and they got no faces, just flesh, smooth and boneless, like eggs. They ain't got hair, either, and when they talk, it's like a dimple opening in this flesh, and their words come out in the same voice, a male voice, but distant, like the voice they use for recorded messages — the time and temperature you get over the phone.

"Bitch done a great job on you boys," I said.

"Rita talked to Grace once or twice about her work down here, and I can see why the subject of romance never come up. Still, you are lawyers; she said that. That means you know the law. I think I may have work for you."

It's hard to get a response from two egg faces. They just stood there, so I told my story. I started from the beginning of it — how I run away from the orphan home and how I come to Gilboa, how I was sick, and how I broke into this empty store. How Elia and me surprised one another, me being sick and him being foreign. He was fresh off the boat and barely spoke English. He took care of me, and when I got well, we started the store up like partners. We sold everything: seed and feed, crackers, candy, lanterns, brooms, piss pots, trowels, and trousers. We slept in the back of the store, and our clothes stank of dried fish, creosote, and lamp oil.

The bitch took all that out in the second draft, but the point of it was that she put that Jewish family into a small Pennsylvania town and kept 'em there while the town got bigger and changed. After World War II, the new suburbs and shopping centers came, and the store went more to clothes. By the time Adam was grown and married to Grace, the store sold nothing but women's fashions, and I didn't have no purpose in it or in the story. I wasn't comfortable around the place — I scared the customers, and they scared me. By that time, I was in my early fifties. I didn't know nothing but the family and this damn town. I was drinking pretty heavy by then, too, and maybe I didn't look too good. I tried to get some other work, but things didn't go right. I strung along doing things for Elia and his wife, and for Adam and Grace and their family — house painting, repair, this and that — and I lived free over the store. I was, in some ways, content. People had quit expecting much from me. I had my habits, which, except for fighting when I was drunk, was not expensive ones. When the Dowben kids was small, I built little things for them — doghouses and birdhouses and toy chests and such.

What beat me was time. The kids grew up and left, the old folks got quieter. Then Elia died. I knowed the family wouldn't put me out of my place or stop the pay they give me, but that changed my life. I was alone. All alone.

And my bad habits got worse — more drunks, more fighting. For that I don't blame the bitch. She only told what happened. For years, Elia had been at me to widen out — keep bees or raise chickens. I could have got a loan back then and gone into something — made a life. It wasn't the bitch's fault. The family could have told her. Two sentences, and everybody would have been happy. The truth is, it wasn't what I wanted. I wanted things to be back like in the forties, to have a store everyone needed with an inventory I knew every nut and bolt of and how to make do with what there was when there wasn't no replacements coming. I had been at home there when the world's lacks and shortages matched my own.

The legal eggs listened on to the end. Funny, we was all standing. A real set of lawyers would have sat down with the client, but since I wasn't figuring on paying 'em, standing up or sitting down didn't matter. When I was done, we all three just stood there. Then the one on the left said, "What do you want us to do?"

"Do? Sue the bitch!" I yelled. "Sue her for

slander, for murder, bodily harm, for twinning eggs
without names so they don't have no faces! This
town is full of monsters! Nothing personal, but we
don't need to look much further than this office. Get
the bitch! Take her to court and get her to give us
lives!"

They turned to one another and started a funny
mumble. It had names in it, this one versus that one,
and appellate decision 242, book six, precedent, ranana, ranana, ranana. They kept it up for four or five
minutes, and then they stopped and turned to me,
and the one on the right said, "I would like to be
called Ronald Calhoun De Becque III." And the one
on the left said in the same voice, "I would like to be
called Ramon Sanchez."

"It ain't only names, it's lives!"

"A class action suit?"

"Right, Ramon, right."

We talked about it, and when I left, I could have
sworn that something was beginning in their faces:
ridges, puckers, features that would be more than
slits and wrinkles maybe, because of their giving
themselves names.

Let me tell you something about light and time and
seasons in Gilboa. The bitch is careful about it, or
tries to be, but since incident comes first, time has a
way of stretching out long and then snapping back
like a rubber band. I never lived in the real world,
but I get the feeling that time there measures out
equal, and each person interprets it for himself. Not
here. We know when Grace and Adam are enjoying
themselves specially or are fighting or are in trouble,
because that's when the time will pull out long,
longer, longer. Then — boing — it'll be next week

or next month or the Fourth of July. Seasons sometimes pass in a day, but the hardest thing is what I
call the go-overs. You're walking down the street or
drinking or drunk or devil knows what, and all of a
sudden it's two years ago or twenty. Then you know
a main character is going back over something again.
That can happen anytime. A couple of times, I got
caught on someone's go-over on the second floor of
some building and was throwed back to before the
damn place was built and fell the two flights. People
in Gilboa don't talk about it much — used to it, or
self-conscious. I never thought about it until I got
crossed out. Then it was all I thought about — that
and getting back into the book. Because I had been
unmade rather than killed, maybe my case wouldn't
be covered. I seen then I would have to go to the
bitch myself.

Easy, you'd think. I know her habits, where she
goes and when. I could've called her up on the pay
phone or wrote her a letter, but I go strange over the
phone — a voice without a body — I reckon it's because of having problems along that line. The mail is
the same way. I needed to see her face-to-face so's I
could watch her look at me with them watering eyes
and thick glasses of hers.

She goes shopping on Thursday — Laundromat,
library. I hung around the shopping center and followed her aisle by aisle in the supermarket, waiting
for her to come and acknowledge, even by looking
away quick, that I existed and that she knowed who
I was. I am her creation, after all. Like a child of hers.
Other people seen me. Even though I had combed
up and put on some cleaner clothes, there was little
looks and shrugs, and people give me larger space to
walk in, like they do. Kings and cripples get that kind

of space. She walked on by, looking past me, probably not on purpose; to her I was just there. And it
made me mad, so I started giving hints, doing things
to get her attention. I mumbled dialogue from the
book, I talked louder. There was a bit in the book
about my voice — the high, whining quality of it. I
thought sure the sound would remind her, but she
sailed on by. My creator. Thinking, no doubt. Her
eye was on the chicken.

Just as she was rounding the corner where they
had the cookies, I cut her off with my cart.

"I'm Arne Karlsson," I said, "born March 8,
1978, died July 6, 1980. How do you do? My hair is
bad, and I'm runty looking and dirty at your pleasure. I can't read or write. I'm a drunk, thanks to
you, and my personal hygiene ain't the best. God
knows when your delicate senses was assailed by a
wino in a union suit, but you give me the torment
of it. I'm like to die."

"What do you want?" she said.

"What the hell do you think I want? I want to live,
or half live, anyway. I want to be in your book, in
Gilboa, as half made as it is."

"You're not as I had pictured you," she said.
"You're smaller, different, somehow."

That level, judging look drove me wild. "Don't
you know what you done, filling a half-formed town
with cripples, tearing time up in rags and sewing it
back together to fit your need, making garbage of
me and, when you didn't like what you made, de-
stroying it!"

People was starting to look our way. For a second,
I thought I had her. She was embarrassed by the stir,
my loud voice. I thought she would promise me
something just to make me stop. Then she said,

"Why don't you come home and we'll talk it over?"
What else was there to do? I went with her, even
helped her load her damn bundles in the car, and we
drove to her house.

I don't know what I expected — a mansion, maybe,
her being a writer and all. The place was a regular
suburban house on a street with seven others, ordinary as hell. She was trying for a big tree in front,
but the thing wouldn't be full grown for another
twenty years, and by that time, the house would be
falling in. The real surprises come when we went inside. The curtains she had was what Grace and Adam
had in *their house,* the chairs and table the same; the
hardware in her house was what Elia and I had put
in years ago when we built *their place,* the houseplants
was the same in the same pots.

She seen me looking at it all. "Surprised? You
shouldn't be. Gilboa is a composite of a dozen towns
I've known, streets I passed or lived on, mostly in
childhood. Oneonta, New York, 1946; Rockville,
Maryland, 1948; Danbury, Connecticut, 1938. The
houses are the houses of my relatives, my grandparents, and my childhood friends."

It put me back some to hear that. "And the
people?" I said. "Where do you get the people?"

"I don't know. I suspect, but I don't know."

"What do you suspect?"

"I suspect they are parts of me, and physically
they are composites of people I have seen but don't
know well."

I got sick, then faint, you know, and dizzy, and
when I knowed I was gonna throw up I looked
around quick and seen the kitchen back of a little hall.
I ran in and just made the sink. When it was over, I

stood there shaking. She come in and asked me if I wanted something to settle me. Then she helped me to a chair.

We was both embarrassed. I think she'd guessed why I was sick. It wouldn't've helped to blame it on bad booze. After a while, she said, "I wish I could do it the way God does, gene codes and all the rest, parents, grandparents, all the generations and everyone complete. I wish I could make everyone on earth the main character in his own story. I can't do that; I haven't the skill."

"But to make us out of parts of *you* . . ."

"I'm the only person I really know well enough, but there are attributes, attitudes, personality quirks I've seen in others. It isn't all me."

"But mostly . . ."

"Yes, mostly."

"Even knowing *that,* I don't want to die."

"Can't you see you don't belong in this book? You're too strong for the part you play. Haven't you wondered all along why you're so much better defined than anyone but the three protagonists — likes and dislikes, habits, history?"

"I know why. It's memory." I told her my idea, about being strong because I was in at the start of things.

She heard me out, but then she said, "It's no good, Arne. Let me move you, bring you back in another form. I'll even keep your name; I'll just put you in another story."

I laughed in her face. "I don't need that! I'm too strong. You erased me and I still ain't dead. You erased every reference to me from every friend and neighbor, and yet here I am."

She looked sad. "The last part hasn't been done."

"What's that?"

"The book itself hasn't yet become real. The people in New York will read it and pock it with copyeditor's marks, and then it will be put into galleys and then finally be printed and bound, and then it will be real. When that happens, everything that isn't written there, all the aborted ideas, the extra people and events that gathered around the writing, all the dreams and energy that illuminated it to me, will be cut away from it, and all that will be left will be what is written there."

"How will it happen? Will I feel pain?"

"I don't know."

"Why the hell did you start me if you didn't mean to let me live!"

"I thought . . . I don't know. Forgive me."

"I'm going to die because I don't fit in your plan! Well, you ain't the only one with a plan. Ronald Calhoun De Becque III and Ramon Sanchez have plans, too."

"Yes, I know. Everything is possible until the words are set and the book printed."

"How long have we got? Will I know when it starts? I mean, will I die all at once, or fade away, and when?"

"I don't know. I'm expecting the galleys some time in the next three months."

"So I got three months to live."

"I think so."

I stayed drunk pretty steady after that. Sometimes I went up to see De Becque III and Sanchez. You could tell them apart now because Sanchez had gone to the five and dime and got him a pirate mustache like kids wear, and he started putting a little Spanish sound in his words. De Becque III had gone to one of them photo machines and had his picture taken twice and said they was De Becque the Second and De Becque the First, and that they was all lawyers come out of Yale Law School. They was still egg faces for all that; he'd whip 'em out and show you every time he seen you. His instant ancestors.

It was the way they took to bear their pain and do nothing. They never did get up a lawsuit.

The bitch come down two, three times a week that first month and just walked around town. She spent most of her time with the main characters, Grace and them, but going or coming she would stop by the Two Charlies or the Ace-Hi or the Payday, where I spent my time, and once or twice happened behind them places where I was lying by the garbage cans or by the fence they put up when the freeway come in. In fact, I woke up once by that fence, covered with papers that had blown there, scraps of plastic and other stuff, and there she was looking down at me. I thanked her for keeping the weather good and warm so's I didn't have to be in the snow or nothing, and she quick shook her head and turned and walked away. Later, she fixed it up at the bars for me to get the booze I wanted, and for me to stay in their back rooms when I was too drunk to go home. After that, she didn't check up on me so much.

As the time went by, the town started to fade at its edges. In the beginning, there'd been a big campground out east where the river came down in some falls, but though it was in the town plan, she never wrote nothing about it or set no action in it. One day, I decided to go up there, but when I walked up

Cleve Road one mile, the road ended, and everything went to fog, even though the sun was shining back in Gilboa. Over to the south, the hills disappeared. They had only showed within the town limits anyway; at their backsides the land fell off like it was blasted straight down as far as the eye could see.

Back in town things got worse. Bitch quit thinking the days and nights, the weeks and months, now the story was done, and so time stopped. It got to be afternoon always, in no particular season. Except for the saloons, my part of town began to get eaten up in that fog of her forgetting. Even folks who'd had faces began to fade away. There's something worse than an egg face, and that's a sort of plastic bag blown into the shape of a person that the air is slowly leaving. You'd see 'em here and there, but mostly the streets was empty. The main characters was all inside their houses waiting to be printed. The last time I seen Adam, he said that the reality lasted for the main characters as long as people read the book and that the shrinkage of printing and objectifying was so great that the town would be nothing like what the bitch seen it as being. Except he called her The Author.

And I'm still alive. The drugstore mirror is gone spidery, and half of the store is fogged away, but I'm still here, clear and ugly, a very old man, maybe five foot six inches tall, and wearing scratchy, filthy underwear under a pair of tore bib overalls. Bitch is putting me in another story, and I got to stay here until she starts it or until the printing is com . . .

THE FLIGHT INTO EGYPT

THEY give little maps at the museum. He hadn't known that. At the door Claude had fumbled. He was faint and winded. The outstretched hand had made him think of being apprehended, and he had shied a little, before he had looked and seen the man offering the map.

Claude was being pursued, a turn of events which had only happened twice before, a thing of nightmares and the fantasies of his very occasional drunks.

He had been walking to the printers, a place on Bisher, for his order of business cards and someone had yelled, "That man — that's the man who . . ." and Claude had begun to run madly, blindly; voices were behind him yelling for someone to stop him.

Two blocks. Three. Claude hated prison but he hated jail even more. He had been in jail four times. When he wanted to stop running, being winded and with a stitch in his side, he thought of jail and ran harder. He wasn't sure he was being pursued. He thought he still heard cries and footsteps following, but he knew that if he stopped and turned around, he would lose his advantage. There was a hedge on his left and as he ran along it he came to a small opening where one of the shrubs had died and been removed. He broke through into . . .

At first he thought he had made a serious mistake. The ground between hedge and building was wide open. His only hope was a full-out sprint to the building and he had no more breath to give. His heart was bursting. There was no choice. He thought he heard voices, a stir on the other side of the hedge. With a desperate last pull of air, he threw himself into motion and made for the building.

He went toward the back of the place, a doorway or some kind of delivery entrance where he could get his breath. It was February, and though there was no snow here, there was a dry freeze that made him shudder the air into his lungs. By the time he had stopped coughing and sobbing for breath he was ice cold. He went around to the front. It turned out to be the art museum. Of course — he had passed the front of it on the parkway. Coming in from the side he hadn't realized how many blocks he had run from Bisher. He needed a bathroom. He was freezing and still felt fear, like a rat's whiskered exploration on his skin.

Going in, he had had that moment of uncertainty, the dip and yaw of panic and release, and had taken the map. He groped for admission money — "Oh, not today," the woman said, "Tuesdays are free days."

So Claude went up the big staircase to the second floor and studied the map for possible hiding places, an old habit, and walked from room to room, slowly easing and warming. It was a pleasant place. The walls were a soft blue-gray, a color he associated with quietness. The place was comforting, room after room a wordless echo of well-being from another time. Claude felt safe enough to sit down. Here the chairs were in the middle of the rooms and faced the walls. On the walls were the pictures and in each room, different styles, he guessed, or from different countries. He allowed himself to rest in the warmth, the pleasantness of the place. These rooms were what he imagined rich people's lives were like.

Claude ran scams for a living. He made money, sometimes lots of money, but he lived too close to the edge to consider himself rich. He did and had done all the modern variations on the Canal Shares Switch, the Stick, the Missing Heir, and a dozen others. He had been inside only once, but he had been in a few county jails. Those trips still gave him nightmares.

This time he had been spotted in the part of town he had kept free for business. Coincidence. It had happened once in Philadelphia, when a Mark turned out to be the cousin of a man he had taken in Tampa. It had happened in K.C. when he showed up there after three artists had run the same scam one after another for three years straight. Funny later, but only later.

Never had he been seen and recognized on the street by a Mark he had once taken. Part of his talent was physical, like a dancer's, a function of his face and body.

Claude could be anyone. Ordinarily nondescript, he could be commanding or modest, scholarly or sporty, elegant or a good ole boy, anybody . . . nobody. Seen without his remembered flavor, he went unrecognized even in the few line-ups he had had to make.

Sitting quietly, having checked for suspicious people as he had learned to do so long ago that he was barely conscious of doing it, Claude found himself looking at one of the pictures.

It was a religious picture called "The Flight into Egypt." He remembered the story and other pictures like this from Sunday School, but this one was special. Its Mary was a radiantly beautiful woman, both virginal and maternal, veiled by her flowing hair. She wore her golden head-circle, palpable as apparel. There was the friendly and docile donkey led by plodding Joseph; a contented baby Jesus, also with his golden circle. What was singular about the picture was the overwhelming atmosphere of sweetness and serenity in the artist's vision. This was not an escape but a stroll. It was set in those few moments between sundown and twilight when shadow, having been extinguished, seems instead to have been swallowed by form, so that it glows out of every rock and tree. Benediction hung in the painted air like bell-sound. In the background the work of farms was going on, succor at hand, but no intrusion in the quiet progress of the Holy Family. And it was Italy, not Egypt, a land in which nature had been domesticated and was tended and benign. In neither Joseph's nor Mary's face was there the pain of hunger — known or expected, the tightness of anxiety, the questions of flight: where to, what next? Claude, oppressed by the sudden need to escape, found himself facing a Divine Escape that was infused with an almost rapturous serenity.

He realized time was passing, but he was content. The longer the pursuers took, the less likely he would be turned in. He could pick up the cards from the printer later, going by another way, carefully. Luckily the Mark had seen him on the street, not in the shop. He had been careful in this city; the incident shouldn't be harmful. In the spell of the museum, the radiance of the picture, Claude reviewed his plans. Looking again, he noticed how honest the picture was; there was no scam to it. No lines of movement guided the eye, no tricks of perspective dazzled or compelled. The Holy Family was simply there, foreground, in this rural Italian scene. He moved his eyes slowly right to left, as though the slow group was moving, too, and he saw the winding road as it led past farmsteads and small clumps of trees, past plowed fields. It was an evening in early spring.

Claude got up and walked from room to room looking for the enchantment in other pictures. There were many nice ones, he thought, and some were silly and some were ugly and some were scams. Some ran scams the way he did; they reached out to the people looking at them and told them how to feel. He had done that all his life. There were some that were themselves, but none of them had the direct serenity of that "Flight into Egypt," that utter silence. He went back and sat in front of it some more.

Claude had grown up with the scam, with talking kids out of beating him up and, in high school and college, out of dope, money, girls. It had taken him years to learn that tapping other people's greed was the second, less important part of the scam; the first was the confidence part, getting them to see the world as what *he* said it was, engaging them. Then, their greed didn't seem like greed, it seemed like justice or fun, or love, whatever he said it was. Scams had given Claude variety and adventure. He had been in two dozen cities in a dozen years. He had also done time, and he had no friends and no real peace.

Here, he was working a variation on the Uranium Retrieval scam, which he called Toxic Waste. In Uranium Retrieval, you sold them a mountain of mine tailings. In Toxic Waste you sold them useless ground, and the more godforsaken, arid, and waterless, the better. It was a good scam because three-fourths of it was legit. The Mark *did* own the land, buying it from Claude. The only phony part was Claude's name, his validation as a private subcontractor of the Nuclear Waste Disposal Commission, and the information that the government was going to lease or buy this land from private citizens to put minimally toxic waste on it. The sites, the maps, the studies were all valid. That the secrecy was only in the greed part of the scam gave security to nervous Marks. Claude was doing very well. He was doing so well he thought he might even pay Charley Quick the $500 a month to reactivate the D.C. phone. This played the recorded message that said it was the office of whatever name Claude was using at the moment. In the two years he had been working the scam, only two people had ever called Washington to check. If he had the number, though, he would make the Marks call. It would help things along.

It was almost closing time, and being winter it was almost dark. He thought he might try to duck back to the printing place, pick up his order, and go. He got up and gave a final glance at the Holy Family at the end of their day. Soon they would move into a milder nightfall and a gentle sleep, even if outdoors, on warm earth and under a generous sky.

Claude always stayed at medium-priced hotels when he was working, and he never went to or took Marks to expensive places. He had to act as though he were actually on contract from the NWDC. When doing a scam, Claude's life had to be more completely consistent than anyone's life is, and while the scam was running, no boozing, no gambling, no girls. Claude was cautious. He had known too many artists who got caught because they were silly or vain or got seen at the wrong places. The act was twenty-four hours a day, which made for dull days and long nights. He usually spent his evenings in newspaper research studying Marks or preparing the maps he would use. Now and then he read things to keep his identity up so he could sound convincing on the scam.

And now the money was beginning to come. He had a new clientele he was working, the result of a conversation he had overheard on an airplane. The new Marks were retired government employees. He culled their names from small suburban papers, along with their clubs and other revealing details. These people were often burned out, and sometimes bitter about years of bureaucratic mediocrity. It was easy to meet them at a church or club, begin to talk, and continue over lunch, giving them the idea that he was only selling them some of that land fat cats would buy anyway before the government leased or bought it. Why not be the one? Why not, after all the waste and incompetence the government shoved down their throats, get in on the receiving side for once? It was easy to scout who would and who would not, early enough to make almost all the leads fruitful after one meeting, a huge saving of time. These Marks had far less money than his usual pool, but there were many more of them, and his thousand acres of Colorado desert was going in ten-acre plots for two thousand an acre. It was a splendid deal, he told them, and a little of a man's own back for all the years of plodding and stress. It was not greed, he implied, it was justice.

He had appointments, lunches, dinners for the rest of next week. His plots and maps were filling with the names of tract-holders. Since no one was applying for mineral, water, or road permits, few of the county agencies in the area would be concerned. Claude had made two trips to the sites and had let it be known there that he was purchasing the land for a religious retreat. The members of his sect valued the wilderness as God-chosen and wished to protect it that way, he said. They would be visiting it only on religious pilgrimage. It was a pure-gold scam and he could buy in huge areas of Utah, Wyoming, Montana, Idaho, Nevada, New Mexico, Arizona . . . anywhere there was waste space. He could pull the scam in every state in the union. He was forty-two, and unless he got bored with it, this thing could take him through the rest of his life.

Claude was not a religious man, but he was, as most people are who live and work on the edges of danger, a superstitious one. The museum had saved him; the Holy Family had befriended him, and fair was fair. He went again, in thanks, and contemplated the scene of twilit serenity. That trip was so pleasant he went again, and a fourth time.

On that visit, the guard who stood at the entryway to the room beyond his, looked through, and seeing him, walked over. "I seen you sittin' here, three, four times. We got some regulars, students and that, but you ain't copying the picture; it gives you a lift, don't it? You *look* at other stuff, but just coming and going to this one; am I right?"

Claude nodded. "This one is nice, yeah, peaceful," the guard said. They looked at it together for a while and then the guard nodded and walked back to his place. It was, Claude realized, one of the rare moments he had shared with another person for no purpose beyond itself. Claude went to church each Sunday because Marks still equated piety with virtue. He met Marks at churches. He went to lunch and dinner with Marks and he played tennis and golf and handball with them. With each Mark he lived a carefully constructed false identity: a family man with a wife and two teenage kids. He said they were shy kids because it made the Marks sympathetic and a little superior, which made them talk about their own kids. Claude had always been amazed at how little detail he needed to give. His wife. "My wife doesn't like me traveling." It was all he needed to say about her. The guard had not been a Mark. They had been quiet together under the spell of the picture. He had given no lie.

Claude wasn't married. He had made a stupid mistake at nineteen and had gotten a poor man's divorce by taking off. Then there had been Louise, when he was twenty-eight. They were going to do a team thing. She had been working the Vindictive Secretary scam in saloons when he met her. She was beautiful and sexy but she had no discipline, she was greedy, and worst of all, her timing was bad. She could never resist cheap stunts, short-changing or picking pockets, *stunts,* when he was on to a Mark for thousands. They had fought because he was hoping for something he had never wanted before — friendship along with sex, maybe, traveling with someone who . . . but she kept stunting and he had left her in Vegas. She was probably doing time now, some place, but he had wanted . . .

He sat before the three quiet people and the serene little donkey, all on the move, and remembered how thrilling that idea had been when he was growing up, going, moving, getting away. Half the thrill of the scam in those days had been that you weren't tied up, tied in, tied down to one dull place and the same people. He had said goodbye to Frackville, Pennsylvania, when he was fifteen and goodbye to talk about the price of coal, foreign competition, joblessness. Where was there *work?* The whole country was heavy with money, tormented by its weight, and begging to be sheared clean. This Mary, this Joseph, strolling in afterglow . . . They stayed away from big cities, too. He had been thrilled with big cities

when he was first on the road. He had realized in the
last ten years that smaller was easier. Middle-sized
cities don't have big bunko squads. People here were
more careful of their reputations and shame was
more painful to them than loss. He had lowered his
sights and raised his income. He had worked harder,
traveled more, six months in each city and only one
scam in each, no matter how tempting. For the past
decade, disciplined by the mistakes that had caught
others, he had gone free and gotten rich. He spent
his month-long vacations at the finest hotels in the
most exclusive resorts. He gambled sometimes. Passing a beautiful home somewhere, he would think of
himself in it, but he knew he would never settle
down. House and lawn were for fantasy; ten minutes
there for real and he'd go nuts. He was road people,
like they were, like Mary and Joseph.

The next time he visited the museum it was to say
goodbye. The plots were filling and the maps were
almost ready to be rolled up. Seven more signatures
and he could be gone, on to New Mexico to buy up
half the state.

He sat in the chair that faced the painting. He wanted
to hold the scene, to count the little people in the
background, place the houses, fix the trails of dinner
smoke from the chimneys on the far side of the
plowed fields. If he counted, located, measured it all,
maybe he could, when he wanted to, summon up the
picture, reconstruct it for himself in his new place.
The guard came over, smiling.

"How's it goin'?"

Claude didn't want to lie. "I'm having to leave
soon. I wanted to remember this picture."

The man nodded. "My brother's work is like that, jobs from hell to Texas. Permanent move, your move?"

"Yes."

"Listen; I should have thought of it before. Downstairs they got a gift shop. They sell prints, you know, photographs, even reproductions, same size and everything. If you can't get a reproduction, at least you could get a picture to take with you."

"Really?"

"Sure; you go down there and ask for this picture."

The gift shop clerk said they had photographs and a Christmas card, too, and they had prints, full size and half size. For a moment, he had a pang of sorrow that the picture, so special, so miraculous, could be made ordinary, replaceable, but he wasn't coming back here, or if he did, not above once. "Let me see the print," he said.

He felt an odd relief when he saw it was only a picture of "The Flight into Egypt," not a copy. The colors were neither as subtle nor as bright and the luminous quality was missing. As a picture, though, it could remind him, spread out in hotel rooms or on trains or planes, when he needed it, the evocation of its peace, the sweetness of its vision. "I'll take the print," he said.

She gave it to him rolled up from a box of them. He went to the post office and got a mailing tube to keep it in. By Thursday he would be gone. Unless someone got suspicious and checked at the NWDC, he would have been away for six or seven months before people began inquiring to Washington about its dump site.

Claude spent the rest of the day at the library researching new sites to buy in four other states. He also began his goodbye calls to the ninety-two Marks, which would give him a longer lead time. He was going back to Washington, he said, to report to the commission. "Of course your names won't be brought in and no one will know you have purchased part of the site. It usually takes a month or two to get the approvals through, but *you* know how the government is. In anywhere between four and seven months, you'll be approached to sell. When you do sell, I'll expect to get a five percent commission on my part in the deal. And it's a good idea not to be too greedy. Hundred-seventy-five-dollar wrenches to the contrary, our agency doesn't like straight robbery. Keep the asking price reasonable and everyone will prosper." In the evening he had another couple, a retired postal worker and his teacher wife. The man was angry at the system and loaded for bear. Claude let no logic stand in the way of the man's rage. The deal had been made almost before Claude was ready. "Let me show you the area," he said.

"I know it," the man said, "I've been in that part of the state."

"Well, here it is," and Claude unrolled the site map. "Your area is near the north end of . . ." He was looking at the couple and saw from their faces that something was wrong.

He had taken the wrong tube — he had unrolled "The Flight into Egypt." Easy to explain, and he did — his wife's birthday and he had seen this and

thought she might like . . . slipped the wrong tube
in his attaché case . . . the other was upstairs and in
just a minute . . . He had learned years ago that
when something went wrong at the crucial time in a
scam, when reality showed like the safety pin on the
call girl's slip strap, the deal died. Marks like consis-
tency, not dimension.

"It's all right," the postal worker said.

"It really isn't," Claude answered. "I do feel ob-
ligated to show you what you are getting." He knew.
He knew it was over. He left the couple and their
check at the table. When he came back with the map,
couple and check were gone.

He had no worries, really. Righteousness and reality
might come with the morning, but it would take
them a day or two to decide, and a day or two was
all he needed to sell off the last few plots and be gone.
They probably wouldn't go to the police. "Your
Flight has encouraged mine," he said to the Holy
Family and rolled the picture up and put it back in
the tube. He was irritated by what had happened, his
own thoughtless mistake, but a month ago — two
weeks ago — he would have gone hot with rage and
frustration. For a moment he wondered if something
had changed in him that would make him lose his
edge. *Marks* lived like that, and until now it had
weakened them in his eyes. A Mark in Louisville had
wanted his winnings to keep his damaged son. A
Mark in Wichita was supporting his unmarried
daughter and two children — love and anguish —
annoyance and allegiance. These were common experiences for everyone but people like himself. Ordinary people were compromised by what they loved
and cared about every day.

*   *   *

The mistake must not happen again, though. He would mark the tube, warning himself, but like family, he would always have it to guard and look after. It would always be there to trip him up. He might never again be so smooth in his lies. In the next place, when the story, the identity, had to be trotted out, he might suddenly forget the carefully plotted wife, the shy teenage son, the daughter who wore braces. He might say, instead, "There's just my brother Joseph, and of course Mary and the baby."

PERSISTENCE OF MEMORY

JURGEN had come to Leonard on the yard and told him there was a visitor. "I don't think it's a relative," he said, and he looked at Leonard oddly. Leonard got up and followed, happy for the change in routine. Media had tapered off; if it was a woman, he might be able to touch her for money. He needed money. With the same odd look, Jurgen let him wash up before he went in. The visitors' room was large and bare, divided by a Plexiglas barricade. There was one person there, his visitor, the oldest, ugliest woman he had ever seen, skeletal, lipless, and wrinkled. Her fingers were working, working over her face and body, touching it, moving, picking, bunching at the ragged dress she wore. He was glad for once he couldn't see clearly. A former visitor had plastered her side of the Plexiglas partition with kisses and the mess hadn't been cleaned off yet. He sat down and looked at her from a lowered head. It was what he did with the press.

*   *   *

The woman watched him and then, to his horror, opened her mouth and gave a piercing cry. On both sides of the barrier the guards turned, but things like that happened here and they turned back. "Lady," Leonard said, "I don't know you. There's been a mistake." She unnerved him.

She gave a cough, trying with physical wrenchings and swallowings to suppress the weeping. She gulped air, and forced back another cry. He was transfixed like a bystander at a fatal wreck. "I need you," she said. "I and the others — all the others — need you," and her hands, like spiders, ran up and down up and down her face, hair, body.

Leonard was revolted and fascinated in his revulsion. "What is it? Who are you?"

"Gehenna," she said.

"Well, Mrs. Gehenna."

Her laughter was more horrifying than her cry. It was a shriek. For the first time in his experience, Leonard saw the guards shiver. On both sides of the barrier they retreated behind the doors and watched through the glass. The woman took another breath. "There's no time for screaming," she said. "It's too late to laugh or scream. Listen. Gehenna is not who I am, although," and a laugh like a hiccup escaped, "Gehenna is where I'm from. It's the other side, and the souls of the punished seethe and fire falls from the sky and nests in our hair. Listen. One day a week, from Sabbath eve to sundown Sabbath day, the law relents, and we are free of it, and Hell rejoices more than Heaven."

"What is all this —" Leonard said. The woman must be mad.

"Listen. On Sabbath eve the fire stops, the lake of flame dries up, and we are free and we can go into the world. Listen — What do you imagine we do, hung upside down the six-days-forever? How do we endure, sheaved like bats in an attic where rags of flame burn us as they light on our fur?" Leonard was silent. She leaned forward and whispered through the speaking holes in the Plexiglas. "We tell stories. In the first millennium we tell our own lives, all the proofs, justifications, over and over. We cry the unfairness of our damnation, we revisit the woundings that we bore and those we gave others again and again and again."

"What do you want from me?"

"Listen! Listen! Why do you think God made man? It was the story He loved. In Gehenna, the instruments of music incinerate or freeze and the notes burn in the mouths of the players. Fine art goes to stinking smoke; sculptors' marble burns to lime. Only the story — Listen! We say 'Listen,' and we tell stories."

"I'm going back on the yard," Leonard said and got up. "I think you're crazy."

"I can get you out of here," the woman said.

Leonard stopped. At the level at which he stood, the Plexiglas was less stained and scratched. He saw her face. Then, he believed what she said. There were no scars on the flesh, only fresh burns, made from a point so close they looked like powderburns, made and remade endlessly. "How can you get me out?"

Her voice was gritty. "You're serving fifteen years, parole in seven and a half. Aggravated robbery."

"It wasn't the money," Leonard said. "You

wouldn't understand. It was a statement against a repressive society, against a society that values property rights above human rights."

"Listen. There's no time for that, for all the reasons and the justifications. I have only this small sabbath, a sabbath you waste, a sabbath of no value to you. You have 2,737 days to serve, and you've served 364, so that including leap years you have 2,375. For every day of those days, I can offer you what you yearn for — unconsciousness, nothingness, or dreams — long, lovely dreams. While you are away, you'll function here in this world and you won't incur the risks or dangers of this place. Listen! You can be conscious for just the time it takes to give to us . . . what we need. It will happen at a time before the prison wakes up in the morning. Then you will decide which of your memories you will give us. It will be your part of what we need, use, desire . . ."

"Memory? Which of my memories?"

"Our own memories burn and sear. The bad ones are all those years of reasons endlessly repeated. Even the good ones get tainted in Gehenna. It's to close those away, to drown them out, that we hang in anguish and cry other stories, take other days and dreams, see other roads, live in other houses. Listen, we say, and we wrap our burning flesh in your sensations, your evocations. Keep what you want; save what you want. Give me, us, the humiliating moments, the times of weakness, cowardice, the fights with friends, the abuse by the ones supposed to love you. For these incidents and the sensations connected with them, for every one, you can have a day of consciousness removed from here, from the hatred, the hostility, from the boredom and danger of this place."

★   ★   ★

She was silent then, but her body thrummed with impatience, her hands picking, smoothing, finding the sparks of her burning world as though to extinguish them before they set her afire.

"Is this . . . job . . . for me alone?"

She laughed. "Gehenna is all day and all night the six-day-forever, and the need never ends. There's a lady in New Jersey who gives all the ugliness she's ever known — a wretched childhood, a hideous rape — and she dreams herself off on a Hawaiian vacation with an ideal lover every time her husband's family comes to visit. There is a man in a Cuban jail — compared to his, your days are days of heaven. We have children . . ."

"Children?"

The old wrinkles drew up her mouth. He couldn't tell if it was a laughter or a moan. "What makes you think children have lives they want to live completely, or that they have no memories with which to pay us? Their sensations are more intense, their memories less blunted. Small ones stand closer to the coiled snake sunning or the peony on its stem. I love their fresher passions, brighter than the later passions, for color, taste, bright red, sweet sugar — yes . . ."

"Why did you choose me?"

"We listen — we can't help listening. The world's everyday sound is a vast roar, but there are voices now and then, that we can single out. Maybe one of us was passing and heard you curse. . . . Listen, time is short; will you or won't you?"

Before him the body began to tremble and the fingers that had been picking by habit for seeds of fire, maggots of fire, went wild over the face and body, trembling and jittering.

"You're willing to offer me . . ."

"Anesthesia against present pain."

"And my body will function here . . ."

"Better than you could function. There'd be no emotion to get in the way."

"Let me think about it."

"That is one thing we can't give. Look at the day — the clock is ticking — there are shadows now that weren't here fifteen minutes ago, and no time. You have no time. Ringnose wants his money and if he doesn't get it, he may kill you."

Leonard gaped at her. It was her knowledge more than her physical presence that made him believe she had power that had not arisen from his need, boredom, or jailhouse fever. He had been stymied by his debt to Ringnose. When he had first come on the tier, the big man had offered him some hash and, being new and frightened, Leonard had taken it, terrified of Ringnose's menace. Now, Leonard owed him for it; money, services, what? He had been hoping for something to change this. He had written to his parents begging for money, but they were too frightened to break the law by trying to smuggle it in to him. He kept hoping that something might happen, someone from the movement whose media had praised him as a hero "making our rotting institutions pay as they go." "You didn't set me up with Ringnose, did you?" he asked her.

"Time — there's no time for that. Listen, you can hear water dropping from the leaky spigot. Each drop is a second, each second rides the world from

east to west and drops off, gone. Give us a memory
and we will give you a day off — nothingness, escape, Ringnose paid."

"Any memory?"

"Any memory strong enough, any incident you
can see in your mind, feel in your head or your vitals,
conjure in vision, know. Sort among the sensations,
the horrors, the joys if you want to lose those, too.
There are plenty you will want to let go of."

Leonard thought he had had enough bad experiences
to supply years of blanking out. "When do I start?"

The Spirit's arms shot up in exultation and her eyes
shone. "Tonight. Get us one. I'll come to you tomorrow, at dawn, into your mind, evoke it, take it,
and the day will be rubbed out, erased."

He lay in his bunk that evening, suddenly conscious
that for the first time since his imprisonment, he was
interested, even fascinated by what he was doing. It
felt good to care about something, to choose, to have
means.

His name had been Leonard Futterman; he had
changed it to Len Future when he was a college freshman. He had wanted a life without past entanglements, nothing to render unclear the loyalty he felt
for the group he was joining, a revolutionary group
that wanted a new world. His parents had marveled
at his energy. They did not know how far it had gone
until his arrest. The jittery movements of the Spirit
had reminded him slightly of his parents' terror as
they faced him in jail and heard his arguments and

the fury he brought to the positions he took. By then he had come to despise their timidity and weakness. Memory. Incident. Choose.

Grandfather Herrman had left a small glass factory in Germany to emigrate to South America in 1932, a year after his father's birth. Leonard remembered his grandparents as nervous and furtive, eternal strangers. He had sometimes marveled as he thought of the old people, how pale and frightened they must have been among the colorful, loud inhabitants of Brazil. They had spent three years there and had come to the United States and were foreign here as well. They had been shamed, Leonard learned, in some mysterious way. Memory: Grandfather on porch, Brooklyn, 1963, crying for his dead wife. It had made Leonard embarrassed even then because it seemed so babyish. That memory was well let go. He wondered if he could recreate it fully enough. He put himself on the porch. He remembered how its gray painted railing was chipped here and there and in the chips showed its hundred undercoats in thirty colors. He heard the sound of the old man's sobs — "Oh, God, oh, God, what will I do?" — shrill as a woman's in the hot, still afternoon. In the bunk beneath him, Milburn Waycross, huge and angry, muttered hate in his evening routine, shot his urges across the back wall of the cell, and withdrew into sleep. Tomorrow, Milburn Waycross and Ringnose and the food and the waiting and the stink and the noise would be gone. If the memory was complete enough, all he needed to do was evoke it and she — they could have it and give it to the fire that sent them burning away on its wind. Remember.

*   *   *

He woke as usual before the buzz-clang wake-up. For the first time since his imprisonment, he felt expectation, even excitement. Would she come walking through the walls? As he lay waiting, her urgent voice whispered in his head, "Memory! Memory!" and then Leonard let her have what he had prepared, the porch, the look of his grandfather in detail, the sense of shame and anger, the time of the year, the smell of the painted wood, oily in the heat of his hand. He seemed to slip back into a doze and again the voice cried, "Memory! Memory!" Mrs. Farney, his third-grade teacher — Fly-Face Farney, who pulled and pulled him to the principal's office, who never let any of them walk but always pulled, pushed, tugged at them, and whose rasping "children" was the stuff of nightmare. The essence of her bloomed in his mind and he gave the days, two separate ones, and dozed again and woke, and again, and again.

It occurred to Leonard that he might be being cheated. He felt he had awakened, given a memory, and slipped back to sleep for a moment, and then given another. When the voice came again, he said, "How can I be sure days are passing?"

She said, "You yourself will leave proof." Every time he woke thereafter, a different color rubber band was around his wrist, or a thread or a shoelace. Then he turned, stretched, sought memory, found it, gave it, and again, and again. Sometimes the memory was fragmentary and her voice, or another voice, would scream out of the place in fire, "Give it, remember!" and he would try harder or give another.

On the sabbath, the voices were still, and Leonard used his rest to dream away the time in fantasy while his body went to his work and served his sentence.

In forty days Leonard had decimated most of his childhood. At first he had imagined he had endless memories to give — his playmates, teachers, Mrs. Teel, Paulie Malone. There was the day he wet his pants because he had played too long at recess and misjudged the time. There were school trips and days home sick and the way the afternoon light lay long knives of shadow across his bed. He had thought all that would fill years. Once, waking, it occurred to him that dreams were memories, too, and for a while he lived off his store of childhood dreams and adolescent sex fantasies, those which were complete enough for her to take.

It was now winter and his wakings to the drip of melting icicles from fifth tier's overhang or the feathery fall of snow past the window made him know that Gehenna was keeping its part of the bargain. He had moments of anxiety about his part of it. Eighty days had gone from 2,375. He had 2,295 left. Did he have as many memories? Did he have a thousand? A hundred more?

His wakings came to be edged with anxiety. Then he discovered he could get better access to his memory if he gave himself simple nouns: pine tree, apple, street. He could remember specific things connected with those. He had sixty more days, but on the sixty-first he hit the blank wall of his bankrupt past. It happened with the word caramel corn. He was remembering a carnival he had gone to, a day for which he had waited, he and . . . he and . . . silence. Nothing. The day had been shared by someone, someone eager, happy, waiting. He and *someone* had gone in the car, laughing and joking, had ridden the rides, eaten the caramel corn. The memory with the loss of that someone lay deflated, spent. Although he got the day, childhood intensity of hot sun and the cooking-sugar smell of the caramel and the oily smell of the popping corn, carnival music, and the colors all around them, he had seen the end. The memories were not to be shared, but given, and when there were no more, he would hit the wall, blank, total, with no face or scenes he knew. There would, when it was all over, be no evocation of anything, no memory at all.

It was too late to stop. The few moments of waking, stretching, formulating his memory were horrible to him, unbearable to smell and see. His cell was small, two bunks, one very low toilet, the high sink over it — a man had to wash sometimes with the stink of a stopped up commode directly under him. The walls were full of graffiti so that the eye was caught by the ugly screed of words scratched in the thousand angers of a thousand cons. He was buying his way out of it with something that had, only one hundred forty-one days ago, seemed less valuable than the smallest coin made. Remember. It caught. They were at the beach, his aunt and uncle, mother and father of . . . the wall again. He remembered his aunt who, for the beach, always wore a kerchief, a white one with red dots. . . . He realized he was working hard, trying to squeeze detail out of a resisting past without giving too much. Memories could be divided, saved, husbanded. The day at the beach, though, was it one or a distillation of many such days? In either case it must be rationed, given in segments like an orange, because like an orange, part by part, his mind was being eaten. The wall told him so. There had once been someone connected with him for whom there was now no evocation of any kind.

On day 150 (2,225 days remaining), Leonard awoke and begged for a rest. The Spirit howled from hell: "Do you know how to lie in fire, to freeze in the shame of your pleasant past?"

"I don't have anything more to give —"

"Then live the rest of your sentence."

"No, please . . . I can't do that."

"Try harder. We fixed it with Ringnose and no one bothers you now. We have done well by you."

"You're eating me alive."

"Listen! You have relatives, friends, you went to school, camp, you are *middle class*. Never in human history have people had more novelty of experience, trips, visits, outings, vacations. It is novelty on which memory is based. Listen!"

"Give me time to go to the library, to get some books, pictures . . ."

"Give it — give it!" she cried.

Some time later he woke and found himself holding his high school and college yearbooks. He opened them greedily, no longer caring to separate the pleasant from the unpleasant, the whole from the fragmented. He knew he would give all he had, wherever 2,225 memories were stored. He started with *The Cougar,* his high school yearbook.

The teams; there were the coaches, the clubs, the green springtimes and the blue-wind autumns. He had once thought he might save the best of these, a simple memory of Willie Madigan, Joe Sperber, Clem Jones, and himself, walking across the far end of the track after school. It was the day they had all decided to quit football. Willie and Clem were first string, Joe and Leonard were third, where no one cared. They were, that day, amazed and proud of Willie and of their friendship. They had made a decision, the first that pitted them against the adult world of expectation. It was a heady moment. The trees across the road were bare, the wind almost cold and whipping the school flags so that their sound was like applause. They were dressed for the cold — Willie was in his letterman's blue and white, he himself was in a trainman's coat he had gotten secondhand and wore like a dare. Such were their bodies then that they could have gone coatless and not really minded. They felt this somehow to be their strength. They gave none of the credit to their youth. Invincible, they were making the choice to step down. For Willie and Clem this had not been possible until they knew they were capable of first-string play. Caught in that memory, Leonard paused a moment in a pain almost great enough to stop it, and then he let it go, evoked it, and it was taken and he slept again.

He used up the high school yearbook in thirty days. He could read it from cover to cover and evoke nothing, no one. Junior high had gone months ago. Grade school was a fitful flicker like lightning at the horizon reflecting itself against clouds — seen and gone before it could be caught.

College. Relatively few of the cons had gone to college and there was a certain envy, felt and sometimes expressed by them. One of the blacks Leonard had bunked with had said: "You jivin', everybody be the same, you be robbin' banks for the poor. That's after you done got all you can get."

Leonard had answered, "Everyone gets what he can," but he had stopped defending himself and then he had stopped trying to alter his speech to be more like theirs.

College was where Leonard felt he had come into his own. It was the time of his greatest excitement and awakening. His activities didn't appear in the year-book, the arguments, the commitments, the people. Nowhere were there pictures of Anthony Lorenzo, of all the talking and the listening that had formed his political awareness, of Barbara and Teri, Don Miller, Ken Seybright. Still, the scenes of the campus, the dorms, and student center brought back many of the memories of their meetings, bull-sessions, the organizing and defining by themselves as a serious political group and by the other students as radicals. Leonard had liked the term *radical*. He enjoyed being unique, separated. Lorenzo was a brilliant leader, a patriot in a way that didn't make Leonard want to gag at the word. He was Len, now, Len Future, and he and Lorenzo and Seybright and Barb and Teri were going to do what the books only talked about. They would shatter and remake, explode and rebuild. They held protests and marches and when they turned around they saw others marching with them. They began to think of more direct forms of action.

In the beginning Leonard had thought he would keep those memories as his own, but now he told himself it would be foolish and romantic to save what had no practical use and what was an unnecessary possession, a mental photo album as trite and bourgeois as the yearbooks he now held. He spent the next wakings on his later days, the robberies.

How Gehenna loved the robberies. There were other voices now, a gabble of them, and when the memory was interesting or special they moaned like lovers. For the slack or incomplete memories, they urged and pulled. "The day, what was it like?"

"It was the night we planned the second bank job," Leonard said. He had a sudden spasm of guilt about giving up the names and faces, invoking them in his mind-voice. They had sworn secrecy. . . .

"Memory! Memory —" They gibbered like bats.

He hesitated. Miller was doing time here, too, but in another building, and they seldom met. Lorenzo had copped a plea, Seybright had escaped, and as far as Leonard knew was still free. The loyalty they had sworn . . . He dove into the memory.

It was a summer night, hot and muggy. They had all felt powerful, in command. Action against property was righteous, Lorenzo had said. Leonard's part had been to map the bank, detail the exits, and later watch how it opened.

"Give us all of it!"

He tried to give the details he knew they craved. Lorenzo's apartment, dank but cool. They drank beer, having sworn off drugs until after the job. Leonard had laid out the bank's floor plan. They were all on a high, a quiet high, like rafting on fast water. . . . That made him remember rafting, another memory, another day's respite, and he slept and woke and gave them the water, sun-glinted as he came toward the rapids, the mile-long sinews contracting and stretching against his boat. I remember . . . and then he slept.

"About the robbery . . ." she said. The robbery itself had been a comedown because they had been off stride that day; he knew it waking up, but couldn't remember specifically enough, and the job had only one strong memory, the moment of their being in 'the bank, of his dropping the attaché case and having to pick it up. He tried to tell her — them — in his mind-voice that it should have been funny, clumsiness when grace was called for — a robbery was, after all, a public appearance — and how he had almost said "oops," but it wasn't funny. The onlookers had been terrified; thwarting him might result in his firing his gun and a red-splattered — "Oh, God!" a woman had cried, and fainted. A new voice demanded that minute and Leonard tried, picturing humor gone cold, the smell of the air just at that moment, hot day, cold sweat, and how they were off rhythm so that no one had thought to plan who went through the door first so there was a scramble and Lorenzo nearly fell.

"Feelings, what were your feelings?"
He knew what they wanted by now, shame, rage, triumph, joy. He had had none of those. "You try for nothingness, no emotion. There's too much else to think of." He remembered the belly-clutch of fear just then. The door. Then he remembered seeing how ordinary the street looked, how out on that ordinary street they had gone back to their plan to split

up. He gave them bright sun, dislocation, fear, relief within seconds. They took that moment.

On the 210th day, Leonard suffered a kind of breakdown. He woke up and there was nothing. He felt no sensation, saw no picture in his mind — none. They came: "Remember. Remember!"

"I have nothing." There was a cry from hell — anguish and rage, the cry of the addicted. Leonard felt their terror and then his own. "I'm dried up. I can't . . . " and then there was only the prison day, bearing down.

For the first time in seven months, Leonard rose resident in his body, heard the wake-up coughs and hawks of the men on the tier, men pissing, groaning, cursing. He smelled the smells. The seven months he had escaped into memory had blunted his ability to protect himself from the onslaught of his senses. He dressed, fumbling, almost weeping, was walked to breakfast, recoiled in the ugly impacted hate and rage of the men around him, paranoid spew, fume of ungratified sex, their sounds their smells their hair-trigger touchiness or obtunded despair. Now and then men came to him and said things, things pertaining to the life his surrogate self shared with them. He answered as well as he could. Once or twice he saw puzzlement on their faces. It was masked quickly as everything was, and he yearned almost to tears for the salvation he was losing — why couldn't he remember? There must be more. During the evening break he went to the library and looked at cookbooks for memories, at catalogues, at pictures, for any clue that would open the magic door again, door through which he had once walked so easily. The day passed. Another, another.

Leonard's search became desperate because somehow he wasn't able to adjust to prison life as he had before. The possibility of an alternative had destroyed his ability to tighten himself against the assaults of its boredom, danger, and ugliness. Three days. She came to the visitors' room again.

If anything, she was skinnier, more withered, tighter. Her hands never stopped their pinching, picking, spidering in her ragged clothes.

"I've lost it," he said. "There is no more."

"Nonsense. Of course there's more. Look around. You don't want to be here — find something. Listen!"

"I'm played out. Done."

Her eyes lit. "You need a vacation," she said.

It was a car ad he had seen years before, a gracious old house among big trees. There was a wide veranda with a rocker on it. A sports car was in front of the house, and in it were scuba things and picnic baskets.

"Wonderful," she said, "go there and rest. The house has everything you'll need."

"How long?"

"A week. We have Ringnose now, for what he's worth, Luchese, Kent. Enjoy yourself."

All the days were sun-dappled. He lay in the meadow in front of the house or rocked and read magazines on the porch. Twice he took the car to the lake with the people who came by, owners of the gear and the picnic things. They were pretty laughing girls and clean-limbed young men, but they were ad people — they had no pasts, no futures, no hopes, no memories. They took him scuba-diving but the lake was silted and the company boring. He made love to the girls and forgot it immediately after doing it. He had vowed he would rest from memory, but a few times he tried it gingerly, like a neurology patient testing for the paralysis that might or might not still be there. There was no remembering and in the old brass bed, open-window cool in the moonlight, he heard rats scrabbling in the walls.

And the days there were unchanging. It never rained; there was no sense of movement through a season, no old flowers dying or new ones in bud.

"You've rested. Let's begin. There's more — of course there's more."

"Something has let go . . ." he said, "I can feel it."

"Only memories."

"Don't lie. I felt it *there,* lazing in the sun, reading, riding, making love. I've sold you my soul, haven't I?"

She laughed the screeching laugh that drove the guards behind the doors. "No one, not even you, gives up his soul."

"What do I give up, besides those memories? I felt something stop and break away and flow away inside me."

"Oh, that — that's not serious — it's not a vital need."

"What is it?"

"If it's gone, it would have been the ability to change, to recreate yourself. It's more of a choice

than a need, and you've never wanted change in
yourself."

"I'm pledged to work for change. The movement . . ."

"Your bunch wants everyone else to change —
society."

"How do people change?" Leonard asked.

For a moment she slowed and went quieter. "They
start with changing their own stories, by retelling
them with new shadings. Are there gentler moments
in memory? Are there crueler? By stroke and stroke,
memory by memory, over time they remodel their
pasts and then themselves, their ideas of who they
were, then are, and then, of who they will be."

"And I have no past. I gave it all to you."

"You hated it; it's gone."

"I'm walking streets without markers . . ."

"Losing *memories* doesn't mean losing your *memory*. Back then, didn't you recognize a friend even
when you had forgotten some of the things you did
together? You still have the friend, you just don't
have the memory."

"And changing . . ."

"You'll get old like everyone else, but you'll no
longer have to labor at rewriting your past or re-
modeling yourself. Give us memory, now, give it.
Remember!"

"I can't take prison. I can't stand these days . . ."

"Find the stories for us. They're there —
hundreds, thousands more. You don't want them,
you don't use them. Give us — give us — and we'll
see you're comfortable, sleeping, reading, rocking on
the porch —"

★   ★   ★

He went back to his cell and lay on his bunk ransacking. Friends, all gone, foods, names, flowers. He got ten things on a list and another ten that might yield — flowerpot, a broken flowerpot. Where was it? When did it happen? He went to the screaming cafeteria, writing all the associations he had, desperately seeking — plaid shirt — madras shirt — whose? It was a kid in school, Prentice. There had to be more. The evening dragged. A washcloth — *injuries*. When? Where? Ten more memories, another ten. Remember the time I shut my finger in the car door and my dad was . . . he slept.

On the 250th day he woke in a dry, familiar desperation, went through a list of one hundred words seeking to evoke — there — nothing to give now. He tried another hundred, hoping for the eye-corner phantom that runs for safety before it can be seen and identified, a moment, a girl, a friend . . .

The past was bare, a twilit plain without the beauty of twilight, and unchanging.

To the screams of anguish he said, "It's over."

"Find it — find it!"

"I'm done."

He rose into the prison morning. There he lay and counted the time remaining to him, the two thousand one hundred days before he could be accepted for parole. Each of those days would be a prison day, a day through which he would walk skin-stripped at the mercy of his senses, uninsulated. He would not be clever because vulnerable people aren't clever and because of that he might be beaten, stabbed, made a victim again. He wanted to cry but the wake-up sounded, raw in his ears. Then the whole tier groaned, and rose in hate. It occurred to Leonard that simpler than what the Spirit had said about recasting life, every prisoner had a small place of refuge through the day. The refuge was memory. The man at the laundry basket piling and sorting clothes might be fishing on a once-seen lake, or simply cruising the main drag in Coffeeville on a Saturday night, with the car radio on and a girl in a tight sweater. Leonard, whose experiences had been more varied than most of the prisoners, had, by choice, given away the geography of his childhood and adolescence. There was nothing left to glow behind the hideous moment and make it bearable.

The days, taken raw, went hour by hour. He had begun to think of suicide. Then Rimper on tier three had a heart attack. Leonard put in for the job at the power plant and got it, there being no other con who wanted it.

The work was simple. He checked the gauges that monitored the lights, heat, and power. Years ago, the job had been vital and heavy with perks. Now, all the systems were on backup and auxiliary power and the job was only boring. Leonard wanted it because it let him be alone, free of having to fake the self he had been while his real self slept.

May. His parents came. They were, as always, cowed by the prison. They huddled and shrank. His mother brought bribe food, and spoke in whispers. "Are you all right?" He told them he was. They began to talk about family news: Aunt Essie had had a stroke. Cousin Brian was getting married. Births and Bar Mitzvehs. For none, not one, had Leonard a memory. He recognized his parents, but they had lost definition and it was hard to follow their simplest talk. "It takes me in the feet — you know me and my feet, all the years standing . . ." And Leonard didn't have a clue to what his father meant or to his mother's sighed, "Betty's upset, naturally. You'd think after all her troubles . . ."

He sat and watched them suffer behind the Plexiglas. He had given away all the cousins and the aunts and the days, landmarks of his childhood, mountains, seashores, clouds, spiderwebs from which hung . . . wait . . . from which dew hung . . . He saw it with perfect, pristine clarity, a memory without defensiveness or self-serving, a simple, stunning picture infused with childhood's awe. The dew was suspended in such a way on that perfect web that each drop carried, weighing and trembling lightly on the suspension cables of the web, a little rainbow. He saw it again, how the light brimmed in the tiny prisms, and prism and drop and web hung in the spring morning where he stood close to the smell of the wet grass, because he was a little kid. Grass touched his knee, cold-green with the morning's cold dew. Then there was a little breeze and the web trembled and the drop suddenly shuddered and the prism scattered rainbow and fell from the web like tears. "I remember," he said. They thought he was speaking of Aunt Essie and nodded.

The ruined landscape had yielded up a survivor. Where there was one there might be others. One by one, they might creep from under the rubble. Hadn't he been seeing someone home drunk one night in college? Didn't he pretend to be drunker than he was so he might look up at the vast spread of stars and yes, yes, he had been wearing a . . . it was a wool jacket, heavy, and a blue knit watch-cap and his friend — a shadow now — had still some part of him that had not been given away. Web and starry-night, warm-jacket shadow friend would be his to use, to remake himself, bit by bit, year by year. His friend was singing away in his ear. He couldn't capture the tune and there was a destination he couldn't place, but the memory, wind and cold and gin and being tired and the stars and the singing . . . dew in the web — Thank God. "Did you ever have long hair?" he asked his drawn, huddled mother; "Was it ever held with two curved combs at the sides of your head?"

FAMILY TREE

IT was March and the storm threw wet, intractable snow on Denver. City traffic was gridlocked, and in the suburbs lines were down. Adam Cik lived on Gilpin Street. He was the only one in the office who walked to work. Today the going was slow and he got there half an hour late. No one had come. He waited. They called in one by one. Adam was senior man at the Denver office where all the billing was done for companies in Chicago, New York, and Detroit. He ran the office, filled out the reports, and kept the statistics. The five others thought him stodgy — he thought of himself as steady. At 9:15, he sat down at the console and keyed in the orders coming from other cities. He logged them. Then he started on Grace's work, checking the orders sent to local outlets against their stated inventories. It took another hour to run down four discrepancies; by eleven, he was finished.

★   ★   ★

He had imagined a slow office today, not a stopped one. He got coffee, went to the bathroom, and considered leaving. He went to the coatrack and then decided to stay. There was a certain excitement in being here alone. Grace's chatter sometimes annoyed him; Tony was sometimes insulting under the guise of wit. Adam remembered that six months ago, Larson had programed in the access number to Data-Tix for sports events, theater, and concerts. They also had the number codes for the Denver Public Library. On a day like this there would be plenty of time to get in. Perhaps he might run his name through their main computer. . . .

Adam Cik. He had had hassles in school because of the name: sea-cik, cik-joke. His father had told him the family had come to America from Greece, but they were not Greek. When he was growing up he had sometimes been stung with envy for the comfortable ethnic identity of his friends. He had had no soul foods to talk about, no evocative holidays, no words of magical specialness.

He was an only child, quiet and serious. His mother had died when he was twelve. By the time adolescence came, he had found himself judged ordinary and dull. It seemed to him that he was only lacking traditions, a past, a rootedness. He thought that feeling should be expressed in patriotism, but when he was in high school, his classmates laughed at him for it. The reputation as dull endured through school and into the army. He liked the order and predictability of the service, and for a while he thought of making it his career.

★   ★   ★

It was in the service that he had begun, tentatively, to seek namesakes. He had looked at rosters, lists, rolls, to find his name. He went, too, to Arlington Cemetery, to archives of World War I and II, and sought among the names there for his own. It wasn't there — it wasn't anywhere. He served two hitches, both in the United States. Then, because he had met Marie, who wanted a permanent home, took the job in Denver he now had. Now and then he was sent on short trips to various cities. He got into the habit of looking at the phone books in the places where he stopped, hunting for Ciks, and he would leave the plane when there was a stop on the way and go to the phone book; he never found anyone.

At his wedding, one of Marie's relatives, a little drunk, had told him he should change his name; it sounded funny; their kids would be laughed at. Adam had looked over at his father sitting alone, a small, gray man, lost in the uproar of Marie's big, loud family, and he had wanted to say something about carrying a banner no matter for how small an army. It sounded silly and he had had a little to drink also. He had turned away from the man without answering.

Two years later, Adam's father died of a heart attack. At the funeral, it had occurred to Adam that now he might be the only Cik in the world. The two children they had later were girls, and Adam, though he had not stopped looking for Ciks, had stopped hoping to find family or to go through any more formal or vigorous research. As he sat at the console in the empty office on this snowbound day, his fingers hovered over the keys. He had already tapped in the access code. If he tapped in his name, what would he find? Perhaps there would be some Cik who was or had been a writer, a poet, a scholar . . . He smiled, and then typed CIK, ALL TITLES, and waited. He found he was eager. He went for more coffee.

In the beginning Adam had tried to make Marie's family his. He liked them and they seemed to like him, in spite of his funny flag waving and his shyness at all other times. Sometimes they did overwhelm him. Because he had no family at all, he and Marie and the girls always went to one or another of Marie's people on holidays. The Beaudines were a noisy, spirited bunch — originally French Canadian and Irish. They had been in Colorado for generations, and they were self-regarding to the point of vanity. Once Adam had asked about the family's migration to America and he got a history that took an hour. "You shouldn't have gotten them going," Marie said afterward. "You know what Claude and Martha are like . . ."

"They're proud of the Beaudines and the Dupuys, the Collerans and the Hallorans and the Hogues. Luckily they didn't ask me about the Ciks or the Peterses."

"Luckily? It was simple bad manners —"

"I wish *I* was able to look back, the way your family does, like a long view through an open door where people are standing. When I try to look through my door, there's no one there."

Marie's comfort had been as clumsy as Claude's pride. She told him it didn't matter. Too many people *live* in their family trees. Adam didn't argue.

Marie, comfortable in identity, had never known a silence like his.

Sometimes she kidded him about his patriotism. It wasn't hard to see that he was using America as a kind of family identity. When Ginny and Lydia were small, he had celebrated all the national holidays with them. Marie seldom went along to the parades, but the three of them were curbside at every one: Fourth of July, Labor Day, Colorado Day, St. Patrick's, and Veterans' Day. They flew the flag on all of them. Marie's family laughed at it — "Flag as big as the one they fly at Arlington." Some of the neighbors said things, too. Now and then at summer barbecues or mowing front lawns, Bob Wylie or Harry Stamps would kid him. "What's the flag out for *today?*"

Once or twice, Bob had implied that Adam's patriotism was excessive and embarrassing. As the girls had moved into adolescence, they, too, began to complain. "Why do you have to hang that *huge* flag out every time we turn around?" "Dad, Bud Callan calls you *Yankee Doodle.*" Later they said, "We want you to change our name — *Cik* — nobody's named *Cik*. Homecik, Cik to Death, Cik Joke . . ."

"Are kids still doing that?"

"Yes; we hate it."

"That ridicule," Adam said, "is what I had in school. Even the same jokes. Savor them. They're the only family tradition the Ciks have."

Adam, at the door with coffee, heard the clicking of the computer as it began to make hard copy. If not for the snow, he probably could not have gotten in to the library's memory banks. He pulled his chair up and watched the paper feed jerkily from the machine. Hum. Stop. It was finished. He picked up the copy, proud of his idea. He had not expected anything, yet here was a list of sorts, items, the literary contribution to the English-speaking world by people named Cik. There were only three of them, but they were in his name, a name he had not seen before except referring to him or his father. Smiling slightly, shyly, he let his eye go slowly down the copy: one was a monograph by a Brother Anton Cik, 1847, a hypothetical plot pattern for a certain comet. *Brother* Anton. No children, then. Brother, you should have been more careful of lineages and links. Plotting stars, you didn't think about your posterity. . . . There was a book on medical conditions of the feet and legs, 1886. Dr. Robert Cik. Chicago. Maybe he had a family and they were still alive somewhere in the country. Adam's eye went to the last item. It was what looked like an autobiography: *Journey of One Damned,* 1888, a translation from the Serbian of the murderer, Joachim Cik, 1740, including an account of his capture, trial, and execution.

Adam tore off the printout and looked at it for some time. Serbia. At least he had learned that. A murderer. The idea stopped him for a moment. Then he thought, "There are murderers named Smith and Jones, too." It meant only that a Cik in 1740 had committed a crime — perhaps in response to tyranny or in self-defense. Perhaps he could find out by learning more of the background. He entered the name CIK again, this time for books, articles, etc., about the *subject* CIK. On the other computers, order, inquiries, and billing had begun to come in from various parts of the country. He posted them, and for two hours he found himself busy again. At two, he ate the lunch he had brought with him and had more coffee from the machine. Afterward, he went back and read what was in the bin from the library.

There were five entries: in a book, *Why Did They Kill: A Study of Joachim Cik and His Murderous Family,* by Julius Leonard, 1963; two chapters in *Inherited or Familial Psychopathy,* a thesis by Lucy Manuel, 1957; the autobiography Adam had seen before; *The Trials and Executions of the Family of Girard Cik,* from the court records of the Assizes of Sarajevo, 1738–40, translated and annotated by Marius Reiner. The last was *The Arrest, Interrogation, and Execution of Euphemia Cik* for witchcraft in Bavaria, 1760, a study in mob psychology by Hans Munck, 1925.

Adam sat stunned, his mind circling on itself in a fog of denial. He kept thinking, "That isn't fair. That isn't right." Then he worked at thinking rationally. People seldom talk about their family backgrounds. Even Marie's people had cousins, uncles around whose names was a silence. Every family has its mentally ill, its criminal . . . look back far enough . . . half the world is descended from the sons of Cain. . . . How many ordinary people are progeny of the Youngers, the Daltons, the Jameses? He was sorry now that he was alone, that he had brought this knowledge on himself when there was no one around to reflect the ordinary routine, to say the platitudes, to give the small talk that would restate the little realities of daily life — You may not even be a relative. There may be innumerable Ciks in Bosnia. In Bosnia, Cik may be as common as Smith or Jones.

★   ★   ★

He began to feel an obscure anxiety, even a fear. "Murderous family," Julius Leonard had said. . . . Still, in every place, at different times in history, war or anarchy made whole families respond by . . . These thoughts came in the slowed-down black-and-white primer words of shock and denial. After a long time staring out at the snow and the lowering sky, Adam tapped another set of numbers on the machine. They would put the code numbers of the five entries on order and have them sent to his library. It was time to close the office. He did this without being conscious of doing it, and only the shock of cold on his face when he was outside broke the mood for a while. He went home, carrying the printouts in his pocket. When he got home, he read them again.

Adam got the books he had sent for and read them the way an alcoholic pulls at his bottle. Girard Cik haunted the Denver days. He had been a huge, brutal man, feared even in his youth. He had taken a woman named Perdita from her horrified and resisting family and lived with her in plain sight, in a village near Jajce in what was then Bosnia. There was no indication that the family was Bosnian any more than Bavarian or Greek. Girard and Perdita had six sons and at least that many daughters, and with them and a host of relatives who were equally voracious, they had terrorized the countryside for miles around. His house was a fortress guarded by dogs and family. For fifteen years, between 1722 and 1737, Girard and Company stole, murdered, raped, committed arson and kidnapping, unopposed. The boys grew to manhood and stole girls to bring to the fortress. Slowly, one by one, in accidents or by being waylaid in secret so as to preclude reprisals, four of the boys and five of the girls died or were killed. In 1737, the baron of the province finally ordered the nest cleared. An army marched on the stronghold of the Ciks, stormed it, razed it, and killing mostly women and children, at last found only two of the Cik men left alive to take: Girard, now old and covered with what were described as "loathsome sores," and the son, Joachim, the only one who could read and write. Girard died in prison. Joachim was saved for a trial, "to make an example," the commentator said, "to all errant men, that justice, though slow, is done at last." The confession, which may or may not have been written by him, was read by him and took two hours. Then he was executed and his body buried at a crossroads "so that it might bear the curse of passers-by until he and his deeds were forgotten." This took five generations.

Adam lost . . . mislaid . . . the spring that year. His present world, its trees, houses, people, its days of work and leisure were passed by as one passes by a window on his way to some errand of greater importance. The trees Adam saw, the people, the sunrises and full moons, were in Bosnia and Serbia in the years of Girard and Joachim Cik.

Adam began to study the pasts of those disputed places. He tried to look across two continents and an ocean, to see the mountains and woods, how people lived, to see past the colorful costumes in the research books to the agonizing history, the poverty, the revolutions, the tyrannies. He tried to follow Girard, to use political and social history, to understand what had formed him, to relate him to the world in which

he lived. He tried to see how it would be with
Joachim and the other unnamed boys and girls, and
finally to Euphemia dying the family's violent death
thirty years after Joachim's. Was Euphemia a daughter? A granddaughter? None of the accounts had
listed all the names of family members. Had any left
the fortress before the final raid? Were there other
kin, nephews, cousins? As they were written of, they
seemed more like a visitation of evil than a family of
individuals with separate personalities and styles. He
had already read everything he could get about the
family and had tried to find more in the German and
Serbian and Croatian listings. For Euphemia, there
was a little more. The records of her trial had apparently been lost in the Second World War; there was
only the account by Munck remaining and *he* had
been far less interested in Euphemia than in the psychology of her accusers. Munck had discounted any
possibility that she could have been a witch, or even
a malevolent neighbor. His writing showed him as
having been very proud of being a modern with a
rational German mind.

Marie, who at first had encouraged Adam in his re-
searches, was now tired and even frightened of the
revelations that had overwhelmed him. Her experience with families was sunny, ordinary, a history of
more or less decent generations and the occasional
stray. It was poor preparation for Adam's devils, his
anger and compulsion in spite of the anger to learn
more and more. "There must have been other Ciks,"
he cried to her when she told him to let the family
rest. "If they had all been killed or captured at the
fortress, maybe there would have been no Brother

Anton, no Dr. Robert. My father said our time in
Samothrace wasn't more than two generations . . ."

"I see you disappearing into this thing," Marie
said, "swallowed up. Those people are suddenly
more important than your own kids, than I."

"Not true — I need to know who we were —
why . . ."

Memorial Day came and went that spring without
Adam's flags or celebration. Marie was worried
enough to talk to her brother, Roger. When Adam
found out, he was annoyed. "Roger is a school coun-
selor," he said.

"He knows that your changing the habits of years
is indicative of psychological tension," she said,
sounding unconsciously like Roger. "He said we
should get help."

"The help I need is from a genealogist. Why are
you upset? Lydia will be in college, Ginny doesn't
care; the neighbors have been laughing at me for
years about my flag-waving."

"And that's why you didn't celebrate this year?"

"Sure."

It wasn't true. He had been down in the family room
ready to bring up the flag and the Memorial Day dec-
orations he had been using for almost two decades
and he had had a sudden pang of guilt and anger. The
Ciks, the ones in Bosnia, were evil, selfish, cruel, but
they didn't accept second best, settle for less, substitute country for family and the acceptable for the na-
ked call of their wills. Their motives were clear,
unmixed. They had no pride in nation, region, cul-
ture. They did not defend anyone but their own.

Their evil was great, but so, Adam thought, was their sense of self. And he had put the flag away and let the day go by without watching the parade or going to Fort Logan and the ceremony at the graves, none of which were kinsmen's.

It was the power of those forebears that held him fascinated. *They* filled their canvas; they had never ceded anything, letting it slip away to others as it seemed to Adam he had done all his life.

In June Adam made his yearly trip to the home office in Detroit. The city was having a heat wave, and as he stepped outside the terminal, the air hit furry and rank against his face. He always planned to use this time to see the city but this time the heat made him decide for the hotel immediately. He had done his work well. In his attaché case were a series of carefully worked plans and reports. He knew he should be confident, but the feeling of having to measure up, to explain his methods to managers who might not understand them, always made him anxious, and as he traveled to the hotel, registered, and went to his room, he felt increasingly constricted and restless.

Because of this feeling, he was preoccupied and did not want to look up Ruthven or Morrison, who were also at the hotel — at least not until dinner. He went up to his room and took out the reports and looked them over, bathed, and then decided to walk the hotel mezzanine and look at the shops. Maybe he could get some small things for Marie and the girls.

He went down the stairs from the fourth floor. It felt good to move a little. At the mezzanine the stairway opened out to a carpeted and rather grand staircase

with the arcade of shops going all around the open
well that looked into the main lobby. He began to
make the circuit, passing idly by the furs and jewelry,
a fashionable cigar store, a women's boutique. Most
of the things he saw were overpriced and too elaborate. Marie liked trinkets which she could put in her
display case, and then give to her little nieces and
nephews. He walked on around to the east side of the
arcade.

He became aware of a noise — a series of noises
around the bend of the arcade, out of sight. Voices
were shouting, glass breaking. Then there were
shots. Two, then another. Because he couldn't see
anything, he didn't know if he should move, stay,
hit the floor. His time in the service had included no
war at all — he had developed no instinctive reaction
toward gunfire. He thought that if he got down on
the floor he would be unable to make any other
move, but the sound of the glass shattering had made
him aware of his closeness to the big display windows. He moved away from them and out into the
middle of the walkway.

Then a man ran past him, a medium-sized man wearing work clothes, a man whose sweaty face was set
in the mask of fear rigidly controlled. He was running almost blindly, holding a gun. The scent of his
passing had terror in it. It was acetic, the smell of
nightmare-wakings. It was this smell that made
Adam afraid and told him to move, but by then it
was too late. Another man, bigger, was on him at
full run. The man had not seen him until they collided and then the man grabbed him. "Asshole —
why didn't you get out of the way!"

"Wait!" Adam said, and tried to extricate himself, but the man now had hold of him.

"You come with me, asshole."

There was suddenly in Adam a feeling of immense insult, of incredulous wrath. "Don't you know who I am?" he shouted, and his voice was like another man's, a wilder, freer, more powerful man's. "I am a Cik — one of the Ciks," and he spoke it into the man's face as into an idiot's.

Shock widened the man's eyes — his pupils went large. He stood dead still for an instant, and Adam began to pull away and then he seemed to go icy with rage. The man hardened his hold on Adam. "Sick — you gonna be dead you don't come with me." They began to struggle, the man pulling, Adam resisting. Adam saw through the red of his rage, the face, and with all his force he sent a punch straight into it and a kind of rage and joy broke in him. He wanted more face to hit, more body to kick. The criminal screamed, "What you doing?" in his own incredulity and wrath. They both fell. Adam was trying to kick, to be as satisfied kicking as he had been with his punch. Blood was spattered. The blood made him roar with happiness. He felt neither of the shots that were fired into him.

They lay side by side in the emergency room. The criminal had been shot himself and later hit in the head by the security police who had had to pry Adam's hands loose from him. The man — his name was Luther — lay tied down. He raged in disbelief at Adam's ignorance of the simplest, the most obvious customs and expectations. "This isn't your beef, man — you tell me *sick* — you *crazy*. He had it com-

ing — it was self-defense — I shot him — this man's
crazy. He's crazy," he said over and over to the
nurses, aides, doctors, and police.

To Adam's complete surprise, they all seemed to
agree with Luther. "Look at that hand — some of
those bones will have to be reset. You shouldn't have
tried to take him on."

"He was armed."

"Did you think you could detain him? You might
have been killed!"

Adam looked at the policeman who had said that, as
he stood filling out his report. He wanted to talk
about the Ciks, the wildness, the madness he had
shared with them. He had been doped for surgery
and it was getting hard to talk. He said, "We would
never have accepted an insult like that. My people are
. . . " But the pictures of Bosnia in 1730 were fading as the pain of the gunshots started to burn along
the pathways of his body, and his broken hand shot
pain into his arm and shoulder. They had told him
he would recover. Marie was coming. The company
had been notified. As they wheeled him away toward
surgery, they kidded him about being from Denver.
"You're quite a cowboy," and as he waited for the
oblivion in the shot just before surgery, he started to
tell them that what he had done savored more of
Bosnia than Denver, but the words came out not as
he had framed them. "Joachim and Girard — they
had mountains, too. I must have settled near mountains because . . . You see, I'm not at home in this
city. This city is too flat, and when they cut the
trees . . ." and then he went through the door
where he thought the paradox was, but it only closed
behind him.

LIKE A NATIVE

ROSE'S parents had come from a place called Eagle Spring. When they talked about it, their eyes turned long-lonesome and little smiles came on their faces. Playing between the houses with Freckles, Tee, and Mary, she had once heard her father talking at the open window. His voice and words sounded different from the people here, people he called "city-born." "Day like this I'd head for Chilion's Grove," he said. "Fishin'd be good, a day like this." She was listening, smiling, and Freckles, annoyed, hit her hand because she had it up, saying something-nothing, caught in listening to what he could not hear.

They were "Deafies," her friends, Freckles, Tee, and Mary. Their parents were *Deafandum.* Daddy said it was a mistake to let her stay so long with people like that, parents and kids all Deafandum, but then, he sighed and said, *"Poor* means you got no choice."

They had moved here to work in the defense plant, to make the electricity that was in airplanes. At first Rose thought they must have been chosen for this work because they were from Eagle Spring, a place connected with flight. When she talked about Eagle Spring to Freckles, she would use the Sign for springtime so that the name carried her parents' sense of its beauty, a springtime of eagles.

Rose's people had quiet voices that didn't move up and down. Their hands and bodies did not move when they talked and they showed no feeling by obvious looks. To read them, you had to look for the twitch of a muscle in Daddy's face when he was angry, or around his eyes, tired. Mama primped when she felt good and let her hair go lank when she was cross or tired. And there were two lines up near the top of her nose that said, "Get gone."

Her friends, the Allmons, spoke with their whole bodies. Each one claimed a space around himself and filled it. They pointed people in the air, "you," "he," "them," and gave them parts to say with body habits that defined them. Their language was all finger, hand, face. Rose sometimes went with them to Deaf church. She had learned their language easily, without thinking how.

When the war was over, the plant changed and began to make television sets. Everyone was happy. Daddy had his job there, Mama was home and kept house. Rose was ten then, and the Allmon children, one after the other, had gone away to Deaf school. When they came back summers, they were full of secret school talk and wit and new Signs and private jokes. They had Sign nicknames and their conversation was about boys and girls Rose didn't know. In her own

school she was shy and quiet in her speech and most
of the time was forgotten on the sidelines.

She had learned long ago not to use any of the
Allmons' language at home or school, not even the
simplest movements, the slip of "who cares" down
from the nose, or pointing to herself — "I think."
The Allmons and their language made people nervous, but Rose loved the long green and golden summers when she and the kids spent days together
down near the river or on past the outskirts of town.
They played games long after the Hearing kids had
given them up, running games or stick games. Their
talk was witty and funny and in it they imitated
people they knew.

But Rose began to notice as she was thirteen and
fourteen and fifteen that their world was slower to
widen than the world of the Hearing kids at her
school. They seemed to know less, about ordinary
things. They didn't read books or newspapers. Their
television was childish.

In ways she couldn't explain, Rose began to feel separated from Tee and Freckles. She began to try harder
to be where the Hearing kids gathered, to follow
their talk and learn their tastes. It wasn't easy to
translate the immediate impressions of a thing from
an air-drawn image, spontaneous joy or sorrow —
to stop the hand before it rose.

The summer she was sixteen, she worked at the five-
and-dime. All day, humid, hungering, moose-faced
boy-men hung around the jukebox playing records.
She learned the lyrics and the boys' "lines," but she
had to be careful not to look straight at them the way

she had always looked straight into the faces of the
Allmons and their friends. There had been trouble in
the beginning because of it.

One day Daddy came home and said, "That's all."
Only that. The factory had closed. He and then
Mama tried to get other work, but there was nothing
to be had. For three weeks in late August, Rose's
income was the only money coming in. They lived
on biscuits and beans. In December the car gave out.
At Christmas Daddy said, "We're going back to
Eagle Spring."

The voice that spoke the beautiful name said it
dead flat. Rose wanted suddenly to Sign to him: *You
didn't fail; things failed you.* It would have been quick
flip — subject out, object in, and the negative defi-
nite as a stubbed toe.

They were unhappy, which puzzled Rose. Where
was the soft stream of memory now? "Winter we'd
get around the fire," Daddy had said every winter,
"and tell stories and roast chestnuts — you know,
nothing's nicer than a hickory wood fire —" She remembered clearly the yearning in the words, fragile
as Signs in the air, gone now, unprovable.

Going back, the miraculous land unrolled itself before her. Mountains and rivers. Even with the trees
bare and black in the winter silence, the places had a
rolling grandeur, a distant-vista sense of space, and a
dignity that made Rose catch her breath. And the
names: Fourways, Hidden Creek — names Mama
had used as lullabye words — Rest Easy and Say-
ward. At Bethany they got off the bus. It was a
two-mile walk to Eagle Spring and another two to
Grandpa's where they would stay. "We'll be with

Granny and Grandpa," Mama said, "but I got money saved to get you gone from this place. Now, you go in when we get there, and you take off them clothes and save 'em for leavin' — all your clothes, you hear?" The tone was winter-bitter.

They started up the dirt road, walking slowly but never stopping. "That's the hill way, you'll learn," Daddy said. "No, she won't!" Mama snapped.

They stayed with Mama's folks, "on The Branch." Rose learned to skin and hang meat, to smoke-dry fish, to can venison. Outside the odorous, bare-floored house, the mountains spread away in fog-sea mornings; winter closed them in. She learned hard and slow day by day. She lost eggs and broke lamp chimneys and made them go black. She spooked the chickens and ruined the cheese, but the strangeness was in more than surface things. It was in the language, the words she spoke, the way she spoke them. When spring came they all went down to Eagle Spring to shop and go to church and Rose knew that an indefinable difference held her from the people of The Branch and the people of Eagle Spring and kept her at arms' length, forever apart.

Mama was proud. "You keep on talkin' nice, like you do. You ain't to get comfortable and stay here!" But the young men and girls from Mountain Meadows and Chilion's Grove looked at her and were curious. Among themselves they laughed and talked and teased, but when she talked, they went quiet and the boys backed away a little, politely, and the girls lost their lightness in her presence. Rose made them feel countrified. When she tried, carefully, to use their words, the boys went shy and the girls turned aside, and went away to be together without her.

*   *   *

She began going to school again as Mama insisted.
Her city schooling impressed the teachers, and they
allowed her to slip ahead and be a senior. When she
was accepted at nurses' training, Mama gave her all
the quilt money and all the egg money and all her
savings and a suitcase with the city clothes, now a
size too small. They saw her away down the mountain and then from Eagle Spring to the bus, and she
was away into what they called The World.

Learning the language. She had to be more serious
than most of the other students. She had to drill night
after night on the difficult medical words, the secret
language of doctors and disease, and slowly she
learned to hear the words and then to speak them
until it was easy for her to say them. She was less
lonely in nursing school than she had ever been except for her years with the Allmons, but there was
something missing still, a place she had not found.

As time went by, Rose began to have a special
identity around the hospital. "Is the hillbilly
around?" "Ask the hillbilly to come, too." She listened for scorn, but there was none. It was interest
and even some affection. Her accent seemed part of
the charm of her strangeness, "authentic," one intern
said, "natural." She couldn't begin to explain how
wrong they were, so she said nothing.

Because she had never been natural or authentic in
Eagle Spring, and with every visit she was moving
further from Mama and Daddy. The words she used,
even their arrangement, were changing. Her language was a new way of seeing the world. "You
think of things I never even heered of," Mama said.

Less and less was possible to express, to share with the people on the high, silent arms of the mountains where Grandpa and Granny's cabin was.

Sometimes in dreams she would venture back to the first people of all, to the primal language, the language that remembered perpetual summer, the language of first intensities and first memories — the Sign. Many of the people in her dreams were not Deaf but Signed anyway, because it was, in the dream, the natural language of mankind.

The psychiatry affiliation came during Rose's senior year. It was three months' service at the state hospital. On the third day, Rose and her partner, a girl named Ellie Metcalf, stood frozen at their posts in the day room on a male ward, "observing" as they had been told to do. After lunch, she found herself, without knowing why, moving toward an empty-faced, shaved-skull man who had been standing alone, one of a line of such men in a denim shirt and soft cotton pants. Her hands came up naturally, her body readied itself for the questioning posture — her Sign quick and colloquial. "You like lunch?" standing so as to ready the space between them for conversation. She might have slapped him, kissed him, given him the electric shock they used here. His head came up, his eyes focused, going wide. "Who?" he Signed, his posture question-and-amazement. He moved away from the wall. "Who are you?"

"Rose," spelling it and pointing to her student's name tag.

It was the pure tongue long dormant in both of them and for both, spoken without thought to the words. "She — Lettie —" He put "Lettie's" place beside him and established it there so as to speak of her the Deaf way. "Did she send you — oh, God, did she send you to end —" He drew the loneliness Sign in long ellipses, large and slow, so that Rose was made to see each day the loneliness, all day the loneliness, day after day the loneliness, to the end of endurance and beyond.

"How long?" she asked. "How long here?"

"I don't know." One single Sign down from a face that showed he had no way of asking, knowing, or measuring. They stood hung together stock-still. They wanted to fall into each other's arms, but such a thing would be misinterpreted before the Hearies. "Once," he said, "on a walk I saw — there's another here, a Deaf — we talked a minute. I looked for him again, but — could you find — will you find —"

"Oh, yes, if I can."

"Did Lettie send you?"

"No, this is part of my training — to be a nurse."

"So it has an end."

"Not now, not now. We'll talk about that later."

He stood, the Deaf way, and wept. They became aware at the same time of people around them, of the head nurse. He went stiff — "Will you be hurt by this?"

"We'll see, soon enough."

He laughed.

The nurses and attendants were amazed. "Saunders hasn't moved so much in all the years he's been here!" "How did you know?" "How did you learn . . ."

She got permission to walk the wards with Saunders. No one had known he was deaf, or how many others there were. To the Deaf, they were irresistible. Here, there, living statues broke from the walls, their fingers erupting in the cry, eyes widened, faces collapsed. Some ran to them, Telling The Story for the first time, Sign coming crude or elegant, angry or fearful; many had the patched and ugly home-Sign of Deaf who had never been taught to Sign and had not had contact with anyone but Hearing families now dead or scattered. Male wards and female wards, chronic and acute, custodial and treatment, they bore their own along, talking to themselves and each other, a passionate, swelling mob, twenty, thirty, whose eyes were now set on one another for the first time. "You here?" "How long?" "I live on —" "My name is —"

And Rose told them about Freckles and Tee and Mary, and Mr. and Mrs. Allmon. She spoke as she had known them when she was five, ten, and fifteen. She couldn't believe how good it felt, how happy, to fill a soundless world with meaning, speaking the true word out of the heart of life.

Rose was allowed run of the wards during her three months' affiliation. She found other, shyer deaf people. Some she found were profoundly ill, their Signs disordered and irrational, but many seemed ordinary to her, and she often spent her days off socializing with them, easy and happy in their company. She spoke to the doctors on behalf of some, and a few times interpreted in staffings. She was not allowed more. When the rotation was over and she was to leave, old Mrs. Sprinkles pulled at her sweater and said, "Come back and work here — you're as good as Deaf. It's for *you*. We Deaf see how your eyes shine, how your face shines when you are

with us. Don't go into Hearie life. They have enough
people already. See how they waste them? Stay
Deaf — we are the honest people. We put our feelings on our faces and don't mouth, mouth and say
nothing." Rose said she would think about it.

But a ward head nurse said, "This place isn't for
you. The pay is low, no city in miles, and in the town
nobody your own age to meet. My husband is sickly;
we live here because it's cheap — that's what this is
for, for people in retreat." She was right. So was
Mrs. Sprinkles.

When Rose went back to her school hospital, news
of her "gift" went with her. She was sometimes
called on to interpret where there were deaf people.
They usually turned out to be hearing people deaf-
ened in old age, who did not Sign and were horrified
by her "gestures."

On the weekend before graduation, Rose took a bus
north, to the city and the friends she had left at sixteen. It was a long trip, and the old neighborhood
had altered. Like the face of a dying friend, it was
familiar in the bone, but not in the flesh. Bad luck,
like a disease, had set in. The neighborhood was
riddled with it. Trees had been cut down or died, the
yards overgrown and uncared for.

She came to the block on which she had lived.
There were many black people there now. Brightly
dressed but ragged children were going up and down
on skates as she had done once. She passed her own
house. A brown woman sat on the steps playing with
a baby. Rose went to the next house, the Allmons'
house, and knocked. The Allmons had had a dog
who used to get their attention when someone was

at the door. Rose waited, then knocked again. The door opened and half a face became visible on the other side. "Whut you wan?"

Rose explained. It took a long time; when she finished, the woman said, "They ain't no dead people here!" Rose explained again. The woman opened a little wider to listen.

"Their name was Allmon; there was a man and wife and three children —"

"Girl, this house done change owner so many time I can't keep up with it, but there's a old woman live up the street, Mrs. Thompson, three houses up. Blue roof. You go see her."

Mrs. Thompson remembered the Allmons but not where they had gone. She turned watering, confused eyes on Rose and said, "Yes, I remember them. They and those crackers who lived next to them, they started all this. It used to be a nice neighborhood — poor, yes, but decent, until the odd ones started coming." She had not remembered Rose's name or introduction. It had taken a moment for Rose to realize that "the crackers" had been her own family.

Rose stood in the sunny street. She tried to think of the names of the Allmons' friends, of the place at which Mr. Allmon had worked. The church was the only other place she could try.

It was still there, five blocks away past vacant lots and vacant factories. She went to the parish house and knocked. "Oh, yes," the minister said, "we still have the deaf people who come to morning service on Sundays. They meet in the basement for social hour. There's an interpreter. The former pastor Signed himself but he retired." The man seemed sympathetic, and she thought she heard in his speech the barest echo of Eagle Spring but she was afraid to ask.

She spent the night at the bus station. On Sunday, she stood near the church door looking at the people as they came in. Except for a faintly familiar face, they were strangers to her. She had grown into unrecognizability and one after another — this couple was not the Allmons, nor this, nor this. People began to fill the church.

The Deaf all walked to the left and took the pews up front. Rose followed them there and sat down, looking hard at them, hoping she would at last recognize some of the friends, remember some of the names. The service began.

The interpreter was an earnest man, serious, accurate, and totally without Shine. The words were Signed large as the minister's voice went up, smaller as it went down, but there was no poetry, no play, no finger-dance or look of the face that commented on the words of the hands. People watched respectfully but now and then as the service went on, they began to communicate: air-quick wit or greetings to new people coming. In their eagerness at seeing one another, one or two people talked through the sermon as though the church were empty.

Rose began to watch these people, relishing their language, their play. At every pause in the prayers the hands would go up, a forest of hands a silent babble of voices, nothing at all to do with the prayers or the minister or the sermon, any more than tele-

vision shows have to do with the commercials that
bracket and interrupt them. Amen at last and up to
go.

The Hearing left with great decorum, nodding se-
renely at the Deaf. The Deaf rose into their talk,
which had it been sound would have blown the four
walls down. In two's, three's, they drifted downstairs to the basement.

As they lined up for the coffee and cookies, Rose
caught the momentary upward-eye-downward-
hand-glide of end-thought of a woman and broke
in. "Please excuse me — I'm from Morgantown and
I'm looking for a family, the Allmons, Mr. and Mrs.
Allmon, who used to live on Sanford Street. Three
children, Freckles, Tee, Mary —"

"Sorry, no, how long ago?"

"Five years."

"I don't know them, but this is Mrs. Oliver —
they've been here longer —"

And again, "Sorry, no, we changed to this church
four years ago, when St. James stopped its Deaf Mis-
sion."

"Who?"

"Allmon. Three children, Freckles . . ."

"Yes, I've heard of them, but I don't know where
they went —"

By now there was a small, interested following walking with her, from group to group. "Allmon? Where
did he work?"

"The   foundry.   There   were   other   Deaf
there . . ."

"That closed, that foundry, or it moved."

"Jenny, wasn't there a woman who used to —
yes, oh, yes, three children —"

So it happened naturally that Rose began to be the
center of the group remembering or trying to remember the Allmons and where they had gone. Until one woman said, "Where do *you* live? Where is
your group?"

"I'm a nurse," Rose answered for the first time.
"I've just graduated, and . . ."

There was a silence not of voices, but of the mole-
cules in the room. Hands no longer stirred them. The
hands had stopped. "You're not Deaf," one woman
said. The Sign tone was not incredulous or wondering, but accusatory. She turned to her friend. "She's
not Deaf," she said, with a finger toward Rose.

"Oh, no," Rose said, "I'm not Deaf."

"Then why do you act like you are?"

"Many Hearing use Sign," Rose said. "The interpreter at services today was Hearing."

"Yes, but he Signs like a Hearie. You Sign like a
Deaf. You act Deaf. Hearies use our *Signs*," the
woman said, and she began to speak. The Signs were
the same, but the grammar, the structure was
changed in a way Rose felt but could not frame.

"It's not my fault," Rose said. "I grew up with
Mr. and Mrs. Allmon and with their kids. We all
played together —"

"See, see, that's a school Sign, residential school.
She's making out like she went to residential
school —"

"I'm not tricking," Rose said. "I need to find my
old friends. I need to know where they went."

★   ★   ★

A man stepped forward from the group that was now gathered around Rose. "Excuse us, please," he said, "you surprised us. The foundry closed five years ago. I remember John Allmon, but I don't know where they went. I don't think they stayed around here because if they did they would be at the social club or some Deaf clubs or churches here that we would know."

"She shouldn't try to act Deaf." The woman beside him put disapproval on her upper lip.

The woman who had begun to ask the other people for Rose touched her on the shoulder. "We were surprised, that's all. Fanny there doesn't like surprises. We should say we're sorry."

And so they did, but guardedly, stiffly, their Signs formal and stilted and more like English. Later, as she was leaving, Rose said, "I talked to all the deaf people at the state hospital. They knew I was Hearing, and they —" But by then she realized that such isolated and lonely souls cut their expectations to a much more modest shape in the air. And she knew, too, as she left the church, that if she ever met Freckles or Tee or even the Allmons again, they would address her in the formal, Anglicized Sign they used for outsiders, the Sign that defined her as Hearing and assigned her and them to the worlds in which they did, in fact, belong.

NAMING THE WIND

IN this season, the wind blew from
the north. Night after night, it came howling and
gusting from the north-northwest, over Windy Gap
like apocalypse. It hit the walls of Warren's house
head on, and his house and barn groaned in the dark.
There were sounds he knew were being made all
day — the house and barn were old and their wood
was weathering away, but on windy nights like these
it kept him sleepless, and lashed cries from his buildings, and with it, bearing in on him, knotted in its
mile-long mane, an army of accusing ghosts — what
he should have done and had not done. All night the
ghosts rode, letting him drift off and sleep only an
hour or two before dawn. He overslept. When Lois
Silverman brought her horse for shoeing next morning, he wasn't in the barn; she had to go up to the
house to get him.

"I slept in this morning. Here it is eight o'clock

and I'm still eating. Come in and have some coffee with us."

She came in and sat down. She looked tired herself — a pretty woman, but drawn and tight in the face now. She and Cassie talked a little. He had teased Cassie about the new people. "You're turning these city folks into towners — gossips and motor mouths." Cassie called it neighbor talk; it was nothing mean. Warren went away in his mind, still hearing the wind out there, moving toward ambush.

It might lie low, behind the nearer mountains, moving like the guerrilla armies he had seen in Korea, there-not-there, green against green, gray against gray, attacking and kill-and-run before you knew it.

Suddenly Lois Silverman cried, "I hate these winds!" Warren was surprised, but he only nodded slightly. She gripped the cup for warmth. "If only they would stop at night. It gets so you can't sleep and you can't get up either, and you just lie there and listen to it. Now the forecast says more of the same."

For no reason he could think of, Warren felt he had to defend his mountains and meadows against her accusation. "It's the season," he said, "can't expect summer to stay forever." She nodded, unconsciously adopting his manner, trying for stoic's patience, stoic's wisdom. Across the table, Cassie was biting back laughter; he could see it in her eyes. They had talked about it — "Martin Jones and Charlie Ruff gripe about everything, but soon as the new people start, you act like you never heard of complaining." He got up. "I'll help you get them horses out of the trailer. Didn't I hear you sold that white mare of yours?"

★   ★   ★

Warren could remember years of wind although it
was worse now because the developers who had built
the houses to the north and west of his place had cut
down so many trees that there was nothing to stop
it and it poured through the pass screaming and
down the gulches to collide with his house and barn
almost broadside. There had always been high winds
on this side of the gulch. He could remember as a kid
lying in bed listening to them tear through the darkness, but when he was a kid, he had been comforted
by his walls and his warmth, snug in his bed, safe.
He suddenly had a picture in his mind of his mother
standing at the stove in her bathrobe, her hair in two
thick braids. On those windy mornings-after she
would sigh into the cooking-fire. "Wind's knocked
out all the stars. Wind's blown the moon to China."
China. He held the door open for Lois Silverman and
they went toward her horse trailer. He was remembering about China, where everything fetched up in
the end. "Your dad sees that mess, he'll whip you to
China." "Pump's lost its prime — water's gone to
China." Then he went there himself, or to Korea,
which should have been close enough, and he had
found none of the lost things there, not the watch,
or the water, or the whippings, or his mother's stove
polish, or his father's axle bolt. Only the wind.

They got her horses out and unhooked the trailer
and she drove away in the car. He looked at her big
gelding's old shoes, which he remembered were ze-
ros. He took off the left rear one, noticing its patterns
of wear; then he fitted the new one, trimmed, fitted
again, losing himself in the work. He wished he had
acknowledged her complaint about the wind. She
had looked drawn and sleepless, that little bit like his
mother standing at the stove, just around the eyes.

She was a nice woman — her kids rode in the Mountain Roundup, which had come alive again up here because of the new people and their kids. It was a rodeo group that did fancy figures; it went all over the state to compete. As he was working, two more roundup people came — Morrissey with his chestnut mare and Hendry with his quarter horse. Warren felt raw and scraped. He was glad the two men had time only to leave their horses, give a greeting, and go. Both were new people, professionals in Aureole. Did either of them lie sleepless and accused in the night, hour after hour, listening?

Warren's wind-nights were often made of what had happened in Korea, things he had done and had not done there, shameful things and cowardly things, in that near-China of all endplaces. He had known no special horror like My Lai, but he had seen and had been involved in relocations, the burning of fields, and looks into the faces of civilians in villages taken and retaken. When he had done these things they had meant little to him. It was only now, years later, lying awake safe and at home, that those remembered moments had grown larger. He had also had instants of bravery and fine generosity, but they were blown away in the wind and his moments of cowardice clung and stank and so did the lust and selfishness that still made him cringe. He had killed a woman out of fear and found later that she had come to spy on the camp. She had had a child, maybe four years old. The child had been ugly and ill-favored. Miller had killed it and Warren had said nothing. The cruelty he and his buddies had done had not come from hate or sadism except for Miller and maybe Carlson. Boredom did it, fear, the stress of waiting for attack or defense. The waiting he did in

Korea was far worse than the actual patrols or engagements, and over the two years he was there, he had experienced an erosion of part of his sense of reality. He realized that the Warren Knowles he called himself could do anything to anyone when meaning had been diluted, dissolved in him, had run out of him. The knowledge had left him hollow in a way he felt but could not describe. Cassie knew none of this, so her laughter at him had a comfort in it. She slept well, wind or no.

He had come home with it, the hollowness and the knowledge of its possibilities. It had made him restless and ugly. His hand shook, he faded out in the middle of conversations, unable to concentrate. His physical condition was perfect but he would find himself standing at the baler, or with the paint gun, his face showing a pain he could not feel.

His dad had been in the First World War, and in the trenches, although he had never spoken of what that had been like. Gently, persevering, he had made Warren walk with him, sometimes talking, sometimes silent. As Warren had opened up, Ken Knowles had heard him out with complete understanding and over the next year had helped in Warren's healing. Later, he had said, "I always wondered what good it all did, my being over there in the war — I didn't even know if I hit anything I fired at, but it made me understand what you'd gone through and what you come home with, and I'm content about that."

Kenneth Knowles died in a nursing home in Aureole. He was too bad off after his stroke for Cassie to take care of, with the kids, too, and the work of the ranch. Neither his brother Tom nor his sister Celia had been able to help. Mom was mind-

wandering and sick herself. The nursing home had
been necessary; everyone knew it. Warren had visited
his dad on Sunday afternoons. In those days it took
an hour and a half to get to Aureole. He spent an
hour and then had the trip back. Two years. It was
a chore without pleasure, Sundays and holidays, sitting at the bedside while his dad cried and pleaded.
On the windy nights, those cries came back as accusations of selfishness and disloyalty because Ken
Knowles's death after those two years had come as a
relief. Korea and Korea's debt to his father were the
first, the usual, the main.

The wind slowed to an ordinary breeze through the
day. Warren shod eight horses and then took the
truck up to see his small herd in the close pasture. It
was January and the winter dark was early. He had
to get feed to the herd each day.

The pasture was at the foot of the mountain and
above him the snow took on tints of the sky, red at
sunrise, blue and blue-silver at noon, purple and red
at the setting sun. He breathed deeply. The air mixed
its scents — pine and snow and on still days, among
the herd, the sweet grass and the tang of manure
were less sharp than at other seasons. Warren liked
his life. He loved Cassie. Their boys were grown and
doing well. His nephew Allen was at Fort Collins
studying ranching and after graduation would be
coming here to make his life. Why did the wind bear
all those accusations before his wide-open eyes?

At dusk, the wind picked up again. As he and
Cassie watched TV they could hear the distant roar
and then air pushing at the unprotected side of the
house on the now unbroken space between Windy
Gap and the ranch buildings. There was a whining

in the wash lines and guywires and TV antennas and around corners making the night malevolent.

Lying in bed unable to sleep, Warren remembered Lois Silverman's curse at the wind, and suddenly he thought about Wilson Peach. Peach had been his grandfather's top hand on the old place. A good man, Peach, a mild man, good with animals, and patient enough to have taught Warren to ride and rope and make the dozen or so knots that were used around the ranch. Warren was nine then. His father was busy with the two older boys; his grandfather too powerful and remote. Peach was Warren's guardian and friend.

When Warren was ten, he saw Peach suddenly changed. One morning he went to the corral and there was Peach, sullen and violent, cursing the horses, the land, the people. His anger was frightening. Two months later it happened again, and this time Warren got too close and Peach turned on him, his face distorted. "Take your goddamn tack!" throwing it so that harness, almost like a whip, flew past the horses' rumps and hit Warren's arm as he backed away from his altered friend.

He hadn't had the words to put the question of Peach's sudden awful changes to anyone, but the leather harness made a long weal, and two days later his mother saw it and asked how it had happened and some little part of the betrayal came out. His mother said, "Mr. Peach drinks some, Christmas and holidays, and then there's anniversaries special to him — when he got married and then when his wife died. When he drinks, he's not himself."

She must have told his father, because later he heard his father say to Jeff, his oldest brother, "Ma said when Peach was drunk he wasn't himself. I reckon it's when a man's *sober* he ain't himself. When he's had a little, his party manners slip away some." Jeff died sober and therefore not himself in France in 1944. He died not by the enemy's hand but of polio, which in his father's eyes seemed to deprive him of something more than his life.

Warren had tried always to bring his public and his private selves together, and but for these nights of wind he might have thought he had done it. Now he knew he would never be able to call himself good. He turned again in bed, envying Cassie her simple acceptances and untroubled sleep.

The winds continued into the third day and more horses came in from the Mountain Roundup people. They were getting ready for their first event of the new year. Lois Silverman brought in her other mare. Warren saw the sleeplessness in her face and body. Jill Friedburg came while Lois was there. Their voices in their greeting and talk seemed roughened from words cried silently, perhaps in defense; their eyes seemed reddened with sights conjured perhaps by the accusing self. Perhaps not — maybe it was all his imagination, his own reverberating anguish.

Then Lois said, half to Jill, half to Warren, "Oh, this wind!" and again, damnably, Warren defended his prior claim to the mountains and the Ute Valley that was under siege by these new people. "Folks move here in summer," he said, "when the climate's easy. Then winter comes and they moan and groan about the weather." He had wanted to say it with a little smile but the words came out grudging and sour. She might have told him his sanctimony stank, but she only laughed a little and said, "I guess we are summer soldiers. I came here from Pennsylvania. We had snow in winter and hailstorms in spring but there never were winds like this . . ." and she dug her delicate hands deep into the pockets of her little down vest. He turned and was moving away and he heard her say to Jill Friedburg, "I lie awake and it's one long Yom Kippur all over again." Jill laughed. "Fifty sins and counting . . ." Lois said, "I thought we would leave Yom Kippur down there, the sins and the regrets, leave them with the old life in the old synagogues." Warren had stopped to listen, standing on the other side of Jill's horse, fussing with its right rear hoof. He didn't understand all the words, but that funny one seemed to be a word that described the geography of his midnight landscape. The women began to walk toward their horse trailers.

Some of the older people resented these new-comers. "Development-itis," Cal Bropes said, "and town's all changed. Bo-Teek. It's all one big Bo-Teek." The new people had brought big changes to the four towns of the Ute. Prices were up. Taxes were up. But they had horses, and Warren's work as a farrier had saved the ranch. Cassie worked too, cleaning houses now and then. In Aureole there were now Vietnamese people and blacks, in Gold Flume these Jewish people, and Christian Scientists. He liked the variety of means and ideas but at the same time he was angry and defensive for the changes they had brought to the land and the towns. The trees had been cut, the wind . . . They weren't bad people — he liked the Silvermans and their kids — he was the one driving the wedge between them, demanding some kind of debt they couldn't pay, perfection to endure, virtues he didn't have. Lois said, "Goodbye,

Warren. Don't get blown off your feet," and again he couldn't bend. He only said, "Hunh," and turned up Melody's hoof to pry off the old shoe.

At first it seemed the winds had died away. The evening was still; the trees near the draw were upright and silent; everything was held after the radiant moments of sunset in total silence. As though to point up the stillness, a cry of argumentative night birds burst from the bush behind the house and was lost in their scattering. When Warren was in the hospital at Inchon, he had become used to the changing hours of the staff. When he came home and heard the familiar creatures begin after sunset, he said to himself, "Night shift," and in that more pleasant form, brought the memory home.

Cassie pointed to the scene outside the window near where she sat. "Moon's up." They stayed silent and watched it. "I got a letter from Andy today."

"How are they doing?"

"Reading between the lines," she said, "I think he's worried. It looks like Marcy's pregnant again. Business is slow." Warren didn't speak. "I been thinking," Cassie went on, "that maybe it's time to invite them all again. It's been three years since we've had all of them together."

Her yearning stung him. "Call them," he said, "it's right they should come."

She sprang to their defense the way he defended the weather from the new people. "They've had hard going, Andy and Marcy. Paul, well, Rochelle's people are in Denver, so naturally . . ."

They both heard at the same time, moving across the hill, the hand, ten miles wide and long as blame, the wind. Warren wanted to cry. Cassie sighed. Warren got up and said quietly, "I'll go check and see everything's tight."

It was surprisingly warm outside and no wonder; the wind had turned more westerly. It was blowing from places bare of snow and had the warmth of stone lately sun-heated and the soft ferny smell of sea-bottom upthrust one hundred million years ago in valleys miles away. There must be a fence at the end of the world to catch all the things blown across his land now that China was no longer taking them. He heard the lowing of a mother cow from the barn, ooooooh, yooooouuuu . . .

He moved toward the loom of the barn's side and stopped amazed in what beauty his night accuser walked. The trees in the sweep of the house bent and spread, a crescent moon had been knocked off round and the stars had been blown rim to rim across the night and scoured blue and hard. They cast a blue sheen on the snow. Ahead of him he heard something lift and slap: some water pails he had forgotten, and the door was not being held with the extra hasp they used to keep it from being torn away when the wind was strong.

Inside the barn were the comfortable sounds of calves breathing and chewing in the near dark. He let himself be guided by the few small night lights, feeling one by one the patient, neighboring rumps of the heifers. He moved over and found Good Girl, their mother, patting her with his hand. Then, suddenly, he bent over her back and gave himself up to long sobs.

In Warren's childhood, his father had been quick with the hard word, the slap, and for serious offenses, the strap that had been hung near the barn door on its own nail. Those buckets now, left out. "Careless!" and there would be a blow. His father did not rage; the blow was struck and then it would be over. Now the punisher dealt it out all night, night after night, and Warren couldn't hold his breath the way he had then, biting back the pain.

When his moment was over, Warren got up and went around the barn, checking, and then the sheds, then back around the house. Upstairs, Cassie was moving in silhouette to and fro, doing her night preparations. Looking in from outside, the room seemed lofty and serene, but Warren knew better. In that room was the bed he had to lie on, the rack of accusation.

This time, three nights into it, the blaming was a ragged, sleep-patched jumble — his sonhood, his fatherhood. He saw his father in the nursing home — "I don't want to be here!" in the slurred speech of his stroke. He hadn't listened to the boys much either. He had only learned a few years ago that Paul, who was youngest, small and somewhat dreamy, had been ganged up on and bullied in school. "You kept coming home with torn clothes — I punished you over that —" Paul had looked at him levelly and said, "You sure did." He had looked at Paul and said, "Why didn't you tell me?" Paul hadn't answered. The waste. Such a waste. He heaved over in the bed, half asleep. The wind was increasing. Now the house was heaving with it.

In the morning there were pieces of siding off the barn and house and shingles standing up on the northwest side of the barn roof, reminding Warren of a horse curried up-hide. He spent the early hours cleaning up, replacing the torn boards, and the after-noon resetting the shingles. None of his foundations had been challenged, but the outer defenses had been breached here and there, and he was more vulnerable than his wood and his stone. His eyes were sore and crusted with unslept sleep and his mind was fevered and sore with the strap of the accuser.

But the wind was gone. The day, a radiant blue, lifted glowing over his barn and fields. From the vantage point of his roof, he looked out over the new houses 360 degrees to the end of sight. It was cloudless and unstirred. The flapping air, broken free, had been seized at its edges and tied down again.

By four o'clock he was yearning for sleep. He thought for a moment he might drape himself over the peak of the roof and relinquish the world like the cat did, in folds over the arm of the chair. The repairs had to be done but the work was dangerous for a tired man. He decided to go down and drink some strong coffee. He was careful and graceless on the ladder because he was tired enough to make a misstep. Cassie had gone to clean for Lois Silverman. Warren went to the mailbox and then to the house. When the coffee was ready, he sat down and thought he opened the *Ute River Voice*. . . .

He came awake stiff-necked where he had slumped over the table. He had been asleep about an hour, dreamless and with no need to defend. He laughed. Maybe he should make his bed at the table from now on.

He went up on the roof again. The light would soon be gone. He was finishing when he saw Cassie's car on the road and then turning in. She got out of the car and called to him, a habit of so long standing, he couldn't remember it any other way. He called

back to her from the roof and laughed when it took
her a moment to locate him. Normally, she would
have laughed back and said something joking, but
this time said, "Come on down. I have something to
tell you." He came down. "I've been trying to call
you . . ."

"I've been up there."

"Lois — Lois Silverman," she said, "— she went
and killed herself last night."

His mind was stupid with it. He said, "She was
here yesterday." He saw Lois clearly; she had been
wearing that little down vest, her hands fisted hard
into the pockets. What was that word she used to Jill?
"She said something to Jill Friedburg. They were
standing right there." He meant to convey the nor-
mality in yesterday's scene, that little-girl action,
pretty even in her distress . . . *distress,* not despair.
She had been talking about the wind.

"She did it in the garage, in the car. I guess she
was keeping it out of the house, away from Bill and
the kids. I got there at ten, and the sheriff and the
coroner were there. Bill asked me to stay and clean
the upstairs and then take the calls and help with
things. Jill came over to watch the kids. They're
going to have the funeral tomorrow — an awful rush
if you ask me."

"I think it was the wind," Warren said, but he
couldn't tell Cassie about the accusations. Maybe she
knew about the sleeplessness, but nothing more. "I
bet she couldn't get to sleep."

"Well, the house does sit high, and it's up Jackass
Gulch."

"Wind in its teeth," Warren said. Cassie had done

some shopping. They began to take the bags out of the car.

In the old days, when a neighbor died, you'd go to the funeral, and later your wife would take over a dish of something. If you had your hay in, you'd go over and cut his, or take a load of wood so the people in the house wouldn't have to work gritting their teeth on anguish's gristle. But these were new people, and some of them were Jews, with new kinds of distinctions and customs, and Warren had underlined their differences to himself and to them again and again. They put the packages on the kitchen table.

"Did anyone come for the horse?" Cassie asked.

"No, he's still in the barn. I figure I'll let him stay, and not charge 'em board," Warren said.

They hadn't turned on the lights. Cassie was nodding in the dark. He could only see her outline. "She left a note."

"If I ever took my life, I wouldn't leave anything," he said. The dark around them had begun to chill. "What did it say?"

"Just those odd words *Yom Kippur* written three times." It was those words he had heard, the words that meant the accusers riding in the wind. "I told Carol Santoy . . ."

"Ladies' Broadcasting Company."

"That's not fair!" Cassie said. "If John Teets or John Cole committed suicide, you'd call Herb and Willy and you'd ask and you'd wonder out loud . . ."

"I guess so. She said it the last time I saw her, that thing — Yom Kippur." "It was a *holiday,* I thought."

The night was still at last. "Don't turn on the

light yet." In the dark, the sound of their talk had a richness of tone with little reverberations after the words like the second sound of the hammer let fall on the horseshoe. "Pretty woman," Warren said, "young, too." He wondered what could have beaten so hard at her that she couldn't get over it. He did know how the torment had come, how and when, and he shivered a little in the dark.

Later, in their bed, Warren lay awake after Cassie, as always, turned once and was asleep. It was still. The wild maples his grandmother had planted were bare now, and tonight not the smallest of their slender withes moved. The maple was a shrub in these parts; he hadn't seen the tree until he went to Korea. His mind lay resting; touching one thing and another. Soon he would sleep. He thought about Lois Silverman and then about the new people. They had moved into all the new big houses in Jackass Gulch and the developer had renamed it Rosemede and put roads with fancy names all through those hills where the north fork of the Ute meandered. In mental protest, Warren had been unable to remember the names of those roads, flower names, mountain names. The trees had been cut on the flanks of the hills where roads now wound and that brought the wind hard, first to them, and then to him.

Next week, next month, from the high gulches and down Windy Gap and Jackass Gulch and among the mine workings, the Big Suzannah and the Do-Or-Die, the wind would roar in with Yom Kippur in its teeth.

ELIZABETH BAIRD

SHE had been born with a very slight cerebral lesion and it produced brief pauses in her speech and the movements of her body, so that she seemed always to be hesitating, fawnlike, before the disclosure of her thought or will. This shy-gentle quality was much commented on and much praised during her childhood in Ionia. The heat of the Carolina summer had only fans to move it in those days. Girls and women wore softly floating dresses of lawn and dimity. There was a picture taken of her standing by a snowball bush. The picture showed her delicacy, but the photographer had no way to get that little wait, the arm halted before rising, the voice stopped, not like a stammer — like the halt of a small animal before venturing into an open field. The townspeople made much of that delicacy. Dr. Baird's girl was what a girl should be. Her beauty wasn't dramatic like her mother's; it offered no challenge.

Her ways were lovely, womanly and modest, and she was tiny as an elf.

No one knew about the lesion then. It wasn't found until she was in the hospital in California where doctors were trying to sort out the ravages all the prisoners had sustained from beatings, malnutrition, jungle diseases, parasites, and untreated wounds. When one of the doctors came to see Elizabeth at the place on the sun porch she had staked out as her own, he moved slowly, sat slowly, spoke slowly. The prisoners often fainted at fast moves. They were all like Elizabeth, now, stopped still, unable to think or speak or hear for the small seconds that seemed lifetimes.

She didn't take in what he said at first. Later she thought she had been dreaming. Still later, she got Sue Garland to show her the records and there it was in the neurologist's scrawl. She went back to the ward and thought long, slow thoughts about the years of her difference. It had been more than the unknown imperfection in her brain. She had been taught her caution all her childhood long.

Dr. Baird had been the only pediatrician in a hundred miles. He, too, was watchful of his surroundings because chairs and the corners of furniture seemed to catch and trip him when he came home tired in the evenings, and often a morning headache made him very cautious where he put his feet.

Elizabeth's mother was Alicia Powell Baird. She had been a celebrated beauty with auburn hair whose braids were thick as yacht cables, a table-dancer with rolled stockings and a fashionable boyish body. In the days of bobbed hair she danced the Charleston with hers long and loose and cascading down her shoulders. What a sad awakening to come to consciousness every morning and find herself the mother of a dream-struck little girl, wife of a gin alcoholic doctor in a small, hidebound town, mistress of a house that fronted the main street and so had to be kept looking nice all the time and of three mumbling, snuff-dipping Negro servants who lied, stole, and did as little as possible because they had no respect for her.

So, in addition to the hesitancy imposed on her by nature, Elizabeth learned her caution until it was bone deep. She seldom laughed and she was the most silent of the children in school, the most tentative in any group at play.

Life changed suddenly when she was fourteen. Her father died. She stood in the hot, flower-cloying church in her pink voile dress dyed black, among the stranger-kin to hear him described in ways she had not experienced him. His mounded grave was not to be given a stone because there was no money. As she examined her life with the new knowledge in it, Elizabeth lay quietly in bed and saw the grave in her mind, the slow town, the grown-over ground that Alicia was too harried to tend. She wondered now if she could even find the place. Years ago. It was to be years also before Mrs. Agnew would say to her, "Why, honey, everyone knew he drank. The better people didn't trust their children to him and the poorer ones couldn't afford a baby doctor. That's why there was no money, but he was a good man for all that, and don't forget his goodness in your need."

It had made Elizabeth all the more cautious, made all the more necessary the stopping her condition imposed.

In the early years of the widowhood, Alicia was frantic with poverty. Everywhere the depression cramped possibility. Even the work she might have done did not exist in Ionia or anywhere nearby.

Elizabeth did better. She worked in the five-and-dime and later at the bank. Scrimping and saving and renting out rooms to the occasional traveler, the two of them got up the money for Elizabeth's tuition in nurse's training.

They were separating, going home. Because of what had happened in the camp, Elizabeth kept apart from the others, women with whom she had spent the three years of her imprisonment. When they all said goodbye, the tears and hugs were not for her. This difference had not been missed by the hospital people, but no one spoke of it. Elizabeth was put on a train, a sleeper, and she was given many medications she was to take for the diseases and weakness she still had. The porter had been told about her, mercifully not about the differences between her and the others. To him she was one of them, that famous group of army nurses, heroines now, who had lived those years in the Japanese prison camp in the Philippines. "I'm gonna see you rest good all the way to Savannah," he said, "rest good and eat good, too, all the way."

She was exhausted still, and dazed with illness. It was a relief to get into her berth and lie down, but she did not sleep. She needed time with the knowledge that there was a secret cleaving, which she saw as being something half-moon shaped, folded in the shining gray folds of her brain.

Had she known in childhood what she now knew, would it have changed anything? Probably not. She had been praised for it in Ionia, loved for it, and she

had, in the arid, cruel years of nurse's training, as
undeservedly been cursed and castigated for it.

Her first year at Savannah General had been a sudden shock followed by a drawn-out misery. Students
were expected to be lightning quick. Her teachers
seemed to think her pauses before action and speech
were caused by stupidity or unwillingness. Miss
Martin cried at her, "Do I wait forever!" Mrs.
Templeman: "Is this a home for the feebleminded?"
And in the long pause, Elizabeth couldn't bring up
the simple, "No, ma'am." It amazed her that some
of her teachers were bitter about their profession.
Amazement silenced her even more; more silence,
more singling out. "Here's a procedure even Miss
Baird can do." "Zombies and the slow-witted, that's
what they're sending us now." Had she had a place
of escape, Elizabeth would have fled. As there was
none, she stayed and slowly, first among the other
students, then waiting out the teachers year by year,
she gained a gradual, grudging acceptance. She was
pretty. One or two of the girls asked her to double-
date with them. She was grateful but said no. She
wrote to her mother, "I want to be independent, to
be free. Girls around here talk about snagging some
rich old man they get as a private patient. I'll take
low wages but I'll choose my place and my conditions." Later she wrote, "Ionia's not for single
women. There are places we can both work and have
a good life. Can you ever sell that house?" She was
working and learning and she spent no money. She
tried not to hate the weakness of her stopped motion
and sudden stillness; she tried to compensate for her
tiny stature that made the patients call her "dear" and
"cute" and "doll-like," like a doll who must click

into action only after the pause in winding before its mechanism engaged.

It occurred to her now that had they known about what was going on in her brain, they wouldn't have accepted her into nurse's training and certainly not into the army, and if she hadn't gone into the army, she might have — she began to chuckle in her berth, quietly, facing the metal wall. She might have been able to help in the war effort.

She graduated in 1939 and two days later, she joined the army. It was the first duty then available. "Why?" cried Alicia from Ionia, "I thought you wanted independence!"

"I want to find a place for us and that means looking around." Unfortunately, it also meant a whole new chain of icy-faced superiors to convince that she was neither stupid nor unwilling. "Good God! What are they sending us!" Major Bradema had cried the first time, the first of many, and always worse in the tension of meetings with superiors.

She was posted to New Jersey. She was posted to San Diego. She was studying possibilities and places, looking for somewhere she and Alicia could settle, work, and be quiet, and owe no one and draw no one's attention. Late in 1941, she was posted to the large hospital on Oahu, near Pearl Harbor, and studying that, it looked as though she had found such a place. She wrote to Alicia with a plan. If Hawaii was good, she would try for something permanent there. Alicia would sell the house for whatever it would bring and join her. Alicia wrote back, labile with hope. "Do you really think we could do it? When you get there see if it would work; I hardly dare to dream!"

During her training there had been rumors of war, but Elizabeth's personal case had been too urgent for her to give any thought to them. Her own life was so near the bone, her arguments with tradesmen over half soles and cleaning bills so intense, there was no room for other struggles. They were two days out of San Francisco when the captain of their ship told them what the world had been up to while their private struggles had been occupying them: the Japanese had bombed American installations on Hawaii. The nation was at war.

At the first shock of hearing everyone behaved with Elizabeth's breath-caught silence, stopped motionless, speechless for the endless catch-breath which was only seconds. Then a roar went up, a roar of rage in which she did not partake. She and the other nurses, caught in midpassage, were suddenly traveling too slowly. Army nurse now had another meaning than it had a day ago. They were forefront, the first line. Silence, stillness, hiding — all her own needs had been blown and burned away.

No one on the ship had experienced war. Elizabeth listened to the other nurses, and they seemed to know the world better than she. They were frightened but also excited in a way that she was not. No longer would they have to hope for challenge and purpose; and suddenly, nothing was routine.

At Honolulu, some of them were ordered to stay; most of the nurses were dispatched to other stations. Elizabeth was sent to the Philippines, where the need was greatest. They experienced the need, but none of the nurses served it long. They were overwhelmed by the invading armies, taken, and brutalized. Those who lived, lived in the hand of the unreadable,

incomprehensible enemy. They were marched —
starved, beaten, parched, and sick — into long captivity at a women's camp near Luzon.

The camp was in miasmic jungle. Their captors
did not function well in such an environment. They
felt it a monstrous loss of face to be used for this
lowest of all purposes — the guardianship of women
— and in the beginning they took out their resentment on the prisoners. Major Naohito Nishimura
was the camp's commander. He had been injured in
training — no dishonor, but . . .

Not for the first two years would Elizabeth know
why Major Nishimura chose her. Simply, at first, she
thought that it was because Ionia, South Carolina,
was twelve miles from Savannah, and that it lay low
and humid and marshy. This had given her an advantage in her adaptation to the tropical heat, to the
dampness and fetor of the jungle prison. She had
borne up better than most of the others. Nishimura
had been looking for someone as liaison. His eye had
run over the gathered female prisoners. They appeared hideous to him. They were overlarge, physically; their size revolted and oppressed him; it was
unwomanly; their limbs were too long, their faces
protruded in a very unattractive way. They were also
dirty, listless, lank-haired, and stinking. That one
there, though . . .

Elizabeth had been standing in a posture as close
to attention as she could manage but she had not been
attending. It was enough, this first day in the camp,
to be standing still, quiet, under the palm hat she had
made for herself, not having to be alert for kicks and
blows from the soldiers who had driven them on and
on like an animal herd. She had received more abuse
than most of the others because of that hesitation of

hers, the half second it took her to begin to move. Time and again she had been threatened with death. Luck had been with her, there. So far . . . She felt a stir beside her and raised her eyes slightly. The woman beside her hissed, "He wants *you!*" Elizabeth had learned about bowing early in her captivity; they seemed to want it as prelude to anything, even death. She bowed. The interpreter was a Sergeant Akimoto. He explained something, but his English was poor. Elizabeth did not understand. Again, more slowly. This time she did understand but fear and exhaustion made her unable to react at all. Her cursed body, never eager as other people's, had stopped working entirely under the new challenge. A question: "Name, you!"

Another long moment. They might kill her. Another bow. "Baird, Elizabeth, Otaii San." (This had been learned at the cost of a torn ear and a tooth.) There was laughter from all the Japanese, but for once it was not angry or vengeful laughter; it was playful, almost. "Ebisu," the sergeant said. They laughed again. Looking up from under her lids at them, she saw that her captors' eyes had changed momentarily. Later she was to understand that they could not catch *Elizabeth,* but that *Ebisu* was a well-loved nursery figure in Japan — a sea god; all the soldiers knew of his exploits and a section of Tokyo had been named for him. The sound of her name made the soldiers remember home, a home shining above the stench of exile — not their lust but their humanity had been stirred. Rapists and killers, deniers of water to the dying — now they had the look of schoolboys: Ebisu.

And it had been her hesitation, her shyness, her lowered eye, her quick intake of breath before speech, everything that had caused Elizabeth pain and shame through school and the army, that represented for these lonely men the qualities they longed for in woman.

Daytime. The train stopped at the stations of prosperous cities and at each one there was a tug, gentle and insistent as a child at his mother's skirts: no one knows me here — there wouldn't be the shackling gentility of her town . . . Elizabeth knew she was still too sick to go back to work. The doctors had said it might be months, but the quiet of Ionia didn't represent rest but hopelessness to her. If only she could find a place, she and Alicia . . . She tried to let the trip calm her; the train was passing land that was nothing like jungle or camp. Once she had yearned to see it; now it seemed unsheltered, fearful, featureless. She turned back to the comforting metal wall. The doctors had told her to try to forget everything that had happened, but they had known only of the suffering, not of the puzzles attending it. Elizabeth — Ebisu. In the interrogations they all had had, others must have spoken of her as a collaborator. The accusation had not been proved, and the doctors had tried, foolishly, she thought, to pave over what they could not understand. . . .

In the camp after the first week of routine, the community began to differentiate itself. A social world emerged. There were Mothers and Bosses and Givers and Takers, Housekeepers and Gossips, Liars, Toadies, and the too-ill-to-care exiles. Ebisu, unique among them, found herself with few friends and many enemies. At first she tried to reason with their scorn. "I have no extra privileges; *they* picked me." It did no good. Everyone knew that the few improvements depended on Elizabeth's good relations with the guards and the major. It was obvious, too, that the more and better Japanese she learned, the easier things would be for everyone, but they were sick and starving and the feelings were strong and ugly and they persisted: anger at their dependence on Ebisu and the enemy and a terrible, despairing rage as supplies dwindled further and new diseases came. Later they were too tired for rage and settled into a dull, intractable resentment.

To Nishimura and the other guards, Ebisu became dearer. She had, at first, unwittingly learned men's abrupt Japanese instead of the gentler feminine tongue. Sergeant Akimoto had to take her education in hand. Many of her manners had to be corrected and of course there were her looks: a face too florid and the fox-colored hair; fox-witch hair was unnerving, but her size and that hesitant grace, that stillness above all, ritual pause in speech and movement, reminded them achingly of the women at home. It was difficult to keep from mistreating the other prisoners; most of them were overlarge and ugly red, they stared, and had no civilized ways. Ebisu was like a loved, slightly retarded little sister, and thus to be protected and furtively given gifts.

It was the third day of travel. They had crossed Texas from the baked plains of the West to what Elizabeth could now identify as being the landscape of the South; she was moving toward home. As the train neared Savannah, the combination of eagerness and fear she dreaded mounted in her. Suddenly she was hit with the tremors of a malarial attack. She carried medication that was supposed to ease the fever and chill that followed it, but even when she took the pills, the paroxysms left her exhausted, sweat-drenched, and weepy. She had been sitting up, dressed. Now she went back to the berth and lay in the fever dream remembering the last days of captivity: eagerness and fear, and the tremors of fever, like the fever now.

Day after day, inexorably, the old rules were ending. The camp felt the subtle anarchy grow and became terrified of Nishimura and the rage of his men. Everyone knew that shipments of food and weapons were coming later and scanter and then not at all. The planned deployment of landing forces near the camp, the arming for further conquests and then for defense, never materialized. Less and less often were the planes flying overhead Japanese planes. Fewer of Sergeant Akimoto's radio transmissions were getting through.

In the camp there had been more dysentery, more fever. The water supply, barely adequate at the beginning, had become polluted. They caught rain-water, which soon soured and grew slime. Rank growth was everywhere. Every morning had to be spent brush-cutting — if the brush were not cut back constantly, it overgrew every trail and would even choke the compound. The prisoners noticed that Nishimura and his men were uncomfortable in heavy forest. While crowding people did not bother them — no American would have packed the barracks as close or full as they had — crowding vegetation made them almost panicky. They demanded the exhausted prisoners burn or cut off large swaths at the edges of the compound to give themselves vistas and open views. This was not to prevent escape; the jungle and the sea were more dangerous than the camp, even with its fever and dysentery.

One day at brush-cutting, the prisoners were startled by noise above them, noise that did not immediately pass over. Looking up, they saw above them airplanes, first one, then another, wheeling and sputtering like huge wasps. They were the fighter planes of . . . in her darkened berth, Elizabeth lay trembling and relived the dogfight, seeing it again in the lurid colors of fever. The planes did not stay parallel with the ground long enough to be identified by their shapes, as everyone had learned to do, and they were too high and quick to be read for insignia by the dulled women. For three minutes nothing moved in the camp; machetes were not raised, bodies were still, prisoners and guards all looked up, held breathless by the sight in the air. Neither knew any more than that The War, which had brought them all to loneliness and suffering in this fetid place, was being waged in miniature, beautifully aloft, like a dance.

There was one plane that had the capacity, it seemed, to drop without needing any lateral or forward distance, and this plane kept getting under the others, and would come up spitting sound that was almost like cursing; words, then silence, then words again. On one of these maneuvers, the two planes that were above him parted and turned like doors opening, and the clever plane went up between them, and they turned and shot, and Clever Plane wobbled and at the same time one of those planes turned away and shot and another plane burst into fire that made a blot against the sky and from which they could see bits falling. Still, no one moved because no one knew which had gone down and from

which side victory was announcing itself. Clever
Plane seemed to be drowning in the air; it struggled
to right itself. The three others circled it and the prisoners caught a glimpse of the underside of one of
them. It looked . . . it was, a P-40, ours. No one
believed it. It was too easy to hallucinate, starved and
sick, in the gassy miasma of this jungle. Clever Plane
was losing altitude but like a leaf, fluttering down.
One of the others moved away and came up at a bank
turn and spoke the words out of the guns, and a black
scarf of smoke spewed out of the clever plane and
it turned sharply but could not lose the smoke
and came roaring down straight for them unmistakable now, to eyes that blinked to blink
away any doubt; they saw the red ball of Japan's
totem sun.

The prisoners cheered. In spite of the obvious danger, a ragged cry went up. The soldiers were always
more nervous when brush was being cut, when they
were surrounded by the forests they hated and the
prisoners held machetes in their hands. The prisoners
felt their guards' anxiety. There were always guns
pointed at them, then. The smoke-plumed Zero dove
as though willing it, into the ground beyond the
camp. There was no fire or explosion but there was
a rending, a tearing sound, and a crash. The sound
was cut off then, as it was eaten by the jungle. At the
crashing sound, the prisoners threw up their arms
and cheered.

Elizabeth had been in one of the brush groups.
She, too, had gaped at the beauty and grace of the
dogfight; she had seen the underside of the P-40 and
was shamed at her weakness lest it be a hallucination.
She had heard her heart pounding out of control
when she saw and blinked and saw again the enemy's

red ball: a Zero. She had put her head back and opened her mouth to cheer, but as the moment came, she was overtaken by that terrible, choking feeling, her head came forward and dropped, the word throttled, while her body trembled and her hands were caught in a bizarre splay at her thighs. It saved her life. Corporal Abé saw the prisoners raising their machetes in hands suddenly unconscious of them; he heard the dry shout of triumph from their parched throats. Hating the cheer, hating them, he had opened fire, raking across the line of them, stopping where he saw Ebisu, head down, standing frozen.

Nishimura, who had come from his office to watch, also saw. He had cried out to Abé, but the corporal had been carried away and was beyond the reach of his voice. He saw the bullets hit and the women go down. And in all of it, Ebisu had not moved or spoken. Nishimura had seen her, had stopped in wonder at her infinite courage, standing, ready to endure whatever came. He began to run toward her to stop Abé. Then Abé stopped. The last bullet must have fluttered the rice-sack prison shirt she wore. There was dead silence. Nishimura turned and walked back to his office. If he offered her protection, the others were sure to kill her at the end, and he no longer doubted what that end would be. He called Abé into his office and slapped him for his loss of control. He did not approach Ebisu then or later.

It was the merest chance that saved Elizabeth from being killed by the zealots for collaborating. The lucky accident was that the small group of brush-cutters under Abé's gun had been separated from the others by a fallen tree. They had not been visible to the others who had been watching the dogfight and had then heard the shooting. Two women near Elizabeth had also been spared because in their panic they had fallen and had not seen Elizabeth as Abé's stopping point. The ones who had seen her sudden freezing, her clutching silence, her inability to share the risk and glory of the cheer, had been killed. Abé had seen her, and Nishimura. The major ordered the women buried decently. Their food rations were now shared among the living, and because of this, the others lived. Elizabeth continued as the necessary, hated liaison between the commandant and the camp. She was the one who bowed deep and, in the high indrawn breath whose climax was a silence, begged the honorable sergeant, beseeched the exalted lieutenant . . .

The prisoners were liberated in the retaking of the islands. One morning they woke without the whistle to wake them and after moments of confusion realized that the Japanese were no longer there. Panic ensued. Five women who had endured years of starvation and abuse died in the three days before the first marines came.

Now she was going back to Ionia a heroine. National magazines had written stories about the nurses, their capture and years in the women's camp. There was to be a town ceremony; the mayor — amazingly, it was still Mayor Seddon — was to greet her at the station. There was to be a band, dignitaries, speeches. She had tried, had begged to refuse the honor, but Alicia had written that the ceremony was on and Elizabeth might simply sit quietly through it. She was too tired and too long out of the habit of demanding or refusing anything, to object. As in the jungle, escape was beyond her. There was only what there had been for three years: power to endure. The train pulled up to a strangely bustling and crowded station at Savannah. Where had all these people come from? Elizabeth was led carefully to a seat and waited with until the local train pulled in. Her head was pounding and she felt dizzy and sick. She was seated carefully for the short trip. "You'll soon be home," they said, as though to comfort her.

Even travel-dulled, ill with a dozen diseases, Elizabeth could tell that the land here, the farms and roads and people had greatly changed. When she had left, the traveler to Ionia had had to go to Marshall and get a jitney bus. Now, the town had its own station, they told her. As she came closer and the land became home-familiar, Elizabeth saw that the well-remembered Negro-tenant fields and poor-white farms were sprucer, more prosperous. At first she thought that she was seeing the old place with prisoner's eyes, that compared to the abjectness of the camp, any American scene looked splendid, but she soon realized that what she was seeing was far more than the difference between the wealth of America and the poverty in which she had lived in the camp. Off the roads the train was passing, the close-in tenant shacks had been replaced by comfortable, painted houses, and there were cars and buses coming and going and new roads, paved roads, cutting through the dark green land. There were many more cars, many more people, fewer mule and cart teams. There had been change here, great change. They came to the Ionia station, a large and spacious structure, roofed over and newly painted. There were flowers planted around it in large painted pots.

Her mother came into the car where she sat, to lead her to the welcoming dignitaries. Elizabeth had

seen Alicia at the hospital in California when she had
first come there, but she had been too ill to notice
how much her mother had changed. Now the differences leaped out at her. The stunned and struggling widow had become a fashionable matron. Her
clothing was expensive and severe. She wore a suit
and the wonderful hair was rolled at the back of her
neck. The change was in her manner, too; there was
authority in her voice, command in her gestures. She
led Elizabeth out to the doorway and down the steps.
When the crowd saw them, the band started. The
war's opportunities for martial music had been no
help to Ionia. Elizabeth bit her lip and thought of
train wrecks. She watched the mayor and others de-
fer to Alicia. This seemed to be in far more than her
position as mother of a war heroine. There were
speeches through which the old Alicia would have
squirmed and even giggled. This woman kept her
jaw clamped on whatever rebellious word might rise
from her throat.

Heroine. American Courage. Mayor Seddon and
Pastor Aycroft spoke ringingly of it. They praised all
the wrong things in all the wrong ways. Elizabeth
sat, stood, bowed her head, outwaiting them. Eventually the ceremony was over and Alicia guided her
to a car. When the mayor and the pastor made moves
to join them, Alicia smoothly, deftly forestalled
them. "She's still sick, and very tired — you can see.
I want to ride her around town for a look and then
take her home and put her to bed."

"Whose car is this?"

"It's mine. See the sticker? Unlimited gas ration."

"Aren't we going home?"

"We certainly are going home, honey, but not to
that mausoleum your father left us. It's a boarding-

house now — most of those houses are . . ." They turned down a new, paved road, a road that had once meandered along the river. They were traveling to some place that had not existed when she had lived here. The road was straight now, the river banked, walled off, and the thickets and woods on the other side, cleared to make a swath a hundred feet wide. "The army built this road and the barracks I live in . . ."

"Barracks?" Elizabeth had a sudden wave of dizziness. For a moment she had a picture of the bamboo-grass. "Barracks —"

"We're coming, you'll see." Alicia went on, driving competently, not aware of her daughter's panic.

They went up the road and Elizabeth saw the reason for the changes in Ionia. They were coming to a huge factory, a complex of buildings big as a town. "Food," Alicia said, "there's a cannery and a drying plant and a processing plant and a slaughterhouse and a packaging plant. We produce field rations and now that the war is winding down, we're going to be feeding all those refugees in Europe."

"You work here?"

"I'm in charge, darlin'. Personnel. I hired everyone who works here."

Alicia stopped the car and both the women sat still and looked at the pile of buildings. People were coming and going from them, moving quickly, energetically. There were white and colored together and the colored people whom Elizabeth had thought slow by nature were moving with the same kind of vigorous purpose. She felt utterly lost in everyone's speed and energy. For three years as she and the other camp people had moved into and away, washing, cutting brush, eating, rebuilding storm-wrecked barracks, all dreamy with starvation and illness — like walkers under water, all the while, back here, the gears of the normal world had been turning faster, faster, leaving the prisoners even farther and farther behind. Elizabeth felt herself shrinking away almost to disappearance.

Alicia was talking. "I always wanted to *get out* of this town; you remember all our plans; but then the war came and I found out about this plant coming, and I caught my chance and held on. Ionia is rich now and going to get richer, and that means more modern. You wait and see. There'll be more stores and schools and entertainment and more professional people will come to live here. Right now, I live over yonder in a Quonset, but I've got money, lots of it, saved and when the war's over, we'll build something nice. I have the land picked out already . . ."

She went on as Elizabeth dwindled away. Her sound was so confident, so competent, as she threw abbreviations and neologisms into a speech already changed, a tone and speed and sweep beyond Elizabeth's understanding.

"Honey, the whole South has gone *forward.* There's no room anymore for shuffling Negroes and mint juleps on the verandah. The New South is going to *produce,* to outproduce the North. We have the people now, people are beginning to come *here,* not go there. Once we change our system, politically . . ." and she went on talking about money and manpower, electrification, coal, energy. It flowed past Elizabeth who was sitting, eyes lowered, stopped still in the momentary neurological shutdown that had been read as stupidity, laziness, demureness, innocence, and most recently, as Japanese feminine modesty. At two periods in her life that body silence had been accepted and praised. She was aware, with a wry feeling almost like a laughter from the deepest places in herself, that such acceptance and praise would never come again unless, of course, she visited the land of the enemy.

STAND STILL, UTE RIVER

GOLD FLUME, A NEW SUCCESS STORY

Once a booming silver camp, Gold Flume de-
clined in the 1890's when the price of silver
dropped. There was another boom-bust — the uranium fever of the fifties, but after it the Ute Valley
was as depressed as anywhere in the state. Now, it
is enjoying a third life as a fashionable ski resort.
Pickaxe on the north and the towns of Granite,
Bluebank, Callan, and Aureole to the south provide
housing for service personnel who work in Gold
Flume, now a year-round resort. Mary Rember,
who was born in Gold Flume in 1926, is delighted.
"We have a library now," she said, "and the gro-
ceries carry foods we only heard about. Time was
when the only doc around was a vet. Now they've
got specialists and a good hospital." Marvin Stopes
of Callan is less enthusiastic. "Sure the towns
downriver have improved financially, but they are
crowded now, the crime rate is soaring, and there
are social class differences we never had when I was

a boy." There have been characterizations of Gold
Flume as a gilded ghetto. Inflated land values have
forced many of the Flume's young people to move
away. Jacqueline Brown was born in Gold Flume
but now lives in Callan and says she can't afford to
get a place near her aging parents who homesteaded
Whiskey Gulch. "I feel like I've been forced off
my own place," she says. Her schoolmate, Lucy
Tyrone, is happy with the changes. "The Ute used
to be full of tailings. Now there are fish. Life
has come back to the river. Let's face it, the new
people are very careful with the environment, better than we ever were, and when Jackie's folks
do pass on, she'll have a piece of land worth mil-
lions."

> — "High Country" section of the *Den-
> ver Post,* September 16, 1975. En-
> tered in Evidence at the Hearing,
> Ute County Courthouse, Aureole,
> November 15, 1986.

VALLEY'S MYSTERY PLAGUE

A meeting including Epidemiologist Michael
Mariani, Psychiatrist Richard Seale, Pastor John
Embry, Dr. Paul Bissel, and Mayors Thompson
and Pratt was held at the courthouse in Aureole on
Tuesday. The purpose of the meeting was to coor-
dinate forces in an attempt to deal with the so-called
mystery plague affecting 200 victims and their families in the Ute Valley since mid-September. The
results of the meeting, though not definitive, should
bring a guarded optimism to the valley which has
experienced panic and sorrow as friends and loved
ones were struck with the illness which still defies
diagnosis. No new victims have come down with

the malady since September 21st, and Dr. Bissel says that the 200 sufferers officially counted are in stable condition. The participants of the meeting addressed the panic of loved ones, and what Mayor Pratt called "unbecoming and wrong-headed accusations" at the citizens of Gold Flume which, with Pickaxe, was almost unscathed. Information from studies and interviews may be summarized as follows:

1. The effects of the "plague" were sudden and severe and began on the 14th or 15th of September. Symptoms were profound depression, sleeplessness, weeping and lethargy.

2. The condition affected entire families, or only one or two members. All ages and both sexes were afflicted, but more men and more older people were victims. Onset was sudden and frightening.

3. The course of the "plague" seemed to tend to go town by town, downriver. It was first evident in Granite, then Bluebank, then Callan, and finally in Aureole, hardest hit with 120 cases. Two cases were reported afterwards in Gold Flume; one in Pickaxe.

4. Current health and social services are inadequate to the challenge posed by the illness. Contingency plans are going to be studied and the implications for civil defense are profound.

5. No new cases have been reported. The most recent victims were the members of the Alderson family of Gold Flume and Elmer Diez of Pickaxe.

6. Water tests of wells and the Aureole water supply continue negative; tests of air and of the water and ground around the Ute River, and of ground seepage, continues negative. All other findings have so far been negative. The federal govern-

ment says there has been no testing of any kind of war or chemical products, past or present, in the mountains around the Ute or near its drainage system.

— *Ute Valley Prospector*
November 18, 1986

Mariani had left the meeting with a familiar sense of frustration, which he hoped he had not shown. The picture was all too familiar: a sudden wave of illness, with consistent symptoms but no clues. Nothing exceptional was showing up in any of the samples he had taken. The area was full of old mine tailings but there was no sign of their leaching any new substance into the river or the water supply. It was negative for abnormal biota, or particulates of any of the heavy metals. Yet two hundred people had been affected. John Embry, the pastor, had taken him into their homes; some he had found standing staring unseeing out of windows; some were sitting in chairs, mute and motionless; some were in bed; but all of them were sunk in unbelievable, black depression. In cases where a whole family had been afflicted, neighbors or relatives had had to come in and care for all of them. Many of the older people had had to go to hospitals. There had been forty-seven suicide attempts among the two hundred victims. No one could or would speak of what had happened. They sat and stared, their eyes holding despair like frozen mercury. He left the courthouse, took a turn around the block to clear his head, and went back to his temporary office in the Health Department to sit down to reports he had already seen.

"Atlanta's on the line for you," the secretary said. It was Doris Eppling of the Center for Disease Control.

"It's about time," she said, "you finally sent us the second group of samples."

He didn't get on well with Doris. Her confrontational style made communication difficult for him. "We had over a hundred feeder creeks and streams to check. What are the readings?" She gave them. "Isn't that pH rather high?"

"Alkaline soil. Borates. There are acetic parts of the water, too; pine needle rot, horse piss, pyrite, minerals, beercan rust, tire tread dust. It's nobody's Perrier, but it's nothing I wouldn't expect."

"Normal."

"If no one drinks it."

"No one has."

That evening in Gold Flume, he lay soaking in Bernard Krolick's hot tub. He had been there several times before. Krolick was an orthopedic surgeon who, at sixty, had left a high-pressure practice in Boston to come to Gold Flume, where he now handled ski and summer injuries.

"I'm fascinated by this plague thing," Krolick said, "and by the work you guys do, tracing clues back. Is it a virus nourished in a snake's eye and vectored in a rat?"

Mariani chuckled. "Those wonderful insights come once in a lifetime. The usual job has no thrilling denouements like that."

"Want a drink?"

"No, I'm just right as I am. My mind has stopped circling on itself. Embry the minister, Seale, Bissel — we've gone over and over the possibilities until I'm tired to death of thinking about your plague."

"Bissel is okay," Krolick said, "but I don't like

Seale much. A cold fish. The pastor, John Embry, is a good man — generous, too; our congregation uses his church."

"Congregation?"

"Har Shalom. It's a small Jewish group, people from all the towns."

"I didn't think there were any Jewish people here."

"There are about twenty families from Pickaxe to Aureole but most of us are singles like me, divorced or starting over, and some young people."

"Interesting," Mariani said.

Krolick cleared his throat. "Telling about the congregation is new for me. I'm sixty-five, of a generation that didn't talk about its Jewish life to outsiders. It was all very separate, very secret. 'To Endure, Be Obscure' was our motto. Things are different now, and I'm trying to change. Now they announce Jewish holidays on TV."

"How does it feel?"

"Still a little uncomfortable for me. I'm self-conscious. Anyway, Embry is very good to us. He makes us feel like a part of the town."

"I liked him, too. His Sunday School class helped me with some of the sampling."

"I know. I've been pumping him for information about the sampling and your methods. He called me an epidemiological groupie."

Mariani laughed and lay back in the tub. The word took him. Krolick was a large man, muscular and commanding, with iron-gray hair. The word *groupie* suggested another person entirely, one pierced ear, green hair, shades, a neck chain. "Groupie," he said, and they laughed. But the word . . .

*   *   *

The next morning he was on the phone to Doris Eppling. "Could this be a chemical like LSD? Think of fugitive signs, nothing in the body after six hours, nothing in the water. Covering their tracks, couldn't they have flooded the river with ordinary water hoping to wash out our test?"

Doris sighed on the other end of the line. "You don't really believe that, do you?"

"I guess not. I was brainstorming, letting go a little. Sometimes that helps."

"Whatever you do think, too much argues against *that*. First, look at the uniformity of response. With those drugs, you'd get a variety of responses, hallucinations, mania, depression, delusions . . . you'd need huge amounts of the drug in the *water* supply, not in the river."

The next day Mariani went to Embry's church where there was another meeting of concerned citizens. The people here were old-timers, ranch people who had lived along the Ute before Gold Flume and Pickaxe had had their recent transformations. Many of the sufferers were family or friends.

"You've got to stay till this is solved," Ev Rember said. He had been at all of the public meetings. "We're scared you'll leave before we know." Mariani had to explain that there were government regs about the length of his stay when a case wasn't moving. There were other jobs to get to.

An older woman got up. He had seen her before, but hadn't known who she was. "I've been nursing these folks. It was in the fish."

"We thought that at first," Mariani said, "and it may be so, but all our tests have been negative."

"It was the fish," she persisted, "and there was something else. People say the fishing that day — those two days when this thing began, that the fishing was — special — specially good. I've talked to people who said that the fish jumped into their boats that day, that they had flung themselves in or jumped, yes jumped onto their lines. They took those fish home and ate them and the next day got up like they are now, desperate and miserable and wanting to die."

Here and there in the audience, heads nodded in assent.

Mariani had heard the stories about the fishing. It was true that most of the victims had eaten river fish, but there had been nothing indicative in any of the fish taken later, or in freezer samples of fish caught at the time of the problem, that pointed to their having been the cause. The woman went on.

"I talked to the Stopeses and they said the same thing. The Collettis, also. Maybe the fish were desperate themselves in some way; sick, too. Maybe how they acted was *their* suicide try." There was a chuckle from somewhere. "I know this sounds crazy — it's why I didn't speak out at the other meetings, but when you've heard the theories going around — communists, hippies, drug addicts — sick fish starts sounding pretty sane."

Mariani asked her name.

"I'm the public health nurse, Jean Heath." He had seen her at the county meeting; perhaps some new information was coming from the patients that might justify his staying another week or two. "The doctors have done blood tests, CAT scans, ultrasound," Jean said, "and they've tried people on all kinds of tranquilizers, mood elevators, vitamins —"

"Has anything worked?"

She looked at him steadily. "We're all friends here," she said. "I've been nursing in this county for thirty years, and I take a refresher certification every two years."

He shook his head slowly. "I won't laugh."

"Okay," she said. "Cocoa works. Hot cocoa in a thick mug with marshmallows. The William Tell Overture works and so does the sound of a rocking chair. Halloween worked very well. Many people were helped by eating Halloween candy and seeing jack-o-lanterns in neighbors' windows. They were able to get up afterward and move around. Some of them recognized family and friends. They're not mentally ill. The mentally ill people I've nursed hated holidays. I think Thanksgiving and Christmas will do these people a lot of good. I think . . ."

"What?"

"Snow. The first snowfall; the falling snow will work and the snow on the ground, and the sound of sleigh bells will work, too."

"It sounds a little . . ."

"I know," she said, "but I don't mean that cocoa in a thick mug cures anyone; it does make most of them talk for a while. Woodsmoke works. Woodsmoke makes all of them better for a while."

As he listened to Jean Heath, Mariani realized why she had been silent at the meeting in Aureole. Seale, the psychiatrist, would have torn her apart. "Have you a clue as to what this is?"

"I know what it isn't. It isn't anything that attacks the brain or the central nervous system. This is acute depression, despair, but it isn't the same as the psychiatric kind."

"Then there's good and bad news," Mariani said. "The good news is that this was a single occurrence that may never be repeated. People are improving and will probably continue to improve. The bad news is that like most such occurrences, we may never know the causes and so we will have to live with uncertainty."

He said the same thing to Krolick when he was back in the hot tub that evening. "I'll finish up the week and then go. You know, don't you, that most of what I investigate is just like this, fugitive effects, idiopathic and unrepeated. Think of *that* when you're wishing your work had more mystery in it. Bones don't disappear. Hand me that glass. I want to drink to September fifteenth and be done with it."

"Was *that* the day? I thought it started on the fourteenth."

"That was a rumor. The first validated case was the Rember family late on the fifteenth."

"Oh — I didn't know." Krolick was silent for a long time. Then he said quietly, "It was a beautiful day. I remember it well."

"How come?"

"It was a Jewish holiday. I took off."

"One hour —"

"Jewish services go on and on," Krolick said. "We finished the morning service around one and then went down to the river."

Mariani felt the quickening of surprise and interest. "Where?"

"Near here, the first bend past Gold Flume." Krolick was looking at him steadily.

"Why were you there?"

"It's a . . . it was a thing we did . . . do, an old custom, very old."

Mariani sensed Krolick's hesitation. "Tell me," he said.

"How good a man are you?" Krolick asked. "How decent are you? How lacking in hate?"

"What are you talking about?"

"I'm talking about a nightmare, about where we were and what people will think."

"What the hell is it?"

"*We* were at the river, all of us, this time, for Tashlich. We stood on the river bank with bread bits, day-old bread, and we did Tashlich."

"What's that?"

"It's a ceremony, a rite of casting away sin, and we said the two or three prayers and threw the bread into the water. It was a lovely day, mellow-warm. We were all conscious of the sweetness of the weather and there was a little breeze and I felt happy to take those wonderful timeworn prayers outside and offer them up in the turning trees and the noontime sky. We're modern Jews, pragmatic people, and we were shy about the ceremony, the primitive . . . well — symbolic — casting away of sin. Some of us laughed a little and were self-conscious and that's why we didn't go to the bridge but to the bend in the river — private, we said, but not secret."

"You say this was the first time you did this —"

"It was the second time I did it. Some people have done it for two or three years now, but most of us weren't there before — this was the first time there was anything like the full congregation."

"What holiday was it?"

"Rosh Hashanah, the new year. Tashlich is a cus-

tom, though, not a law. And why we were doing it,
why we had not done it before, is bound up in what
I was telling you last time — about how it was
and is —"

"You mean about how you are freer, more open
now?" Mariani knew a few Jewish people but little
about their ceremonies.

"Yes. It suddenly seemed all right, acceptable, to
stand on a riverbank wearing a shawl and do that
symbolic thing, without fear of accusation —"

"What accusation?"

"You don't know, do you?"

"No."

"I forget there are people who are not part of our
nightmare. The accusation is medieval. The accusation would be that we poisoned the water."

Mariani began to laugh. "I've heard of Jewish
guilt; by now it's a comic turn, but you don't seriously think your bread poisoned the river —"

"We have an old religion and a long history. Prayers are powerful. My medical mind says no, but with
this happening —"

"And now you're not sure, that the accusations
weren't true, that your people don't have the power,
to affect nature with your guilt . . ."

"Sin. Nature is affected by other sins — by greed,
by sloth . . ."

"The word is inaccurate and that's what's causing
the confusion. The sins had already been committed.
What you were ridding yourself of was the guilt, the
shame for the sins."

"I'm so afraid someone will connect what he saw
or half saw, passing by, a bunch of us in prayer
shawls throwing something in the water . . ."

"When did you start thinking about this?"

"When you told me about the fish — I'm afraid someone will start the nightmare again."

"Well, I won't blab. No one has so far. Why are you worried?"

"Maybe our souls do affect nature. If not, why pray? If so, could we have unknowingly — all those generations."

"You can't be serious."

"I'm a trained physician, but I've seen things that defy reason . . . ."

"I don't know what was in the river or in the fish. I don't know what happened high in the mountains, what chemistry caused this. I do know, and this is my, pardon the expression, cross to bear, that fugitive effects, sudden, unexplained changes in a very complex biochemistry and electrochemical matrix happen. I told you before that people want answers they can't always have, chemical answers, which most of the time cannot be proved."

"We've been accused so often of so much. Growing up when I did and where I did, there were lies I heard — perhaps I came to believe, or half believe some of them. I see now that it's why this lovely ceremony, standing together outside in the blue air and the warm sunlight at the bend of the river — why we were uncomfortable. Would someone see us and remember, accuse . . . or do we really, with our well-known comedy-turn guilt, have the power our detractors say we have . . . ."

"Did it happen in the Middle Ages?"

"No."

"Why not last year, or before this?"

Krolick had been sitting up, hunched forward in the tub. His posture looked strange to Mariani until

Mariani realized he had never seen anyone in a hot tub tense and distracted. Krolick caught his look and made a conscious effort to lie back. The effect was disconcerting.

"Why not?" Mariani asked again. "Surely you've thought about it."

"The guilt was different. The people who originally did this ceremony knew much more than we do. They were completely familiar with all the words, and the proper formulae. They had only so much pain as their sins gave them. We have the additional weight of our ignorance, that we have to copy the words, learn the prayers, be unsure and blundering. Has something been left out? Was there some other prayer to say before or after, some part of the ceremony? The Jewish exile is a double exile that way, not only because we left Jerusalem in A.D. 37 but because we left *ourselves* somewhere, all those words, all that knowledge."

"I'm not a theologian," Mariani said. "I study what's catching. You'd be surprised how little is catching, how little gets through the body's nets and goalies. We all have TB bacilli in our lungs. We get contaminants in food. Water carries a thousand viruses; why not Despair and Remorse, too? Is it in a virus so small that not even the electron microscope sees it?" He laughed.

Krolick laughed also. *"Algovirus hebraicus."*

"Name it for its density; has it settled by now?"

"Gravovirus hebraicus."

"You don't believe it; not really; you can't."

"Then why am I scared?"

"Not of a possible virus but of your dead-certain neighbors."

"And of our own exile from our own faith."

Mariani stretched and got up out of the tub, lifting himself with his arms. "That's what you were trying to do at the river, wasn't it — be better Jews? If what I saw in two hundred cases is the guilt you people carry around inside you, I can only wonder how you function at all."

Krolick didn't answer but came out of the tub and they dried themselves. Mariani said, "Viruses are named after lots of things but the diseases they cause are named after the doctor. This is going to be Mariani's malaise."

"What about Krolick's complaint? Do you want a sandwich? I have some good cheese and there's beer —"

Mariani was tired and wanted to go home. The bath had relaxed him. "I need to make some calls," he said, "and get some sleep. I'll leave you with this: Hansen discovered the bacteria of leprosy in 1871, and leprosy became Hansen's disease. He died in 1912, so for forty-one years he heard people associate his name with horror and anguish. His name fell like doom on thousands. Hodgkin — his is a disease kids get, and kids find it even easier to confuse the messenger with the message. During their own lifetimes, which were full and not marked with special pain, these doctors . . . ."

"I know *hate* can't kill, because if that had been so," Krolick said, hiding in the sweatshirt he was pulling over his head, "many peoples would have disappeared from the earth generations ago."

Mariani left the next week for a conference in Dallas. The river samples were unchanged. The fish were not unnaturally active. Everything else remained normal. In the houses of the afflicted, people would be reacting to the voices of friends and Mrs. Heath's cocoa and marshmallows. It would soon be Thanksgiving and then the snow would come and Pastor Embry's Sunday School would bring sleighs on the roads between the houses with horses and bells, memory before words, and then it would be Christmas, and they would get better. People who needed answers at any cost would blame him for a government cover-up of secret tests in the mountains. It was all usual and ordinary. Fugitive and/or random phenomena would get another listing for its computer file and some day someone might be able to put it together with other phenomena to tell doctors yet unborn, the story.

Two months later Mariani was working on a parasite infestation in Landry Parish, Louisiana, when a letter came, forwarded to him from Atlanta. It was in Krolick's arresting medical scrawl:

> I am no longer a groupie — I've been cured. Give me a boottop fracture any time. You people have too many phantoms to fight. Now the talk is that the same bunch who mutilated cattle on the range last year were involved in this. Extraterrestrials. The government — that's you, buddy — is hushing it up.

Mariani smiled.

> I figured no one was smart enough to tell you how it all came out, so I will. Jean was right. Christmas did it. Trees in the houses. It was amazing; people got up just like that and walked into

town to see the lights. The church choir is full again and sounds no better, but they're all back, even the older ones who had to be hospitalized. Jean was right about it not being ordinary mental illness — there seem to be no sequelae — not even convalescence.

But are they back to normal? Not quite. Embry told me that Luke Brown (you remember, that whole family was down) comes to church and prays but refuses to speak God's name at all. Ev Rember stands up all during the service swaying back and forth, witnessing, he calls it. The people who had whatever it was are touchier, angrier, Embry says, and more intense. They're more quarrelsome but also more aware. I told him it was probably the pain they've all been through — He said the oddest part of it was how vocal they all are about it. These are folks whose families seldom heard a personal feeling expressed by them from one year to the next; now, you can't shut them up. Their talking about their experience has spread to other parts of their lives, too. Last week there was a soapbox set up in Bluebank and three of them made political speeches extempore that went on for as long as forty-five minutes. Ray Stopes has begun writing a bill of particulars against God. He says, "The Lord has a lot to answer for." People are writing *books* — at least ten of them are doing that. Four are writing songs. So far there have been 166 lawsuits begun, 120 against the government — city, state, and federal; 32 against doctors; 14 against the local ministers as spokesmen for the Almighty, would you believe *that?*

I'm urging you to keep silent about what I told you. Everything that moves is getting sued. I won't leave Gold Flume, but neither will I tell another soul that I recognize what those people are doing. Embry says there was one other odd thing. Many of them come to church now in cowboy clothes. He has no idea. I do. The fringes; it's the fringes.

INTRODUCTION TO SEISMOLOGY

THE picture had been in the bedroom where his wife Lila kept a wall full of pictures of her family. It was the only one Paul had of his people, that first American generation on his mother's side. There were twelve of them, energy personified. They were so eager they were bending toward the camera, uncles and aunts and cousins. Three of the women were pregnant and they were in no grouping a photographer would make; it was a clump, a mass, and all of them but the children were grinning, gap-toothed and round-faced, bursting out of clothing and pasts too small for them, all hands, cheeks, teeth, and go and do and be, all wide-open in the new land, alive, alive.

He brought the picture to the house of mourning where his grandmother sat. The little girl she had been stared from it. Five years old. She wore a checked dress, obviously someone else's, and a big kerchief that almost overwhelmed her tiny face.

Through the old woman's thick glasses, Paul saw the same shocked world-wonder as the little girl had had, looking out through the heavy folds of the wool.

She took the picture and held it for a long time and then began to identify face by face. "I didn't know you had this — Here's Mendel and Aunt Rina — Mama, Papa. It was before people started to separate, to spread away, out and away into the wide world — America," and her hand made the gesture of dispersion — not as seeds are sown, as something is lost.

"And you ended up in Gold Flume, Colorado, of all places." She nodded but didn't add anything.

Paul was used to her silence about those days. His friends' parents seemed to like reliving their hard times from the vantage of present comfort. Perhaps it was because the times had not really been so hard. He did know that Imah seemed happy living in Denver near her son and that though there had been other children, his uncles and aunts, they had all gone away also, scattered like the people in the picture. Paul's father had been a good son to her and now that he, too, was gone, Paul and Lila were all the family she had left out of the six children she and Abner Bronfman had had.

"Are there more pictures somewhere?"

She sighed. Her husband's parents and brothers had stayed in the Old Country and had all disappeared in the Holocaust. He had died years ago. Paul had begun to realize that the worst attrition of age is its depopulation. Imah's world was going as narrow as her vision. "Pictures?" she said. "I took some — your father took some when they were first married and when you were a baby."

"I've seen those," Paul said. "Don't you have any from your and Grandpa's early days?"

"No. None."

"Were they lost in the move from Gold Flume?"

She had once told him that boxes of things had disappeared in the move they had made after Abner's death. She said, *"Your* father lived long enough to see you successful and married to a fine woman. Your degree — it was a blessing."

When Paul had gone up to get his Ph.D. last spring, he had grinned at his father, whom he had spotted with Lila in the mass of spectators. The old man had gone to all Paul's ceremonies, from B.S. to Ph.D. in seismology — it was only later, when he recalled his father's posture as he stood, that Paul saw the stance as rigid and thought he must have been in pain even then. Leonard Bronfman had been proud of his son's success, a secret, deep, silent pride. The family had been desperately poor in Gold Flume, Paul had known that, and that his grandfather, Abner Bronfman, had been a miner. Sometimes he had thought about having inherited some call toward the earth from that unknown grandfather. The earth moves, shifts, goes to putty or quicksand, slops, heaves, shoots mountains, cleaves asunder, pulls sinkholes, and drops canyons sometimes in a day. When he was in college and studying geology, he was sometimes kept awake by the knowledge of the instability of what should be most stable of all: bedrock. He couldn't admit such anxieties to anyone in his classes, but once when he was working with his father, laying pipe in the cellar of a new house, he said, "Don't these give way in tremors?"

Leonard Bronfman had paused in his work, brazing a joint, and answered slowly. "You'll lose more in the activity of freeze-and-thaw than you will in tremors. In quake areas or sinking areas they plan. Here we have freeze-and-thaw and that can shatter rocks."

Then Paul told his father what he couldn't tell his friends or classmates, of both the fear and the excitement he felt about what he was studying, the vast dance of the earth, the upthrust of mountains being born and then of their washing away, of seas coming and retreating, of the cataclysms of volcanos, and the long, slow attrition of wind and water, weights compressing, folding, plates as big as countries moving and grinding against one another. He admitted that he sometimes sat in class lost in the excitement, the simple wonder of it.

His father didn't answer. Paul knew he wouldn't, but Leonard looked at his son and nodded his head slowly. Something had pleased him in what Paul had said. Paul wondered what it was.

Leonard Bronfman was not a man whose thoughts or feelings it was easy to know. Paul had worked summers and holidays with him in the plumbing business. He had been doing it since boyhood, but still knew almost nothing of his father's inner life. There were habits only. He always wore a white shirt, even at work. When he was frustrated or angry, he would stop, go dead still, scarcely breathing. His anger would be like confusion, a confounding that would stop all his motion and seemingly his senses. Time would pass and then he would breathe out and could move again, but he would have to go and rest; he was dulled as though after a seizure.

Paul's mother had died when he was a freshman

in college. She had been full of stories of her people, their coming to America, their settling, their habits. His father's reticence almost to muteness he took as a habit of gender. Men were reticent and didn't tell all they knew or felt. They showed their love in care, their mythos in action. They fixed and repaired and studied and predicted. They sent their wrenches around pipes in nets of lines but never made the metaphor of a body in whose ducts and vessels fluids moved in and out. When Paul did once, his father stopped for a moment and shook his head — it was wonder, but not scorn. Then he sighed and reapplied himself to the pipe before him, listening but not responding.

They had grown apart slightly when Paul was in college. Words separated them, thoughts, theories. Paul began taking his vacations at earthquake and volcano sites and working a night job to pay for graduate school. When he met Lila, whose parents were professors, he felt a quick, sour self-reproach at his shame, that his parents' lives and talk had been so much less cultured than Lila's parents'.

Yet, it was his family and not Lila's who were formal and restrained in their visits, quiet and self-effacing. Paul sat with his grandmother and spoke about his father's quietness. "He was so dignified. Do you know, I never saw him with his shirt off? Summers, working on jobs, it might be broiling and I'd be working with no shirt on, but he always wore something — he wouldn't even strip to his undershirt, not even at home."

Imah nodded, "Yes, he was a good man, a good boy, too, when he was young. That's why . . ." and she stopped and sighed.

★   ★   ★

They didn't keep shivah for the full seven days. Imah was tired and Lila had to go to work. Friends came from the union and a few from the neighborhood, shyly because they weren't Jewish and didn't know what was expected in a Jewish house of mourning.

On the fourth day there was a call. A man with a light tenor voice asked for his mother. "I'm sorry, she's no longer living." There was a pause. "Is there a son, or daughter, then?"

"I'm the son, what can I do for you?"

"I know this sounds odd — I saw the name in the paper, your father's name, and I had been planning to write anyway. It's too late to write to *him,* but I need to write to you —"

"What's this about?"

"Some memories, I guess — things I need to say. He did go to school in Gold Flume from 1933 to 1944 . . ."

"Yes, he did."

"Well, thanks." And the man hung up.

The letter came three days later:

I'm on a twelve-step program, hoping to con-quer my addiction to alcohol and attain sobriety. As part of this program we are encouraged to search our pasts and ask the forgiveness of people we have offended. Your father, whom I knew as Lenny Bronfman, was such a person. We laughed at him, the other kids and I. The very ones who should have protected and befriended him made fun of his misfortunes. Because others did it also is no excuse for my having done it. Some of the teachers did it, too, although Mr. Seeger, who taught the math and science subjects, tried to stop it. Your father has probably told you about those days, which were supposed to be happy childhood times and were for him the opposite in every way. If he was cruel, realize that he had been taught by masters, one of whom, to my shame, was I. I hope he has and you will forgive me. I hope he found success and happiness in life in spite of all he suffered. Sincerely, Eliot Nostrand.

Misfortunes? A cruel man? "Imah?" He had stopped by her house on his way home. She took the letter, her glasses glowing over it, her lips moving, reading carefully half aloud. She turned a vague and troubled look at him.

"What does he mean?"

"I thought *you* might know. Neither of you talk about your days in Gold Flume. Dad's brothers and sisters — I never even met Uncle Herman or Uncle Jules until the funeral. When I asked them at shivah about those days, they said they didn't remember them."

"They were hard days," Imah said. "We were very poor. Maybe people laughed at your father because of that. Maybe it was another brother and this man here confused it."

There was an evasiveness he had never seen in her before. She had gone pale as she read. Under the thinning skin and hair, under the old-lady pallor had been a quickly passing blue tone like shock.

Gold Flume. It had been one of the booming Ute Valley mining towns in the 1860s and there were trains and wagon trails, schools, churches, lots of saloons, but by 1910 it was bust and beginning to die and by the late '20s it must have been a place of narrowing hopes and torn shutters and a few miners working the exhausted claims not for gold but for whatever could be recovered from the mountains of tailings that leached yellow alkali into the Hazard Creek and Indian Creek washes.

It seemed to him suddenly that the reticence of his father and grandmother wasn't a passive disinterest but an active closing away, and that childhood curi- ·osity about the place, and the people there, had been quietly but persistently warded off. His mother had said of the Bronfmans — "They were poor and I guess they didn't want to talk about the ugly town and what they had to do to survive."

"Were there other Jewish people there?"

"I don't know if there were any. Someone taught the kids Hebrew — your dad can read it. I think the family was kosher by default — too poor to see meat or chicken from one year to the next."

His father had once said, *"These* are the days we should be thinking about, not those. You can't change the past."* When he had gone skiing at the ski area near the town, now revived and fashionable, he saw the beauty of the mountains there. Even in poverty there were summers, golden autumns — while his father was alive, he had not thought about that paradox. What had Gold Flume been like back then?

He wanted to know more. He remembered having mentioned it once to McKinstry at work. McKinstry's people had come from there and he was a local history buff. "Jews? Sure. There were Jews in Denver and the San Luis Valley in the eighteen fifties and sixties. The oldest religious building still standing in Denver is a synagogue and there were single families, miners and storekeepers, in all those canyon towns, the boom towns." He thought he remembered McKinstry having told him that his grandfather had been a teacher in Gold Flume.

When he went back to work, he stopped at the table where McKinstry was eating lunch with the other people from records. "Yes, he was — Grandpa taught in the high school in Gold Flume from nineteen thirty until it closed in nineteen fifty. I got my interest in local history from him."

"Is he still living?"

"Oh, yes. He's eighty-six and retired, but very sharp."

"And he remembers those times?"

"Sure — I've been taping him, doing oral history."

Paul felt wonder, and a little envy, something rooted, something secure and wise in the possession of all that past. "Was he Mr. McKinstry?"

"No, his name is John Seeger — he's my mother's dad."

Paul found his heart beating quickly. "Do you think he would see me?"

"An old man with a hat full of reminiscences and a new ear to listen — are you kidding?"

The house was on Elati, near the high school, and they sat in the handkerchief-sized backyard and heard sounds from the school's playing field where Saturday practice was going on. Paul had noticed the grilles on the windows and doors of the neighborhood, although the houses were neat and well cared for. It was almost too late in November to be sitting outside. He felt the cold a little and wondered how the old man was taking it.

"The family says move away," Seeger said, "but I'm near everything and when I want to go out at night, I call a cab. The neighbors are nice, though it's supposed to be a high crime area. The kids — I guess it's my destiny to be where young people are." He looked at Paul engagingly. "My grandson says you want to talk about Gold Flume and the school there. Are you a writer?"

"No, it's actually about my grandfather, Abner Bronfman — well, about the whole family."

"Oh —" John Seeger said.

There was a stunned look and an attempt at a quick recovery so that Paul would mistake the cause of his response. "I'm sorry — I haven't heard that name for so long — it evokes so much — all those years . . . the thirties, the Flume —"

It didn't work. Paul saw he had evoked something confusing, even shameful. He told Seeger about the letter. " 'Mr. Seeger tried to stop it,' it said. Stop what? What did he mean? He said for me to forgive cruelty in my father because he had been taught by masters. Who were those masters? What was that life?"

"Was your father a cruel man?"

"No. My father was reticent and secretive, and I never knew how secretive until I married and got to know my own father-in-law. A kid takes what's given and that's the world. My whole family shut the past away and I realize now that we've lived like shell-shocked refugees whose lands have no geographies, no histories, whose milestones gave no numbers. Now my dad is dead and I feel stunted. I've read about Gold Flume — I've even been there, significantly, without telling anyone."

"Is your mother still living?"

"No, only my grandmother, but she's as bad as he was and there's no one else. Two uncles surfaced at my father's funeral, but only for the day. They said they didn't remember."

"I've always been an advocate of telling the truth," Seeger said, mostly to himself, "full disclosure. I've been a little sanctimonious about it now and then, but these are not my truths to give."

"I'm not asking any more of you than how you saw my father and my grandparents. The letter said, 'Mr. Seeger tried to stop it.' "

Seeger took a deep, sighing breath. "You have to remember that those were savage times. It was a savage place, then. Mining, especially in those days, was a bitter business. The work is hard, dark and oppressive. The shafts there were small and unventilated. If the miner was working tailings, they had to be treated with acids and the fumes got in the miner's lungs and ate them away. Prices were low, wages were lower, and kids — even little kids — worked alongside in the shafts or in the slag. Your father — he —"

"What?"

"I'm trying to tell you. Fathers beat kids in those days and it was accepted. Severe beatings. Your grandmother gave more and your father took more, that's all. They all took — more. When it was . . . when he had to be, he was out of school, and then he'd come in and he wouldn't have the lesson and the others would laugh at him."

"As a dummy."

"Yes."

"There were six in the family. What made my father so memorable?"

"That boy had a strong mind and he wanted to be in school. The others quit at ten and eleven — the law said they had to stay until they were thirteen, but in the mining camps there were no truant officers, and there wouldn't have been any trouble unless someone stepped out of place and made it."

"You —"

"For some of them, yes. Jenkenson was principal then, an officious man, scared of the miners and with good reason. Sometimes the labor of those children made the difference between survival and ruin for their families. Your grandfather had the boys working when they were nine or ten. Did they ever get any more education than occasional visits to the fifth grade?"

"I don't know. As I said, only two of them came to Dad's funeral and I couldn't ask them any questions."

Seeger was working hard to be careful, to be tactful. "He had a keen, inquisitive mind, scientific, I thought. Did he ever finish school?"

"I don't think so. He was a plumber. He read quite a bit and yes, he liked to read in science. I remember one day I couldn't find my high-school physics text and Mom got it for me. He'd been reading it. I couldn't think why a grown man would want to read such a book."

A gulf suddenly opened before him, an awareness, physically, of his father's hunger, pain, and need; his father's thirst for respectability. He saw the white shirt now in a new way. "He always wore a white, starched shirt, even at work, in the summer."

Seeger put his head down so that Paul couldn't see his face. "The beatings were, as I said — uh — they must have left heavy scars."

"Oh."

They sat in silence and Paul wondered why he had stopped hearing the sounds from the ball field all this time. He had noticed their absence by their presence now, shouts, cheering. He felt cold. The sounds rang hollowly in the chill. He was oppressed by the weight of what he had been hearing and shifted his body in the chair.

"I guess it is cooling off a little," Seeger said. "I planned to bring coffee out because I love these fall days and I like to enjoy them till I can't stay out anymore, but it's too cold now. Come on inside. It's ready to drink and I can put a little something with it. I think you could use some."

They talked about Gold Flume in its days of depression, of failed mines and trapped people. "Some of them mined gold to live, working on bootleg claims for the eight or ten dollars they got from the flakes of gold those old mines or tailings yielded. There was no welfare money or food stamps to help out. It's a mistake to judge those people by today's standards. No one thought what he did with the strap was child abuse."

"But my grandfather . . . went beyond that."

"He was a big man, a fierce one. Usually, when men beat their wives or their kids, someone would take them in until the arguments were over or the drunk was over. Father Cleary would take them in. There was usually someone. Your grandfather was big as a house. He was an angry man — and he didn't drink. We were all scared of him. I tried to stop the kids from laughing at Lenny and the other children. The family lived in fear."

"Weren't there police?"

"No. There was a county sheriff, but what your grandfather did at home wasn't against the law in those days."

They sat for long moments without speaking.

Paul was trying to imagine his father as a child, his grandmother as a wife in those days.

"I've given you a lot to think about," John Seeger said.

Paul nodded.

"By the way, who was that man, the one who wrote the letter?"

"Nostrand," Paul said, "Eliot Nostrand."

"He was on a twelve-step program?"

"Yes." It was difficult for Paul to talk.

"I remember him — a skinny kid — there was something the matter with him, too. He had a gray look. His father ran some cattle so they weren't badly off. About the alcohol, I'm not surprised. Everyone drank more then. In the absence of central heating, it warmed you up, or seemed to. Most people judged heavy drinking differently than they do now. Some miners made their own and they put turpentine or kerosene in it and if they or their friends went blind or mad or died, it was just one of those things. No one went to law about anything."

Paul was still silent, wondering when the feeling of being overwhelmed would leave him.

Seeger said, "When you called I thought I might have a picture. I went into a carton of stuff I kept from those days. Would you like to see it?"

Paul became aware of his unresponsiveness. "Oh. Yes. We have nothing — she didn't have or keep even one picture."

"Too poor, probably. Lots of people didn't have the few cents for a print."

Paul thought of the single picture on his wall — Imah's parents and uncles and aunts. They were poor also, but they had gotten someone to take that picture, wanting to be caught in their moment of hope and optimism. That, not the poverty, was the difference.

Seeger went away for a moment and came back with a framed school picture, a little faded. Paul took it gently. There they stood on the schoolhouse steps, stiffened and grave. There were three teachers, the principal, and the full student body — elementary through high. Most of the children were smartened up for the photograph. Here and there a white collar gleamed and jackets were buttoned for a neat appearance.

"Where are *you?*"

Seeger pointed to a lath-skinny young man with straw-colored hair and a large Adam's apple. The old man's laughter freed Paul to laugh as well. "Quite the fellow, wasn't I? I was courting then — a girl from Aureole. She died a month after this picture was taken — pneumonia. It would be my last year in Gold Flume. As I look at him, I don't even remember what his ambitions were. Your dad — here."

The boy bore the wide-eyed, stunned look of his grandmother, the same look. "How old was he here?" Paul said this so he wouldn't cry, having seen his father and grandmother looking out of one another's eyes. Did he, too, have that look, taken unawares? When he stood on the heaving shoulder of a fault as it yawed away and buckled, as he had done three times in aftershocks of earthquakes, was this his face?

"Ten or eleven, I'd say. His father wanted him out of school like the others. The boy held out till he was thirteen." They were both silent, looking at the boy. Paul wondered what that choice to stay in school had cost him. "Do you have children?" Seeger asked.

"No, not yet. We think in a year or two. It makes

me sad now. Dad would have made a good grandfather."

Seeger put the picture away. Paul got up to leave.
He told Seeger he was grateful but there was the
slowing of heartsickness in the sound of his words.

"I hope it was all right," Seeger said, "or that it
will be."

Paul waited a week, two. He did his work, remembering the image of the little boy who looked out at
him from the picture. He told Lila about Seeger but
not about what Seeger had told him. He felt raw with
the knowledge and obscurely ashamed. Now and
then memories took places in the half-light of what
he now knew. His father, an observant but not religious Jew, had always been infatuated with Christmas stories, and the more cloying and saccharine they
were, the better he liked them. Paul had used to
laugh at that when he was in high school, his father's
sitting intent before the TV, his scarred hands with
their broken nails and solder burns hanging over his
knees. He would watch all the little children praying
for dogs or horses or the lives of their parents. "How
can you stand that stuff?" Paul would laugh. Leonard
Bronfman had never answered and now the thought
of years of sleds and puppies and sudden wealth magically appearing on Christmas morning made Paul's
chest tighten with sorrow.

Mostly he remembered those dumbstruck moments when his father stood without words or motion staring at something beyond his present rage or
frustration. Did he see his own father? Was he afraid
of what he himself might become? His mother had
known all these secrets. She had seen the scarred
body and perhaps had listened to him say, "My

father had too many children. We will have only one. I might not have patience for more than one." How much of his father's life had been determined by that looming, damning presence behind him?

He went to Imah at last. "I visited Mr. Seeger, the teacher, Dad's teacher. Do you remember him back in Gold Flume?"

"Was he tall and very thin?"

Paul remembered the man in the picture. "Yes, and he had a great big Adam's apple."

"I remember," she said, but said no more.

Paul persisted. "He told me Grandpa beat Dad; I don't mean spanked or hit. I mean beat."

Silence. Then the old woman's eyes swam, filled, broke tears. The lines of them followed one after the other but she made no sound. He was appalled, then ashamed.

"You don't understand," she said at last.

He had wanted to be gentle, but he had also wanted to know. "What don't I understand? Ma is dead. She can't tell me. Dad is dead; Grandpa is dead, and I never knew him. I'm a stranger to my uncles. You knew all the things I was left out of. I never saw my father bathe or shave. I never saw him any way but fully dressed. The undertaker knows things about my father that I don't know. Why was he like that? Was it because he was scarred? That badly scarred?"

The glasses were fogged. She had not taken them off. Now she did. "You're really asking me why I didn't go away," she said, "why I didn't take the children and leave."

"Tell me that, then. Make me understand."

"Times were bad, then. People starved. He came

all by himself from the Old Country, a boy fourteen, from poverty even worse than ours. Slapping, hitting, beating — it was like a language to him — he used it instead of words. I don't think he wanted . . ."

"Imah —"

"You asked me. You shame me with your thinking. I tell you, these times are not those times. Think about your own Lila, so liberated, who says: I plan, I think, I need. Sometimes I want to yell at those women because they criticize us with their thoughts; why didn't we leave? Those women slap our faces without lifting a hand. Where would I have gone? Who would take us in, to stay where and do what work? Your father defied him. He beat your father more than the others, more than me. I begged Leonard when he was thirteen to run away if he couldn't submit, wear his face right, quit school like the others and go to work, and then when he was grown enough, find a way to get an education. The others were already leaving; one by one they slipped away and escaped him and then they were lost to me forever. Sometimes they wrote, sometimes they didn't. They hated me for not protecting them, for not saving them all that pain. If your Lila knew —"

"My mother knew — she must have, seeing my father's body."

"She knew and didn't know. He never talked about those days, or let her ask him a single question about his childhood."

"It meant she had to be silent about hers, too. Don't you see that closed off both their pasts?"

"We did talk about it, once, your father and I. It was long ago, and I told him I had found a way to stop more cruelty. It was the only time we talked about what happened, only we didn't mention any more than that — we said, 'About what happened.' "

"You mean not even the two of you?"

"Especially not the two of us. If that wasn't a secret between us, a secret we kept from one another, how could we look the other in the eyes?" She had been fussing with her glasses and her hair, pulling neglected ends into a bun she no longer had.

"What did you tell Dad?"

"I told him there would be no more born after him. I saw to it, too. I told your grandfather that I would kill the living ones as well, if he didn't stop."

She got up. She had been sitting next to Paul on the small couch she had moved near the fireplace. He thought idly that when the city got an anti-woodburning law, this ordinary furniture placement would change. A need meets another need and pushes it aside, and under the earth plates shift and pressures build. A century ago no one drank clean water here or breathed clean air, and this lady, abused and despairing, carried the wood in and ashes out, and split kindling with a hatchet. Did she ever want to . . . He shook the thought away and looked at her, moving purposelessly around the room, putting her hands out like a blind person to touch for placement and direction, a curtain, a light switch, a dish, a monkeypod server he had sent her from a field placement.

More memories would only hurt her. "Let me put up some tea for us," he said. Suddenly he wondered if there were any scars on *her* body. He had to stop that thought as well. He had a feeling then of how it must have been for them all those years — stop this thought, that one. Don't go here, there, even in dreams. He saw how she needed comfort. She was unable to tell him the things he wanted to know, how his father had endured the unendurable and how he must consciously have overwhelmed his anger, swallowed it, taken it deep as his core so that it wouldn't discharge against his own wife and son.

She didn't let him get the tea. She used the excuse to get away and lose herself in hospitality, bustling and dithering happily as she had always run to do through the years, cloth napkins and little paper doilies on the underplates, fruit cut and cored for eating, delicate cookies.

She had a habit of asking about his work. Years ago he had tried to explain the intricate math and physics of shifting earths, of compression, liquefaction, stress and fault. When he saw she didn't understand any of what he said, he wanted to stop, but she had kept asking and he had recently begun to give her single facts in the smallest, most discrete units he could, and these she had taken eagerly, appreciatively, as sharing his work with him. He had looked on it with indulgence, but during his last visit, she had said something that surprised him with its mastery of the subject. When a baby comes, he thought, that will be how I will do it, bit by bit, fact by fact, and he felt a little curl of pleasure beginning though there was no child yet.

Now they sat in her favorite room, sunny and white-curtained, and she smiled and said, "Annie Carson is coming to take me shopping. Before she comes, where's my lesson, my Introduction to Seismology?"

He looked over at her, pert and eager. He began. "As you know, seismic activity is constant —"

"It keeps you in work," she said, a joke, rare for her.

"The earth was created with seismologists in mind. You know about the rhythmic waves in their absorption and about their interruption by various thicknesses and densities of rock." She nodded. "Occasionally, a series of waves begins in strata that don't bend or fold or heave because they have been shattered by past waves many times before. We see how powerful the activity is, but there has been no fault or upthrust because the earth has been disordered so many times that the effect is like tiny pills in a bottle being shaken. It settles closer and becomes more stable, not less."

"What's that called?" she asked.

"It has a few names, but there are special phenomena there which I am studying, and if I ever write about any of it, I'll call my word the Bronfman Effect, after Dad."

"It would have pleased him," she said.

Paul looked at his grandmother in the glowing room. He thought of old Gold Flume crouched in its dark canyon, of its shack-houses with few windows, the necessary sacrifice of light and view for warmth. She, too, had made the rest of her life day by day, choice by choice, a repudiation of cruelty and squalor. He wondered if he would have had the endurance to put away rage, to bank it deep and then to offer himself to his wife and child with such desperate love? "I'd have to tell them which Bronfman it was," he said.

RETRIEVAL

THE first time Wreford saw the woman she was standing with the other witnesses backed against the windows of the shop, leaving as wide a circle as they could around the dead boy and all the broken glass. The robbery had been the bungled, stupid work of bungling, stupid kids, he thought, shooting the glass out of the store window and reaching in to snatch at the jewelry there. The burglar alarm had been set off and the watchman had come running and had shot it out with the kids and here lay one of them on the marble floor of the mall, his handful of loot lost in the heap and throw of shattered glass.

Other officers were moving with cameras and notepads to get evidence and statements. The coroner had been called. The witnesses (they always appeared as though by magic — even though it was 2:00 A.M.) stood and stared, hung stock-still in this moment of drama. Wreford noticed the woman because she was the only one who was not staring down at the corpse and the glass. She was a substantial old lady, short and wide, and she had bundled herself against the icy weather in scarves and swathings enough to keep warm in the bitter cold. He went over to her with his notebook. "Were you here during the shooting or before?"

"Before," she said. "I was walking and I heard glass break so I came over."

He questioned her in his routine way. She had little to add. Her vision and hearing were not acute enough to have caught the details in which he was most interested, but her mind was clear and she corroborated the statement of the watchman that the young men (there had been four of them) had been rooting among the jewelry in the showcase when the watchman came on the scene. He had called out to them to stop and put up their hands. One had begun to comply, but another had begun shooting. The three ran away. She didn't see whether or not they took jewelry with them. There had been bullets flying and one or more must have hit the thief because after the shooting he just sagged over and fell in the glass.

"Where were you standing?" Wreford asked. She showed him. He looked at her incredulously. "Why didn't you move back? You were in the line of fire — you could have been hit."

"I'm small," she said. "Most if it went over my head. I thought it was smarter just to stand still."

"Well, you're one lucky lady," Wreford said. "What were you doing out here at this time of night?"

"I had a headache," she said, "and I was out of aspirin. There's an all-night store at the end of the mall. I was walking through here to keep warm."

He got her name, Violet Scheinfeld, her address, and her age, eighty.

"Miss or Mrs.?"

"Mrs.," she said, "widow."

He smiled down at her. "Well, you stay home next time. Shoot-outs are no place for nice old ladies." She gave him a quizzical look. She was an engaging woman. He thought of dispatching a uniformed officer to take her to the drugstore and then home. "How's your headache?"

"It's all gone. The walking cleared it up."

"Are you sure you'll be all right?"

"I want to walk home by myself."

"Be careful. It's icy, and don't go out at night anymore. The streets are full of scuzzos."

"Is that a police term?"

He noticed as she walked away that her bulky upper body fined down to slender, even skinny legs, and that she wore a pair of snappy fur-topped boots.

Wreford spent the rest of the night doing his paper work. Now and then he thought about the old lady. His precinct had once been working class, with two-family and small houses. Now it was deteriorating into a poverty area and turning dangerous. In the last ten years, the crime rate had trebled. He was sorry for the older residents still trapped there. Random crime against persons took an increasing amount of his time.

Three weeks later, Wreford was investigating a bus-truck wreck. It was ten at night, and he had just come on duty. The bus had been crowded with people coming from the Arena. Besides medics, the police had radioed for detectives; a juvenile gang had come on the accident and had begun robbing the victims as they lay in the wreckage. A patrolman reported as Wreford got out of his car. "We've got two of them. Apparently an old lady was walking along, saw what was going down, dove in, and started yelling and flailing around. By the time the kids got over the surprise, a couple of other bystanders had joined in and someone called nine-one-one. They could have killed her, but in the dark — they didn't want to stick one of their own. They punched at her a few times but nothing much seems to have landed. We've got 'em in the cars and ready to go."

"I'll see them at the precinct. Where's Wonder Woman?"

"She's resting in my car."

It was the old lady from the mall robbery. At first he was sure only that he had seen her before and then he looked down and saw the neat, fur-topped boots, and he remembered. "Mrs. . . . uh . . ."

"Scheinfeld," she reminded him. "Violet."

"You shouldn't have done what you did," he said. "You're a civilian. You could have been killed."

"I'm a sweet old lady, too. You said so the last time."

"But you can't go wading into these things."

"I caught them, didn't I? I got the other people so embarrassed they came in to help. Years ago that would have happened without my doing it. I remember in the twenties there was a gang — we called them toughs, then. Once they tried to . . ."

"Never mind that," he said. "The twenties are gone. People carry guns now —"

"What do you think they had then, stone axes?"

"Did they get to you? Did they hurt you?"

"A little here, in the shoulder."

"Where?"

As before, she was bundled in clothing, but her coat had been cut, the fabric sliced as neatly as though on purpose. "Good God, you've been stabbed," he said. He turned to call to the paramedics.

"No!" she cried. He felt her violent tremor through all the clothes she was wearing. "It's nothing. I'm all right. I don't want anyone poking at me. I don't have money to throw away. I'm one of those sweet old ladies on a fixed income who eats cat food."

"You've been hurt —"

"Nonsense." She undid the two top buttons on her coat. Under it was a sweater, which she also unbuttoned. A man's oxford cloth shirt came after that and then a T-shirt. "Is there any blood?" she asked sarcastically, moving each garment aside to reveal the next layer. "Is blood pumping out?" There was no blood. The knife slash had gone through the coat and the sweater and the man's shirt. The T-shirt was undamaged.

"You could have been killed. Why can't I get through to you how dangerous this is?"

"It's more than dangerous, it's sad. All those clothes ruined and I can't see well enough to mend them. Ten years ago I could have saved them all. I was a good seamstress. To stabilize the cloth I first used to —"

"Never mind. Is there anywhere else?"

"They punched my arm and tried to hit me but nothing landed. By then there were people trying to pull me off them."

"Well, go home and make yourself some tea. And

stay away from —" he shook his head, "from toughs."

Scheinfeld. The name stuck in his mind. Cat food. Fixed income. Where did she live? It would be in the records of the mall robbery. He went to the terminal and tapped it out. Toledo Street: 1413 Toledo. It was a side street off Bisher, an old street, running down. The houses were row houses, simple but substantial. *Gideon* Scheinfeld. The association came suddenly. It was a name from years ago, generations ago in the neighborhood. Gideon Scheinfeld had been a legend then. How many working-class neighborhoods had a recognized mathematical genius? People had once talked about a Nobel Prize. Wreford's father had been one of the many boys who had been to Scheinfeld's garage to see him use his computer. He had been interviewed by top science magazines and during World War II he had been consulted by the army, yet he and his family had stayed in the old house on Toledo Street. He must have died years ago, and the widow, Violet — he had her name and the address already on the screen. Idly, half aware, Wreford hit the retrieval collate keys. Maybe after all this time she *was* poor. Maybe the house was all she . . . The screen began to grow and multiply with names, dates, and places.

Wreford looked on in amazement. Three years ago, in June, Violet Scheinfeld's home had been broken into. She had been menaced by the gunmen but not hurt. They had taken: ITEM: ITEM: ITEM: The usual. They had not been caught. The next July she had been witness to an assault on Vandalia Street at 2:00

A.M. and had given helpful descriptions of two young men. In September she had witnessed two incidents. Last year — he counted six. He looked at the places the crimes had taken place: deserted malls, deserted streets, places where the lighting was poor, three in Vandalia Park, four outside Bittner's — a saloon where there were so many fights the police had it on a special computer code. Most of the incidents had occurred in the early morning on streets old ladies should not be using. The computer's retrieval clicked away. There had been three incidents so far this year. Wreford's two and another one he had not known about on Vandalia near Lester, a gang rumble under the railroad trestle at 11:30 P.M. Three incidents and it was only February.

It suddenly occurred to Wreford that these were only the incidents occurring in his precinct. She had said at the first time he had seen her that she was going through the mall to get aspirin for a headache. An insomniac. Someone who had to walk off sleepless nights. He thought of those boots, the sporty, fur-topped boots she wore. It was crazy. He typed in the code for city-wide and pushed the print-out button. The machine began to give him the fruits of its memory like a long, long tongue: INCIDENT, INCIDENT, INCIDENT.

He took the printout and went to the precinct map and he saw then why no one had picked up on Violet Scheinfeld before. The incidents had taken place in four precincts and their distribution — it was as though she was visiting, planning random visits in high crime areas. The insomnia theory did not hold up. Some of the crimes had been miles away.

★   ★   ★

He took the printout to Luebbe, his superior, who looked at it and said tiredly, "Get the old broad in here. I want to tell her we're on to her."

"What do you think it is?"

"I *know* what it is. They get robbed. TV, the silver, but there's always more — a pin their husband gave them, a picture in a nice frame. Maybe it's the only picture they have of him looking the way they remember him and the crooks took it for the frame and the picture is gone. The victims don't see any justice. For people like her who've lived all their lives believing certain things about the law, reality is a terrible blow. A man I know walked the city for weeks looking for the thieves who had stolen a three-dollar candy dish his dead kid gave him for Christmas.

"I'll admit I've never seen it this bad, and never in a person as old as this old lady is, but my own cousin did it. It almost cost him his job and his marriage, agonizing, looking for the guys who mugged his daughter. This one —"

"She has nothing else to do, is that what you're saying?"

"Well, she isn't cruising Bittner's at two A.M. for her health. I want her down here. She's got to stop."

Wreford brought Violet Scheinfeld to the station in his car. He had invited her, without warrant, but she was far from being intimidated. Wreford knew Luebbe was depending on the atmosphere of the station house and the detectives' room to frighten her. Luebbe gave her the full treatment, taking her in the back way and past the desks of uniformed officers, past the holding areas and the interrogation rooms. She seemed completely undaunted, trailing her shawls and scarves and bundled in the coat which had been machine mended, probably at the dry cleaners — and not too well. Her little fur-topped boots followed Luebbe's heavy earthshoes with a certain panache. When they got to the detectives' room, it was obvious to her that she had been taken the long way up. "Sit down," Luebbe ordered.

The interview did not go as Luebbe had planned. Violet began by commenting on the offices. "Those computers you have downstairs — they probably ask Gideon's questions. You know it was the questions, the way you have to ask the questions that opened up the computers. That was years ago. Gideon used to tell me that what people need most in the world is the right questions."

Luebbe tried all his methods. He tried to enlist her as an ally. He tried a heavy-handed sympathy, he tried bullying. She parried them all. She was a citizen, she said, and free to treat her own insomnia. "When you're old your bones ache. When you lie in bed you count your bones. It's better to get up, to walk. It's dark and quiet in the streets at night. In the daytime, there are too many cars. Everyone wants you to move fast, to get out of the way. Do you know how little time they give you to cross a street before the lights change nowadays?"

"It's too dangerous downtown at night," Luebbe insisted. "It's too dangerous for you to be out at all!"

"And whose fault is that?" she said. "Is it my fault that my own city can't protect me? Yell at the criminals; don't yell at me."

"Stay away from Bittner's," Luebbe was shouting now. "If you don't, I'll run you in."

She looked at Luebbe and then at Wreford, who

was sitting off to the side, his eyes fixed on a report he was supposed to be reading. "Did you know," she said, "that a computer can never foretell how or when a bad thing will happen, even at Bittner's? A computer can plot the course of a spaceship and how many boxes of Kleenex an army needs in a year, but —"

"Stay away from there," Luebbe growled.

"Bittner's lies on my way," Violet said, "but I'll take a detour. No more Bittner's. Do you know it's more dangerous for me in this building than out there? The stairs in the place are terrible and the banister — a person can't get a hand on it; the rail's too wide. Try it and see."

So she finished with the last word. Wreford drove her home. She asked him in for a cup of tea. He would have liked to talk about Gideon Scheinfeld but he didn't have time — there was too much work. He wondered if anyone could keep a valuable piece of scientific equipment in a rickety garage anymore. He watched her walk up her steps and into the house. The steps were steep. She had to negotiate them one at a time, like a child.

In March, the precinct had a rapist working near the hospital and the candy factory. Wreford was busy with that investigation and with a drug ring working the school. Now and then he remembered what Violet had said about asking the right questions. Although most of what he had to do was routine, now and then he was able, in his interviews of witnesses and suspects, to work on that idea. At the end of his interviews, he began to say, "What questions should I be asking?" He got strange looks for this from his partners and sometimes a curse or an incredulous look from suspects, but occasionally the question yielded surprising and fruitful responses, and once, a confession.

And Violet Scheinfeld was busy, too, apparently. He saw the boots twice in the background during the ten o'clock Instacam news. Once they stood behind the head of a bank robber, once at the side of the victim in a knife fight. Twice her name came across his desk at the precinct on a list of witnesses. Others had picked up on Violet also. She began to be something of a joke at the station house. "Is she an old groupie?" Bridger asked. "An accident junkie?" There were people who liked accident scenes, who got some kind of thrill from the blood and drama, others who were stirred almost libidinously by the uniforms and power the police wield.

"The woman is eighty years old!" Wreford protested.

"Hope springs eternal," Bridger said.

The possibility made Wreford sad, although he still believed that Luebbe was right, that Violet was stalking some now half-remembered punk, guiltily, self-consciously, but compulsively, in the pain of a loss that must seem silly to others.

He heard in the jokes the same patronizing words he had used about Violet. Now they made him cringe: "Street-Scene Grandma," Halloran said, "the weak-eyed witness."

"What did she witness?" Bridger asked, rising to Halloran's bait.

"She forgot," Halloran said. They laughed. "Midnight Violet" was the name that stuck.

"Midnight Violet has bloomed again," Bridger said when Wreford came to work one evening. "A car chase and shoot-out practically in her lap. Tenth and Institute. Fifteen bullets fired. No injuries. Amazing how panic spoils the aim."

Tenth and Institute. That was Fourth Precinct. It was on the other side of town. Had Violet worn out the local possibilities? She couldn't have walked that far. The buses ran so sporadically at that time she must be taking a cab to her scenes. He talked to Luebbe.

Luebbe shrugged. "The old dame's got us. She's a citizen. If she wants to walk the worst street at the worst time, it's her right. She knew I was bluffing about Bittner's. The street there is a public way. It's her right as an American to get pumped full of lead."

"If she's looking for the criminals who broke into her house, we might get her on interference."

"Impossible," Luebbe said. "No proof."

"If I could get the proof?"

"Go to it," Luebbe said, "if crime is so slow around here that you're bored with your regular work."

Wreford was busy all shift, but later he sat down at his terminal and tapped out an inquiry about Violet's address. Did they still own the house? Yes — Gideon Scheinfeld and Violet Perski Scheinfeld. On a hunch he accessed master files to retrieve Perski, any notation. The machine hummed with feeding.

In a moment the screen began to show what they had. Luckily, Violet and Gideon had been local kids, born and bred in the precinct. Otherwise, he couldn't have . . . A Perski, Ephraim, had been killed at the age of twenty by a stray bullet in a gunfight between rival bootleggers, April 6, 1919. The fight was on Van Allan. He was on Bisher, almost a block away. His address was 114 Bisher. Brother? Cousin?

He tapped the file number into the machine. Any arrests? Any convictions? As he read the printout, he realized that the case had never really been investigated. Accidental homicide. It was a corrupt town in those days. The railroad people were deep into the distribution of bootleg whiskey. They worked out their problems while the police looked the other way.

A family trauma years ago, no care taken, no investigation made. It must have been an embarrassment to the force, one which the investigating officers would have handled gruffly because some of them must have had the decency to be ashamed.

Justice delayed is justice denied. Years later, after widowhood had made Violet feel vulnerable and fragile and old age had compounded those feelings, the break-in came, the menacing, the robbery of treasured things. Again there must have been the feeling of nothing done, no suspects, no closure. Added to this must be the fear that the robbers were free to return anytime, that the streets were no more dangerous than her home. If there was to be no justice, there might as well be vengeance.

It suddenly dawned on Wreford that he was assuming Violet had no gun. All those clothes . . . For all he knew she might be carrying an arsenal. For all anyone knew some of the unidentified bullets imputed to escaped gang members might have come from a gun she carried. Or guns. She was a fearless woman — she had faced Luebbe down, and Luebbe had been formidable. With her eyesight, if what he was thinking was true, *she* was the danger, not the criminals.

★   ★   ★

Before Wreford went to Luebbe with his suspicion, he thought he should defend himself from his boss's laughter. He tapped another request into the computer: crimes committed in the precinct during the last ten years by people eighty or over. He was surprised at the printout: thirty-eight, and everything from stealing social security checks to homicide.

"You know you have no evidence for any of this," Luebbe said, "but go over there and talk to the old broad and get her out of your system."

"I'll see her tomorrow morning on my way home."

Luebbe winked at him and grinned. "Be gentle," he said.

Wreford brought all the printouts Retrieval had given him, all of Violet's appearances and Ephraim Perski. She opened the door and then, recognizing him, smiled. "There's coffee and sweet rolls," she said. "I thought you worked at night."

"Yes, I'm just going off."

The house was old. The rooms through which they walked to get to the kitchen were shabby and threadbare and, in the corners where the light was bad, rayed here and there with cobwebs. There was a musty smell of mice and closed rooms. The kitchen was light and clean, though, a cheerful room. Violet bustled over coffee and a frozen Danish.

They chatted for a while. She asked him if he were married. Yes. Did he have children? Yes. "We did, too — four of them. They went to the coasts. Two of them are retired and grandparents themselves. Good lives — they all have good lives."

When he told her about Mellie's job, she shook her head.

"With your wife working at the jail and you a detective, you must think the whole world is criminal."

"Circumstantial evidence," he said, and they laughed. Then he said, "Which is what I have on you." She looked at him levelly and said nothing. "I think I know what you are doing."

Wreford got the printouts from his briefcase and handed them across the table. She took them and got another pair of glasses from her pocket, murmuring, "You'd think with bifocals . . ." Then she looked the whole sheet down like a stockbroker checking the morning's business.

"How many more times were there?" Wreford asked softly.

"I don't keep track." She read the other paper, the Perski case. "How did you get this?"

"Retrieval," he said, "police work." She looked at him, her eyes swimming in the heavy lenses. It made her look so frail and helpless that he was suddenly ashamed. "I've got you," he said, "and you know it, don't you?"

She shrugged, but with none of the anger or bravado he was used to seeing.

"I've got a woman looking for justice, or what she thinks is justice. Maybe a little vengeance, too."

"Vengeance?" Her eyes went wider behind the immense correction of the glass. "Maybe you're right. I never saw it that way."

"Listen," and Wreford took a deep breath, "what happened back then was unforgivable. Those were corrupt times — you know that. The police were up

to their necks in graft with the bootleggers. Your
. . . was it your brother?"

She nodded slowly. "They never investigated it,"
she said.

"I know," Wreford said. "As a law officer I have
to apologize for what they — for what happened
. . . that there wasn't justice for him. The other
time — when your home was broken into and you
were menaced —"

"I was frightened," she said softly, "I was so
frightened, all I could do was stand there like a fool
and look at their guns."

"I guess I have to say we're sorry for that, too,
because a person wants to feel safe in his home and
we can't really promise that either . . ."

"I know."

"If you know that, why are you going out in the
street to find the ones who did it?"

Her eyes blinked once, her mouth dropped in
amazement. She sat staring at him across the table.
Then she laughed. "Is that what you think I do?"

"Isn't it?"

She took a deep breath. "Years ago, when Gideon
and I were courting and I still lived on Bisher Street,
the police came one day and told us about Ephraim's
death. When we saw the body, we were amazed at
how easily he had gone from us, how he had slid
away forever in an eyeblink, not even a minute. It
worried me later, with my own boys, that in such a
moment . . ." And her fingers made a gesture as if
squeezing the time between them.

"I explained," he said, "why the police . . ."

"It was partly Gideon's fault," she said, looking
softly at Wreford, "Gideon and his computers. He

used to be so excited about what mankind could do with them. He used to say that with the memory function and the counting function no longer a burden, we would all be free to create, to think. He didn't know, until the end, what the computers had also done."

"What does this have to do with your scouting the streets?"

"Gideon was in the hospital and dying of all the accumulated things people have to die of nowadays, because pneumonia isn't enough anymore. He kept dying and they kept bringing him back, all by computers monitoring, listening to his heart and the electricity of his body charging it. Three times they brought him back, and each time there were new sufferings and new losses and the computers, his computers, watched him with their cold fingers that count suffering but don't feel it. They had taken over all the counting, all the memory. When they left us so free for our thinking, our creating, there was nothing there to think or create from any of the minds around us, or from Gideon's mind or from mine."

"Did you go to the streets because you felt that the streets were safer than the house? At least in the streets a person can cry out, can run." He thought of those little boots and then of her age, her frailty. "What about the break-in?" he asked.

"I told you how scared I was," she said, "too scared to do a thing. After the holdup kids left, I cursed myself for days. I had let them go. They could have helped me die as easily as Ephraim had, shot dead — because two of them had guns, and all of them were frightened. What did I do — I let the chance go by. *Fear* made me miss my chance, and now maybe I'll have to die like Gideon did and not like Ephraim."

They sat for a while. Then she got up and poured more coffee. "It's a terrible thing you're telling me," he said, "that you're haunting the streets to make some young man your murderer."

"Those young men are not very nice. Some of them have murdered already. I figure they owe the rest of us some service. A few years from now, when the computers get even better, those boy-men may be our only way out and then they'll be hired by people and maybe do pro bono work like lawyers. However awful they are, they are better than the machines. They wouldn't listen to Gideon or me, those machines. We were powerless. Sometimes I lie in bed and remember how powerless we were month after month."

"Why not suicide, if you really want to — if the pain is so great or the disability so awful —"

"It's a sin. Besides I can't even get sleeping pills from my doctor. I don't know how to shoot a gun. I'd spoil it; I know I would."

"Is that why you attacked the robbers in the bus wreck?"

"Oh, them. No, they were terrible young men."

"Why do you stay around afterward?"

"Well —" and she looked at him almost coyly over the cup she was lifting to drink from, "I'm a taxpayer still, a voter. I have to be a good citizen."

They talked about other things. She showed Wreford Gideon's picture and the awards for things he had done. "He worked for the army during the war, did you know that? It was very secret." There was

pride in her voice. "This house was convenient and
very safe during the war. We just stayed on. You
know, when he was dying, every time the machines
got him back — I would curse them. Then he would
laugh at me because I was treating his machines as
though they had will. I knew it wasn't so, but I
cursed them anyway. I thought of them the way a
person thinks of a well-meaning idiot child, gratefully saving a father without knowing why. Their
memories are long, much longer than an idiot's, but
there was that same awful gratitude . . ."

"Citizen, taxpayer, voter," he said. "I can't stop
you, can I?"

"Don't be sad. I bundle up carefully. Nobody will
get *me* with natural causes. Besides, everyone walks
for his health these days."

"And if I should see you at another crime
scene . . ."

"Bring a Thermos. We'll have coffee," and she
held out the plate with the sweet rolls.

HELL IS A CITY MUCH LIKE SEVILLE

THERE was no reason why the damn car shouldn't be an accomplice. John had bought it secondhand but he had had it repainted and his whole first year with it, the best year of his life, he had driven it as he imagined its driving through the gates of mansions and up to Hollywood studios and into New York to parties. There fame was, cool rooms, long vistas, soft voices making plans that included him.

The car had been a lemon. In addition to what he soon learned were the Jag's endemic problems, lights and wipers that failed in the rain, short circuits that couldn't be traced, rusting, other problems arose in the car and his life with it. That first year it threw a rod, the second, two teenagers stole and rode it around and then abandoned it, and after that it was in the shop more than it was out. It was as delicate

as an ancient invalid. As each new cause of breakdown unfolded itself in the long misery, John would
watch passersby kick its tires with envy. The car
seemed to him to be a metaphor for the rusting out
and wearing down of his own possibilities. He had
been trained to think in such metaphors. He was a
writer. He had had the car for ten years. He had
bought it in 1979 when *Hell Is a City Much Like Se-
ville* had been accepted and then had been optioned
for a film. There was talk of a big paperback sale.

There had been a paperback sale but no film. His
second book, *Banner in the Dust,* was a better book,
he thought, but hadn't done as well. It was a post-
Vietnam novel about men he had met in the vets
hospital. It had an exciting plot, interesting and
memorable characters. It had seemed to him to be an
improvement on some of the sloppy writing of *Hell
Is a City.* He couldn't understand the lackluster reaction of the publisher's people, who had greeted his
new book with so much less enthusiasm. Many of
the staff had changed. He told his agent to try another house with *Upward in Wonder.* The book paid
for his divorce from Faye and got him out of the
apartment that had caused so many of their wrangles.
He had realized his selfishness and was ready to grow
up. The Jag, she had said, the damn car, had been
symbolic of that selfishness. He knew he should have
gotten them out of the apartment before buying the
car that had symbolized so much to him. The lesson
had been learned too late. *Upward in Wonder* made
someone's critic's choice list. His agent said later that
it hadn't lived up to its potential. He didn't know
what that meant or how it could be changed.

Ramparts, Lot's Wife and Mine, and a story collection, *Defender of the Peace,* closed out of town, as it were, unmarketed, unadvertised, unreviewed, and unread.

He was making the money he had made when he was writing *Hell Is a City* fifteen years ago and working for a nonunion glass company. The paint job on the Jag had oxidized to an unattractive brick color and its sounds, to which he now listened more like a doctor than a lover, were coarse and stertorous. When he began to think about suicide, and when he began to think about how, it occurred to him that he could do it with the Jag.

He was thirty-four and he had all but stopped writing. His marriage was over; his ex-wife was now married to a man in Richmond. His parents had split up and were living in the Sunbelt in houses to which he had no link of emotion or memory. His sister lived in Europe, his friends had fallen away in the falling away of his hopes one by one. He knew it was his own fault, that self-absorption in failure is an illness whose odors are ranker than gangrene. He felt defeated, destroyed. Settle for the glass company? Hope for what?

The suicide wish, which had at first been at the periphery of his thoughts, caught his scent, sniffed, and moved closer. He looked at it, measured it, studied it. He lay in its breath and ate in its gaze. It became a possibility, then a series of plans, then a single plan. On a Monday in late October, he made his purchases and the next day he drove up into the mountains, the Jag hacking and spitting as its carburetor adjustment rebelled against the differences in altitude. He had his glazier's circle scriber, a tube of caulk, and a length of hose he had picked up at a junkyard. He had a blanket and little pillow to stuff into the space between the bucket seats so he could lie down. He had a small quilt that would cover him, though he would keep the heater on also. He had a brick and a roll of masking tape. He had a Thermos of coffee and some things for the wait. He had a flashlight and a Swiss army knife.

The aspen had all turned and gone black in the sudden frost. No gold trees trembled and burned in the blue air of the higher mountains. There would be no tourists wandering the backroads, and by the time he found his spot and fixed things it would be evening. He would wait the hours until it was dark, his car prepared, and then he would turn on the engine and die in the damn thing, a better hearse than it had been an engine of splendid arrivals.

He found the place, up an old mining trail off one of the many derelict roads made when the mountainside was full of eager prospectors. The road had been unused for years. Pine needle duff and brown leaves lay deep in its hollows. There was a profound and welcome silence.

John found himself content for the first time in over a year. He measured the hose diameter, adjusted his circle scriber on the flattest part of the back window, masked around it, and knocked out the glass circle cleanly. The day was cooling. After he had set the hose and caulked it to keep it from working free, he put the other end over the exhaust. He had measured everything carefully. It was satisfying work.

Then he sat quietly and waited for the long-shadow afternoon. It came and then there was afterglow and foredarkness and in that a sudden clap of release of sound, like the applause of a well-bred but deeply moved audience, and a cloud of bats flowed from the adit of the mine. The sight thrilled him; he wanted to applaud them in praise of their speed and sureness; it was an unearned, unmerited gift. He poured and drank the last of the coffee, which he had brewed carefully. It was delicious. He got into the car and turned on the motor.

The engine coughed raggedly and began its sputtering run. He settled himself with the blanket between the bucket seats. It was almost dark now. He thought if he ran the car too quickly the fumes might make him sick and then he might vomit and die of drowning, a thought he hated, or half-conscious, he might open the door and ruin the plan. He set the brick on the gas pedal at an angle just enough to keep the idle slow.

Breathe. He breathed. Wait. He waited. The fumes made his eyes water slightly, so he closed them. When he opened them again, he saw people bent down and staring in at him through the windows. There was a light. He was relieved when he remembered he had locked the doors, although it bothered him that the people were all around the car and would be watching him die. There was a murmur of voices and then to his horror the car was being picked up. He was powerless. They were taking him somewhere, even as the motor continued to run. As the car was being taken along, two of the people kept trying to open the doors on either side. John thought, "Why don't they break the window if they want to get at me?" But he didn't want the window broken. No one removed the hose, either. What kind of people were these? Once he shouted at them, "This is my business, not yours," but the car was making noise and all of them were talking, too, some murmuring, some quite loudly.

They were inside a structure now, a barn or garage, and his head cleared. Someone was picking at the lock of the car and then it gave and hands, many hands, pulled him out. He kicked at them and scratched, struggling as they carried him like a bundle to the middle of the place. "This is my choice — you have no right to interfere." There was a voice at his ear. "Settle down, boy. We'll do what we came here to do and then you can go and do what you want." The voice was rough, a whiskey voice, his father would have said. He closed his eyes and went limp. There must have been fifteen or twenty of them. Struggle was useless and he didn't know what they wanted.

They set him upright clumsily, the way a heavy, inert item is set on a floor, with finality. "I was committing suicide," he said foolishly. "You broke in . . ."

"That's all right," the whiskey voiced man said. "I told you you could take up where you left off after we're through."

He was standing in a darkened, barnlike space. The car had been carried in, too. "It's so dark . . ."

"Turn on the lights, there, Louise," the man said.

The room sprang into hard light. It was an old firehouse or garage of some kind. Wide doors had let the car come through. The place looked familiar but John couldn't have been in this one. Perhaps it reminded him of a place he had been as a kid. He had lived in lots of places. His father had been on the move during much of his childhood: Nebraska,

Wyoming, Colorado . . . He let his eyes get used to the garish light. The room was large but there was a good-sized crowd of people — maybe seventy — and they were dressed in a bewildering array of styles and qualities of clothing. They were different kinds of people, too: fashionable matrons, waitresses in uniform, a nurse, cap and all, laborers, a few who looked like skid-row denizens, and even some children. The group around him — the older man who had spoken to him and four or five others — were watching him. The others milled and mixed talking to one another and that was strange, also, because the matrons were talking to the skid-row people and the nurse to the waitress and there were five men in camo who were talking to a boy who was about twelve. A young man in designer jogging clothes was laughing with one of the laborers.

The whiskey-voiced man was grizzled, but he had a lithe, spare body. He whistled through his teeth for silence. He was dressed in denims that were worn through in places. "Listen up, folks — we'll get 'er done and then we can all go back to our business and let Johnny here get on with his. Let's get in order."

The kid said, "I want to stay with them," and he gestured at the soldiers. John had registered the fact that they knew his name. Somebody must have looked at his registration and insurance in the glove compartment.

There was a clamor of voices. The old man whistled again, an earsplitting sound even in the large space. "We've got business here. I say we do our business first and go to socializing later."

One of the soldiers yelled, "Who died and left you in charge?"

"You want to pursue this thing?" the old man asked. He spoke in a deeper voice so the sound would carry. "You tell Johnny why we interrupted his business."

The soldier gestured him on, "Okay, Pops; it's your show."

"Then let's get on with it."

The people regrouped themselves, muttering, and the boy, whom John had been watching, went over to stand with a well-dressed woman and a man in the expensively casual style of a professional at leisure. There was another couple with them, both in vaguely nautical dress, the kind that hobby-sailors would wear ashore. Other groups had formed — twelve in all, some large, some small, some expected — the soldiers were together and the old man joined a group like himself, hard-worked men, some younger than he.

They stood arranged before John as though for a photograph, not smiling but expectant, waiting for a flash, a click, a moment passed. "Dammit," the old man said, "he don't get it."

"Get what?" John asked.

"Who we are."

He looked again. A group of soldiers, and a nurse, the boy's group, the laborers — "You're different sorts of people — you're not really a group, not a social group, church outing, school bunch, neighborhood . . ."

There was laughter among them. "Good God, don't you recognize us?" That from the nautical man.

John peered close. There was an aggressive look to many of them — they looked too . . . he fought for the word, too mannered, too consistent within their models. The smartly dressed ones were too smartly dressed, the men in camo too perfectly sized. They looked more like a drill team than a squad of soldiers. He looked at their faces.

There was no one from college or high school or the two summer camps he had been to, the jobs, the army. Still there was a familiarity — eyes, a sudden expression. It was like identifying the family smile on a distant cousin. "What?" he asked. "What am I seeing?"

"We're in your books," the smartly dressed woman standing next to the boy said, "you're our writer."

At this point most of them laughed. "Our cre-a-tor," the miner said, putting his hands together. The laughter became general. "You're not real," John said, "and if you ever were, you're out of print now, remaindered, shredded."

"Don't get melodramatic," the woman said. She was Doris, he realized, from *Upward in Wonder,* a somewhat brittle woman, disappointed in love. She would be — had been saved by the boy; this boy. Why hadn't he recognized these people? They were born of his imagination, built, piece by piece through writing and rewriting, details accruing one by one, in incident, as he worked to visualize them more and still more clearly.

But he hadn't and they realized it and were disappointed. It seemed finally to be his fault. It was his want of some essential of care or energy or realization, his lack, that had kept them from the immortality of Hester Prynne or Raskolnikov or Lily Bart. It was why even their writer did not know them immediately.

"I'm sorry," he said, and shrugged. "I gave you the best I had."

"Well, maybe so," the old man answered.

Then, John recognized him. It was Sandy Brown, the miner in *Ramparts,* a novel of the early mining days in Colorado. The local papers hadn't even reviewed the book, but one Wyoming paper had said, "Interesting and well researched, but it's ground we've mined before."

It hadn't been; he'd looked up what there was in fiction and nonfiction about the lives of those men in the early camps. Bret Harte and Mark Twain and even O. Henry had talked about camp life but not the work. His people had lived the days; he had taken the story into the mines day by day — shafts opened, shored, flooding, the chill, the dark. He had drawn his people's lives carefully, and shown them truly. Oh, God, what was the use of arguing? The book had lasted for two years. He had had letters from geologists and two from retired miners and three from miners' wives who had appreciated it. It had been reviewed here and there. Some reviewers had had mining experience and quibbled with small points in the work, presiding over its early death with the limp handshake of faint praise. He had loved that book and had bid those people — Sandy and Joe Springer and Pete Blaskovitch — a regretful farewell when the thing was finished. What was the use of arguing the merits of the books — they were all here, all their principal characters, even people in some of the stories, and they were going to accuse him, to get their piece said before they allowed him to die.

★   ★   ★

"I have a few things to say in my defense," he began. Lafe Andrews, Captain Andrews of *Banner in the Dust,* began to laugh. "A few million well-chosen words. How many words are here, I wonder, all the writing and rewriting. If you haven't been able to say it by now . . ."

"Then what is it you want from me? Apology, something abject? I won't do it, even for you."

"We know what's going to happen," the nautical woman said. It was Syl Van Norman from *Lot's Wife and Mine.* "How hard it's going to be. It's happened to us, you see. It's not fair, and injustice is hard to face because you really were pretty good."

"I don't understand."

"You've been fair to us — even to me." The kid was Bobby Bordereau in *Upward in Wonder.*

"Hi, Bobby," John said.

"Hi. Like I said, you've been fair to me and very few writers are fair to kids. They make them too cute or too smart or too innocent."

"Right!" It was Pete Blaskovitch who did a thumb up.

"Hi, Pete."

"Yo."

They were coming to say goodbye. John was moved. The people to whom he had given reality in whatever form and for however long were acknowledging him for the last time. They had been finished in the form they had, in the clothes they were wearing, all of them now out of print. He was not to blame for that. They were telling him they understood. "I think this is a fine tribute," he said.

The laughter started with a woman but which one he couldn't tell; it was someone in a middle group,

and the groups had moved together again slightly.
Here and there was light talk. The laughter was
spreading and as it did, it got louder and John felt his
face go hot with shame. They laughed according to
the people they were; the miners gripped their sides
and gave way. Claudette Sandifer from *Lot's Wife*
dabbed her eyes; Murph Johnsen sniggered; Sam
Barlow guffawed. Captain Andrews held up his hand
and then shouted and brought the squad to attention
and the laughter shredded away. Sandy Brown said,
"Sorry; we weren't out to rag you — not above a
little, but when you come out with that we seen what
you was thinkin' —" There was a brief reawakening
of the laughter.

"Why are you here, then, if not to say goodbye?"

Claudette Sandifer came out of the group and moved
close to him. He remembered her beginning, a stock
villainess, his fictionalized wife's mother, but as he
had come to write her, she had grown into the role
she played, a woman of capacity who loved her
daughter and didn't want to see her waste her life.
Claudette's values were wrong, but she did truly love
and want to protect the daughter who had been weak
and dependent all her life. She had ended well drawn,
clear, and believable. "We haven't been fair," she
said, "because you are at such a disadvantage. When
one is terminally ill, in intractable pain, beset by a
mob, facing torture, suicide may have great dignity.
In a healthy man acting out of pique — you will have
to admit, it's ludicrous."

"You're fictions — how can you understand the
complex emotions — the conflicting — you're *characters*."

"Whose fault is that?" Sandy snapped.

"Wait a minute, man," Joe Springer said. "Don't let him lose it in the argument. We're characters and that's the point, and if he does this, he'll be a character, too. Tell him that."

"Yes, tell him that." A voice from the back. It was Ned Valentine in his tight silk shirt and tight black pants, smooth and self-aware, sleek as a ferret. "He trivialized me and I've lived longer than any of you. I was his joy, his acceptance, his good times, but I was more of a caricature than the rest of you. He learned on me. He got better but I was written stunted."

"Then you lack the skill to tell him."

"Tell me what?" John said.

"Tell you," Sandy said, "that if . . . when you kill yourself, you'll be a character, too, and your friends and your agent and your ex-wife will trivialize you. She'll say, 'He ran after fame. His values were . . .' "

"Tawdry," Doris said. "I think she'd use that word."

"Your agent will blame America," Captain Andrews said, "the legacy of the American Dream," and they all laughed.

"Carol Bester will blame it on a faulty muffler." She had been his last girlfriend, a sad, rather simple girl. He hadn't thought of her since they gave up on each other.

"I always knew he was needy, psychically, spiritually." "That'll be Bud Kingsley," Alex Rudenko said. He was the nautical man from *Upward in Wonder*. He captured the slightly prissy tone of Bud's disappointment.

"You're telling me my wife and my friends are stupid and given to banal judgments," John said.

"We're telling you that suicides are punished by being trivialized, categorized, their motives and lives cheapened, explained away, pictured in terms as simple as a kindergarten painting."

"Why should you care about any of that? I'm wondering why *I* should care." But somehow he did.

"We owe you because you tried not to do that when you wrote us. It makes us sensitive to the process. We thought we'd better warn you. They're going to figure the act, define it, and you in it — tawdry dreams, victim of false values, the whole thing, even in the praise they'll give, the trivializing will ring in your ears."

"I won't hear them."

"We do. You will. It will be a part of you unable to do any more than listen and cry aloud at the injustice of it."

He looked at all of them. They were familiar now and he realized he was seeing them not as he had first conceived them. They had, all but a few, developed in some way. "What gave you the power to step out of the books and tell me this?"

"You made us real," Captain Andrews said, "and we'll be read now and then, and remembered much the way living people are, like acquaintances, people encountered somewhere, met on a train or plane, perhaps."

"The books are gone, out of print, shredded."

"That melodrama," Doris said, "is a literary fault and now I know where it comes from."

"We ain't about to stop you bumping yourself," Sandy said. "We seen the thing happening. We figured we owed you. You done a good, workmanlike job on us. Your folks, even Ned over there, know what's to come when you get made into a character. We wanted to warn you. We done that. Now it's time to go and let you get on with whatever you decide to do.''

Some of them were already starting to leave. The original book groupings separated and one by one, some with a wave or a smile, the men and women John had imagined moved away. Someone turned off the light.

John got back into the car. The motor had been turned off but the key was still in the ignition. He could start it here and be dead before whoever owned the place came and found him.

He thought of what they had said — other people's judgment — Faye's, her new husband's, his agent's, the neighbors'. The thought overwhelmed him. He had wanted to complete a private act, something like a disappearance. He hadn't thought of being found. Even if he burned his I.D., the damn car had plates, a serial number, and he would be made a character by people who weren't writers trained in giving their creations depth, freedom, and the benefit of the doubt. He couldn't do that. He got out of the car and pulled the hose from the window and off the exhaust pipe. It was freezing in the place. He got back into the car and bundled the quilt around him and looked through the open door of the barn. It must give on to a road of some sort. He would drive until he found a state road. He started the car. It sighed and chuffed and went through the open door and off an embankment. Inside the rolling car, the turning car, John was a captive. He hadn't bothered with a seat belt. The fact of his becoming airborne was sudden. He had time only for wonder and horror as he was slammed this way and that, pounded against edges, knobs, and hit by the brick, free, in the closed space. Slam. Again. Slam. Again.

And suddenly it was over and he lay in the dark, whimpering with fear and pain, unable to locate himself in position. After what seemed like a long time, he realized the car was on its side. Magically, the windows were still intact, the front glass was crazed but still in place. He felt around in the back. The hose was still jammed into its hole. The appearance of the characters must have been a gas-induced hallucination. As his death began, he must have nudged the shift into neutral with his knee so the car had rolled backwards and gone down off the hill. He might still end his life if he could get the motor to run. If not that, he could take a shard of the rearview mirror and get his carotid arteries. The pain wouldn't be any worse than what he was having now in his elbows, knees, thigh, head, and face.

But he quailed at cutting himself. He reached up ahead to the roof. The head-liner had been torn. He felt. There was nothing there. His arm went through into the night. The car was open on that side. He moved painfully over shattered glass and twisted metal. Rust must have eaten under the cracks in the paint and the roof had broken away in the fall. He thought suddenly: "God, I could have been killed," and then he laughed, and thought, "cheapened, trivialized, misunderstood." He crawled out of the car. It was lying on its side like a dead bug. If the car hadn't been rusted out, he might have died of monoxide poisoning even as it was rolling over and in fall.

★   ★   ★

"Good Lord, man, where have you been?" said the trucker who picked him up an hour later.

"An auto wreck and a literary discussion." ·

"Which was rougher?" the trucker said, smiling.

"The discussion was rougher; the wreck saved my life."

John watched the trucker. He was a medium-sized man who had the ironic style of a loner. What, he wondered, was such a life like? What kind of woman would such a man need? Would he love certain small routines within the long, drawn hours of his constant, infinite mobility? Would he . . . Was he . . .

TORCH SONG

THE day was echoing cold, and so still that the flags at the lodge all lay limp, gathering frost in their folds. The cold only made for better skiing. Six inches of powder had fallen during the night, a powder so dry we skied on edges that were almost silent in the stillness of the day. We skied better than we ever had before, and by lunchtime we were so tired and exhilarated that we broke precedent and got a bottle of wine, which the five of us shared. A year before, when Mimsy, the last one of us to turn fifty, announced she wanted to go back to her given name — Louisa — Cookie, Zizi, and Putt followed and went back to being Clara, Jean, and Martha. I'm Ruth. We had been skiing together for six years, comfortably, improving our style and speed. Suddenly we had become aware of how good we felt, so we toasted ourselves, the snow, and the day.

We had all been on hand in 1984, cheering the Olympic torch as it came through on its way to the

Summer Games in Los Angeles. The whole town of Aureole had turned out to stand at the side of the highway; some ran, following the torchbearer through the canyon until they were winded and had to drop back. Aureole loves sports, especially winter sports, and especially skiing — there are two ski areas nearby, and most of the town's economy depends on skiers. We follow that sport the way some towns follow football.

"Wonderful snow," I said.

"I wonder what our times were," Louisa said.

"Let's find out."

We decided to go on the timed run after lunch, and before the light was gone.

So we waited behind the hot-doggers and the kids. Martha surprised everyone by making the hill's best time of the day; I was almost as good. In our elation we started kidding about Olympic skiing and how we looked like downhill racers.

"I would love to have skied in the Olympics," Jean said.

Martha nodded. "My secret dream."

"Mine, too," I said.

"Compete in the Olympics? What else?" That was Clara.

Jean protested. "I didn't say *compete,* I said *ski.* Right now I'd like to go over to some little country that doesn't have a ski team and apply. We wouldn't have to be winners or even try to win. Look at what happened at Sarajevo last time. The Albanians were skiing when everyone had gone home."

"So —"

"So they were there, part of it all."

I punctured the fantasy. "Read the rules. A competitor has to be citizen of the country he competes for. We're Americans. With the team America puts in, none of us would qualify to sew on their buttons."

"I would like to walk in the parade," Louisa said, "and ski for the Galapagos Islands, skiing well, but not dangerously, after the winners and the press had gone home so we didn't embarrass our families. I would like to carry a flag. I would like a lovely and becoming pastel outfit — a soft blue, perhaps — nothing black. I look washed-out in black."

I said, "Unless we all renounce our citizenship for another country's, sea to shining sea —"

"What about Ireland? Dozens of famous people live there because of the taxes —"

"I said citizenship, not residence. *Read the rules.* It is in no nation's interest to sponsor five rump-heavy old broads in the Olympic downhill race and open itself to international ridicule."

"Ruth, there is a streak of cruelty in you," Clara said.

We drove home fantasizing about being in the Olympics and marching in the parade and following that wonderful torch to its place.

That was after Thanksgiving. We skied a lot before Christmas vacation put all the schoolkids on the slopes. We work, so we're free to ski only once a week. Louisa is a legal secretary for Burlow, Jones and Tyne here in town. Her husband died three years ago. Jean has a successful catering business. Her assistant takes over on Tuesday when she skis. Martha is the busiest of all of us because she volunteers so much. I'm Ruth Telfer; you know, Telfer's Dry

Goods in Aureole. We're at the new shopping mall. It's hard sometimes, but I try to take every Tuesday off.

The season got even better — cold weather and lots of fresh powder. We were all skiing well. Soon after New Year's, on our regular outing, Jean met us at the church parking lot where we car pool. She said she had a letter for us.

"Us? Who's it from?"

"It's from the Holy Father."

"Who?"

"Holy Father. The Pope. In Rome."

I laughed. "I hope he's well."

"Does he want you to cater the next conclave?"

"I'm serious," Jean said, "and so is this. Get the skis loaded and I'll read it on the way."

We got out on the highway, and Jean began: "The letter is dictated," she said, "but it *is* from him. When we were talking about being in the Olympics, I thought I would write and ask him to sponsor us. The Vatican is a state; it has ambassadors and boundaries — it's even got its own stamps. Holy Father loves to ski. All I did was invite him out to Aureole if he was in America during ski season. I described the powder here and told him that since the kids had grown and gone, there was plenty of room at our house. Then I asked if he couldn't give us temporary Vatican citizenship so that we could ski for the Vatican State in the next Olympics."

"What?"

"Ski. In the Olympics. For the Vatican."

"What did he say?"

"I got his answer yesterday. Here's what he says. Uh . . . well, he thanks us for the invitation. He's

heard about our powder skiing . . . would like to
come, but his pressing duties, et cetera, et cetera."

"Write back and tell him —"

"Shhhh!"

"Okay, here," Jean said, reading from the letter.
" 'It has pleased us to consider your request for temporary citizenship with much interest. We have discussed the issue carefully, as important political and
humanitarian principles arise from it, regarding the
law of sanctuary and other forms of political asylum
within our state. This precedent we hereby establish.
It has pleased us therefore to extend to you, as a
team, temporary Vatican citizenship to begin when
you leave the United States for the Olympic Games
and to end one day after your competition. All your
arrangements should, in the future, be made with
Brother Sylvestro Mudarra, Monastery of San Igna-
cio, Irun, Spain. He is to serve as your Olympic
Committee. With hope of success to you and prayers
for your continued spiritual and bodily health, your
friend . . .' "

"There's something more in the envelope . . ."

"Five cards: two team, two alternates, one trainer.
They're all signed by him. We're — we will be — it
says, under the care of the Papal state as citizens."

"So we're going to . . . do it?"

"Training?"

"The *Olympics?*"

"I guess so."

We began to stamp and cheer in the back of the
car. I cheered, too, although I didn't really believe it.
Finally I said, "We have only two years to get
ready — ready to compete *in the Olympics!*"

"Not compete," Jean said. "Ski."

"Oh, yes. I forgot."

We cheered again.

But we couldn't help taking ourselves more seriously, skiing harder. I don't know how word got around, but Aureole is so small that people find things out as if by magic. Of course I told Arthur, my husband, but he laughed so hard I don't think he would have leaked the story. Clara, who is a psychologist, has learned to be closemouthed. Martha is shy. In any case, before we knew how it happened, the *Ute River Voice* called Jean and said they wanted to interview us about our Olympic plans. We had been practicing hard every week. Our times were being pared, although we had not made best run again. (Louisa's daughter Dee Dee, who lives in Seattle, had had a baby; Louisa had to go there, so she missed two weeks.) The interviewer from the *Voice* was Marcie French. I hadn't seen her any more than to say hello since she came back from college.

The interview was simple: we each gave a kind of statement. Martha told about how we got the idea. Clara talked about how inspired we had been by the torch coming past Aureole. Jean told about writing to Pope John Paul. She showed his letter. Everybody knows how religious Jean is; it was natural that her mind would have gone to that solution. I said that we represented an older Olympic ideal; the games had been started for amateurs with little backing or sponsorship, for the love of sport.

Marcie is a nice girl, but the *Voice* is only a small-town newspaper, and she hasn't learned to hide her emotions. She said, "I never thought you were serious. You can't be serious!" We said we were. "But *look* at you. You couldn't *win!*"

"That's the part that people don't understand.

We're not going there to win. We're going there to compete," Martha said.

"Ski," Jean corrected her.

"We want to show our gratitude for the sport and the people who developed it."

Marcie looked bemused when she left. I guess young people aren't as flexible as they think they are.

When the piece appeared in the Aureole paper, it was better than I thought it would be after the way Marcie looked at us. There was a picture of the four of us (Louisa was still in Seattle), and the headline read: "Aureole Women Make Bid for Olympics." The article gave our names and said that we were going to ski for the Vatican. It included our times and said that we expected in the next two years to cut them even more.

It was a small item, but as we read it and all our names, it made us more aware than ever that we were really going to do it — to try, for the sake of the sport, to do our best.

If I was not bothered by Marcie's article in the *Voice,* I was certainly shocked by the letters column the following week:

Who do those old biddies think they are? Let them wait till they are 65 and join some senior Olympics. Meanwhile, they should stay off the steep slopes; they only get in the way. . . .

I thought Mrs. Telfer was Jewish. I know Mrs. Protheroe is Protestant, although I never see her in church except for funerals. What are they doing competing for a Catholic state? Does that mean they are turning Catholic?

Who is putting these women up to this? Vatican banking interests and Jewish international moneymen have been quiet. Remember the Banco Ambrosiano? What was that but an international plot? There is more here than just skiing. When will the country finally wake up to what's happening?

Letter number one was from the Corson boy, whom I'd seen bipping down Thunder-shoot out of control. Number two was Mrs. Plumacher, poor thing. Although the last letter was unsigned, we all knew it was Denson Sprague, who's the security guard at the bank.

That week when we met to go to the hill, Clara said to me, "How do you like representing international banking interests?"

I answered, "How do you like representing fallen Presbyterianism?"

Martha didn't join in the laughter. "I didn't know half of those feelings existed in Aureole," she said. "Maybe we ought to stop."

"You knew about Denson. Everybody knows about Denson." I laughed now, trying to reassure Martha. "This will blow over because it's the coverage they envy, the publicity, not what we're doing — not what we do at all, but what we're seen to do."

"What's the difference?"

"We'll just need to avoid publicity — keep a low profile."

But the next week when we stopped at the ski lodge to eat our bag lunches, Ernest Timbrough, the manager, came up to us and asked if they could take our pictures. They took shots of us holding, then getting onto, our skis, and then getting ready to go up the lift. He said the pictures were for the little newsletter the ski areas put out as PR. We got him to send a couple of copies to Brother Sylvestro, our Olympic Committee in Spain. The snow was wonderful that day, and so much fun that we soon forgot about the pictures.

That was March, the height of the season. We were skiing hard, but the slopes were crowded, and some days we couldn't even get close to the timed run. One evening Louisa called and asked if I could leave the store on Thursday at noon. "I got a call from a ski company. Viking. They said they wanted to meet with us."

"Why?"

"I don't know. It's for lunch at the Prospector."

Viking Ski Company: you know their commercials. They're on the radio during the ski season and on all the rock stations the young people listen to:

What's it like when you're bashin' the chute down the toughest run they've got? What's it like when you're up to your hip pockets in powder, lookin' down on the eagles and pushin' for broke on the longest, meanest pair of skywalkers made? Viking [clang], *that's what.*

The man who reads that copy sounds like he just ate a crocodile. And you've seen the picture, too. It hangs in all the ski shops. A beautiful young man, underdressed I think, is caught in midair all alone, looking down a huge mogul-heaped hill out past his Vikings. It makes you wonder who took the picture.

Clara and Louisa have Vikings. Clara got hers in swap meet. One eighties. Louisa's had hers for years. I have Hawks. One nineties because I'm on the pudgy side. Martha has Spartans, which she says are lemons. Jean has Contrails. Boots are another big thing, and we all have different ones, some new, some old. We had no idea why the Viking people would send someone all the way out here to see us.

So, the next Thursday afternoon, Louisa, Martha, and I got dressed up and went to the Prospector to meet the man from Viking and have lunch. Clara was busy; Jean was catering. We went into the Nugget Room — it's the place where they serve the same salad they have in the coffee shop, but in fancier dishes, and they charge three dollars more for it. Since we were being treated, we were hardly in a position to point this out.

There were two young men seated who, when they saw us, rose for introduction. They were in their thirties, tanned and active-looking, almost aggressively so. Both of them looked as though they spent all their time skiing. The Viking man's name was Carl Williams, and his companion was a man who said he was from Gustafson Boot. When I shook his hand I told him I had Gustafson boots. You remember *their* commercial, surely:

It's tough, it's brutal, it's a war between you and the mountain moguls and slab and the dirtiest chutes in creation. Beat the mountain. Conquer. Win. Any good ski, any good binding. A Gustafson boot.

"Nice boots," I said to him. "I especially like the way they hold my foot without pinching. The last boots I had —"

"Hmmmmm," he said.

When we were seated and had ordered our seven-dollar salads, Mr. Williams said, "You ladies aren't really . . . this is a joke, isn't it?"

We told him we were serious. We explained the whole thing. They sat absolutely still and listened.

We told them how hard we were working. "We've almost halved our times this season."

"You do timed runs?" Mr. Williams sounded impressed.

"Yes. We try to do at least one timed run every day we're out."

"And what are your times?"

We told him. He sighed; then he took a breath and let go. "That comes to about thirty-eight miles an hour. It's fast, uh . . . yes. But an Olympic-caliber skier skies in the eighties, and the differences between first place and last place are measured in tenths of a second . . . you'll wash out before you get there. In pre-trials you'll be eliminated."

Martha gave him a searching look and said, "Mr. Williams, you know that the trials are *within* the competing nation and put on by the National Olympic Committees. Our Olympic Committee is Brother Sylvestro Mudarra, with whom we correspond. He says that since there are no other entries in this event, our times are those for the Vatican."

"The *Pope* skis faster than that," Williams muttered.

"That's beside the point," I said. "You know that in this event there is no pre-elimination. Why are you trying to discourage us?"

"Because you're being silly," he said.

"Maybe it's because we're being silly on your skis." I had suddenly remembered the shot Ernest Timbrough had taken of us. He had posed us with our equipment. Anyone could see the name "Viking" and the logo — a warrior whose long hair streamed down the front of the skis. Anyone can identify a Gustafson boot. Louisa got the point then.

"You don't want us seen with your equipment," she said. She sounded hurt.

Williams couldn't lie. He was stuck. "We're prepared to offer you a fee of five hundred dollars apiece to let us take the skis and — well, blank out our names."

"Gustafson" laughed. "You girls don't even have racing equipment."

Girls. That did it. "Well, you can buy it for us," I said. "Outfit us. In the latest. Plus, we want travel money from here to the Olympic Village. Brother Sylvestro said our Committee has no money. Or —"

"Or *what?*"

"Or we'll stand there in our Viking skis and our Gustafson boots and our Arrow bindings for every sports magazine in the country."

"You can't —"

"We own those skis; we ski on them. *Ski* magazine. *Sports Illustrated.*" Louisa didn't like being called a girl, either.

The two of them sat and stared at us. Then they paid the check and stood up. "We'll be in touch," Williams said.

"We'll let you know," said "Gustafson."

They left. We looked at each other and grinned. That evening we met to tell Clara and Jean what had happened.

Two days later the Contrail Ski people called. We listened to their offer and told them we'd get back to them. I ski on Hawks. It's such a small company, I didn't know if a representative would call. Three days later one did, with such a small bribe I was almost too insulted to say we'd consider it.

The boot and binding companies came next. We figured "Gustafson" had been calling everybody. We never dreamed — Summit, Arrow, Alpine, even DuCange. Louisa says her DuCange poles are so old nobody would recognize them anymore. It didn't matter. By the time it was all over, we had ten companies, ready to pay money or give favors if only we would blot their names, logos, or outlines from our equipment.

"Holy Father would take a dim view of this," Jean said. I shrugged. "I say we write to Brother Sylvestro," Jean persisted. "We owe him that."

We wrote a long, careful letter to our Committee Chairman, who, when he was not busy with our problems, was praying for world peace in a Spanish mountain monastery. While we waited for an answer, we practiced. Life was getting more hectic. Some of the townspeople and others nearby who read the *Voice* wanted us to be guests at various meetings that needed speakers. We were also skiing harder, trying to get our times down. Frankly, what the Viking man said had shocked us. We had no idea the speeds were so fast in the downhill event. On TV they never said that the skiers were going over eighty miles an hour.

One day on the lift, I asked a young man how he got up his speed. He said by quickening his rhythm with a Walkman, so we borrowed Martha's son's and practiced with it, but we hated the tapes he gave us so much we replaced them with the Brandenburg Concertos and my Handel's Messiah. By the time the season ended, we were clocking a respectable 2.52 on the long run, which translates to about forty miles per hour.

Viking caved in. Gustafson caved in. Eureka caved in. When the snow coarsened and the days got longer, their representatives came bearing gifts:

unmarked skis — long, slim, stiff racing skis; special
gaiters to cover the telltale boots and bindings; and a
promise from Eureka that they would help us with
racing helmets — plastic, they said, but tasteful, that
would show none of the company's distinguishing
marks.

At first the racing skis were a disaster. Because of
their length, cut, and flex, there seemed to be a complete sacrifice of stability for speed. We shot downhill
on them like ball bearings down a bumpy shoot,
ringing off the smallest dips and rises and going airborne at the slightest provocation. We fell innumerable times. The next time we went out to practice,
we made a date with Clara's nephew, Buzzy, who is
an instructor.

I never liked Buzzy. He was the assistant high-
school phys. ed. coach when our kids were going to
school. He thought we were going to compete as
some kind of stunt. When we lined up, he looked at
us the way a motorist looks at a dead cat on the road.
"You ladies are seriously out of shape."

I shot back at him, "I wondered where all the
wrinkles and flab came from."

Irony is lost on Buzzy. "That's right," he said,
"you need a physical program to make you look
better."

"Sorry, Buzzy," I said, "just show us how to
work these skis."

He did, or tried to. At first, we lost speed — we
were nervous about our control. It took us weeks to
drop our time back and then cut it further, second by
second.

May came. We were on spring snow, almost closing up the area with the diehards in shorts and
T-shirts. We felt we owed it to Brother Sylvestro,

our Olympic Committee. We had been writing weekly reports to Brother by then. A typical letter went like this:

Dear Brother:
This week we clocked 2.40 on the long run and 2.36 on the short, which puts us at an average of 40.8 miles an hour. We are sorry we cannot convert this to meters, but as you can see, it is a distinct improvement in the short sprint time even though we are having trouble getting our speed up on the longer slope. We know we must soon make our choice of first-team members and alternates. This is a difficult choice. Clara's mother was ill last week so Clara had to stay home. Everyone else was in attendance. Ruth's strained leg is healing well.
Faithfully,

Brother's letters came regularly also, complete with the Vatican's stamp:

Beloved Daughters:
Be of good cheer. Your times are improving and it seems you have adapted well to the racing skis which were so generously donated. Thanks be to God your health remains good and your spirits high. Prayers will be said for the mother of Clara; may she have a perfect healing. In regard to your problems of precedence, it is well to remember that contemplation of the perfection of the saints so diminishes both pride and fear that they assume their proper proportions in life. Try to remember also that not only does Our Lord praise all offerings made in purity of heart, but to sacrifice He is most attendant.
Yours in Christ,

P.S. Leaning forward from the knee down, rather than from the waist up, drives the ski forward rather than downward. Learn this and you may suffer fewer falls and note a gratifying increase in velocity.

That Thanksgiving we were nagged by the necessity of selecting firsts and alternates. We had been practicing since October, when the area opened, on man-made snow. This was something I had never done before, but our speed — or lack of it — was worrying Brother Sylvestro, who must have finally transposed miles per hour into kilometers and been shocked at the numbers ("Could you not include an extra day of practice, dear daughters?"). Brother Sylvestro was going for the gold.

So, early in November we had begun collecting our times as individuals. There had been two good snowfalls since Thanksgiving. The snow was slow but very forgiving, and we had been, somewhat guiltily, skiing for fun. Then one day at lunch, Louisa surprised and sobered us. "I love this group," she said, "but no woman can serve two masters. I'm not fit enough, and it's showing in my work. I'm alone. If Rufe were alive, things would be different, but if I get hurt now — well, there's just me. It's given me nightmares. It's making me cautious and fearful; I'm taking myself out of the competition. I'll be the trainer."

"But you'll still ski with us, won't you?"

Louisa began to cry. "You're not fun anymore. Ever since we got those damn racing skis. Skiing for me has always been — don't laugh — meditative, like prayer. I don't want to compete in prayer."

"Mimsy —" I reverted to Louisa's old name.

"It's all right," she said, "I'm donating my un-marked skis to the team. Will we ever be just skiing again?"

We didn't answer because we didn't know. "After" had never occurred to us. Then Jean said, "We'd better start."

Louisa tried to perk us up. "Oh, yes. I also have the design for our outfits."

"Show us."

"Black and red are the Swiss Guard colors — but they would look awful on us. Instead . . ." She took a piece of poster board out of her parka.

It was a simple tunic made to wear over the fancy stretch ski clothes as we walked in the parade. It was velour in a soft French blue, with a hood, in case it was snowing. Louisa remembered the bad weather in Sarajevo. On the front of the tunic, wings outspread, was the dove of peace, in ecru, with golden rays coming out of the wing feathers. We said, "Oh —" with pleasure. I said, "I can whip these up, if you'll help me with the dove. What do you think, Louisa, appliqúe?" Louisa nodded.

Then and there, with a light snow falling, we stood on top of Barrel Roll Run and chose Clara and Jean as Olympic team, Martha and me as alternates, Louisa as trainer. There were some tears, but I was proud of us. We were still good friends.

Aureole gets the news of the world on five chan-nels. There is a radio, and we have the *Denver Post* and the *Rocky Mountain News,* and our local paper, the *Ute River Voice,* to tell us who died and what was served at the Grange potluck in Gold Flume. Some-times the word from outside, which is always bad, makes us think we should pull the mountain walls closer, block traffic on the highway at both ends, and bless the natural isolation that has preserved us so far. We don't. We only sigh as we turn on the woes of 5:00 and 10:00 P.M.

My interest in the outside news rises and falls inversely with my own troubles. Things in the retail business have changing radically, and Arthur and I have had to take a good deal of energy and time thinking about how we will adjust. I only half heard the story about the priests in Bukovina.

Apparently, some individual Polish churches were sending missionary priests to other Eastern Bloc states. The priests were preaching to large crowds and kindling popular religious sentiment in such countries as Hungary and Czechoslovakia. The Soviets, of course, were upset. If I wanted to think or know more about this, I was to be disappointed; it was one of those items that surfaces, pops, and dissipates into the air, never to be heard of again; at least, not soon enough to matter.

As the time for the competition came closer, even though the games were almost a year away, pre-Olympic media buildup began. Because we were competing for another nation we were spared the attention the American athletes were getting, but we did have three articles written about us in diocesan papers and magazines, and we appeared in the *Monthly Rosary* under the headline: "Holy Father's Downhill Team." The photograph was not our most flattering. Prayers were said for us in at least five churches.

Arthur had stayed out of most of our plans, but I knew that he, Ned, and Bill, the Official Olympic Husbands, had been on the phone to one another. Bill works in the Aureole National Bank. Ned is a mining engineer. I knew they were worrying about us working too hard, going too fast, and maybe being hurt. We and Brother Sylvestro were only wishing we were faster ("Heads down, my daughters, your arms and elbows must be close or wind resistance will defeat you"). The racing skis had made a big difference, and we were doing times that seemed speed-of-light to us but worked out to only 44.16 miles per hour, far below the slowest Olympic times, unless you go back to the 1930s.

And then, suddenly, there was a breakthrough. It started when we saw an old film on ski races. I was ironing and watching TV as the narrator told us the skier we were seeing would have a near-fatal accident. Luckily, Arthur was still at the store. In order to make clear what had happened, there was footage of the man before he went over, showing him while he was still in control. I stood watching, concentrating intently, my iron up like a gavel. I was watching the shift of his weight, which seemed extreme. His position got him off the flat of his skis, reducing friction and clatter that would slow him on rough patches. I had learned about keeping off the flat years ago, but with the new skis, we had not adapted. I could hardly wait to call the team. They had been watching also. The next time we were out we began to experiment with an aggressive hip thrust. Like hula dancers, we bong-bonged down the hill, and we tried to remember what our big-shouldered, slim-waisted, iron-kneed competition had done on the film. It didn't work. We realized we were a separate creation.

And so we were forced into a new set of laws, one made, as Martha gratuitously said, for hens, not hawks. We didn't have their shoulders, but they didn't have our low center of gravity. Why should

we not use that advantage — settle just the tiniest bit
butt-sprung, or with our skis the slightest bit apart,
to account for our obvious anatomical differences?
"Buns for ballast!" we cried, and flew down the
slopes trying for hell-bent. Our times went down:
2.10, 1.58, 1.50. On the sprints we were doing 46.1
miles an hour.

Martha and I finished our parade outfits and we
all went down to the store to try them on in front of
the big three-way mirror. It was about 8:00 P.M., and
Bud Bourneman was patrolling the streets in his police car. When we saw him we flagged him down and
told him where we were going. He said he wanted
to come and see us in our Olympic outfits.

"Give us ten minutes." We had a camera, to get a
picture for Brother Sylvestro. Brother had written
that he would bring the Vatican flag for us to carry
in the opening ceremonies. He hoped his trip to Canada might be lengthened to include a trip to Gethsemani Monastery in Kentucky, because he was a
great admirer of Thomas Merton, who had been a
monk there; and he also wanted to go to Disneyland.
Did we think those trips might be done in two days?
His last paragraph was, as they had all become recently, urgent and a little irritated, or at least as irritated as being a religious allowed him to be. He
hated losing, and it was beginning to tell on him.
("You are not working hard enough," he had written
last week. "Sloth is a sin that must be strenuously
fought and conquered.")

I lost my temper. Martha wrote back: "Dear
Brother, so is pride."

The tunics were perfect for us. French blue is very
flattering to our gray hair, and the style was right for
our figures. The doves had worked out especially

well after Martha's sister, Lillian, had hand-embroidered their eyes and the golden rays in chain stitch.

We looked beautiful. Even Bud said so, and so did the other deputies who came in the other car. I guess it was the store lights being on that got Mildred Anthony and Del alerted, and they came over. They work cleaning up the mall at night. People say they are insensitive because they used to set mousetraps in the window displays and there were days when the morning would reveal the mannequins in La Boutique looking coolly down on a dead mouse or two. They certainly weren't insensitive to us. We got a hand, standing there. Marcelline — that's Bud's wife — listens in at home on the low band, the police frequency, and she came by and took a couple of pictures, too, and when they were developed they were our first formal Olympic pictures, because in the excitement we had forgotten to take any.

Our only pictures. That week, two of us broke 1.30, which is forty-nine miles per hour. It can get you arrested on a mountain road in bad weather. We were exultant. We were so exultant we were drinking Black Russians in the Après Ski bar at 5:00 P.M., when we should have been home watching the news.

I got back at six and started dinner and then a bath. I had just taken my clothes off when the phone rang. It was Buzzy, Clara's nephew and our would-be coach. "You heard the news?"

"What news?"

"Well, you better get the ten o'clock, but I think your Olympic days are kaput." He sounded happy.

"What's this about?"

"Just catch it," he said, and hung up.

I had just put the phone down when it rang again. My sister-in-law Francine, just as vague. As I got into the tub, the phone rang again. Four or five times.

So at ten I was watching, and so were the rest of us, as the announcer said, in the neutral voice that has given us so many years of hurricanes, wars, sweepstakes winners, and group nightmares:

"The Vatican representative walked out of the pre-Olympic conference today after announcing that the Vatican would boycott the 1988 Winter Olympic Games, in which it has an entry for the first time in history.

"Brother Sylvestro Mudarra protested what he called the reign of terror against Catholic priests in the Communist bloc. 'Its most recent outrages,' he said, 'the silencing and house arrest of four priests in Bukovina, leave us no alternative but to remove our participants from the contest.'

"Brother Sylvestro praised the Olympic contestants the Vatican had fielded and expressed his sorrow that they should be made to suffer for the wrong-doing of others."   .

Those contestants were Clara, Jean, Martha, and I, with Louisa as trainer. We got Brother Sylvestro's letter three days later. Our work and sacrifice could, if properly seen, he said, ennoble the remainder of our lives, that our intention in its purity was as much a delight to God as its execution would have been. He made no mention of his own sorrows, the loss of Gethsemani and Disneyland. To our discredit, we did not mention them either in our letter back to him. We thought that he, as our Olympic Committee, should have told us before he told the media.

Viking sent us a bill for the skis. They said we were not using them for the purpose intended. We sent them a copy of Brother Sylvestro's letter and added that their intention could be as delightful to the Lord as ours, and that there was surely enough glory in sacrifice to extend to everyone at Viking. We made sixteen copies of that letter, one for each of our sponsors. We would need all sixteen.

Meanwhile, we got hundreds of letters, from all over the country, cursing us for various things: mocking religion, church, and state; letting America down; attempting to get into the Olympic limelight; bringing women's liberation into disrepute; and being radical feminists.

We're going to take photos to send to Pope John Paul. They will be of the full Vatican ski team posed on the Thunder-shoot Run wearing its Olympic tunics and its unmarked gear, Louisa standing by with a clipboard to register our times.

At first we thought we would all go to Canada for the games, but Louisa's daughter is due again, and Mary Alice, our mainstay at the dry goods store, wants to go in for elective surgery then.

We do know that our skiing has improved. And the five of us did vote that if His Holiness ever came out to Aureole for the powder, his lift ticket would be on us. Brother Sylvestro skis on his own.